BEHIND THE WALL

She was breathtakingly beautiful, so beautiful that with an electric jolt of shock and exhilaration Blaine realized that this was an *Image,* that he was dreaming, dreaming at last the lucid dream, the deep astral fantasy of the collective unconscious.

She was slender and erect, with dark eyes and thick, dusky hair. Her smile was a child's, though she herself looked in her late teens—delighted but tentative, shy, as if unsure whether she should be smiling at him at all. The small, bare foot thrust over the wall was high-arched and perfect.

On an impulse he took a step forward and caught the girl's foot in his hand. It was cool and smooth as silk. Through her foot he felt a sudden jerk, as if something had yanked at her from the other side of the wall.

He heard her fall heavily to the ground. Then a heavy, sickening blow. The girl screamed.

Blaine stood rooted to his spot, head swimming with horror. It was a dream, he reminded himself—not real, just a lucid dream. The girl was screaming incomprehensibly and there were more blows, the bone-breaking thud of fists and boots on a living body. . . .

Tower of Dreams

TOWER
OF
DREAMS

JAMIL NASIR

BANTAM BOOKS

NEW YORK   TORONTO   LONDON   SYDNEY   AUCKLAND

TOWER OF DREAMS
A Bantam Spectra Book / January 1999

SPECTRA and the portrayal of a boxed "s" are trademarks of Bantam Books,
a division of Bantam Doubleday Dell Publishing Group, Inc.

ISBN 0-553-58089-2

Published simultaneously in the United States and Canada

Bantam Books are published by Bantam Books, a division of Bantam Doubleday
Dell Publishing Group, Inc. Its trademark, consisting of the words "Bantam
Books" and the portrayal of a rooster, is Registered in U.S. Patent and Trademark
Office and in other countries. Marca Registrada. Bantam Books, 1540 Broadway,
New York, New York 10036.

PRINTED IN THE UNITED STATES OF AMERICA

OPM 0 9 8 7 6 5 4 3 2 1

The rivalries for things of this world
Divert you,
Until ye visit the graves.

The Glorious Quran
Sura CII

1

By 11 A.M. the morning breeze that had rustled the coarse leaves of the fig trees had quieted to baking stillness. The daybreak sounds of roosters crowing, transistor radios blaring Arabic music, and the voices of the village children, remote but clear in the oasis silence below the mountains, had given way to the crunching passage of an occasional car on the road outside the high garden wall and, from the villa next door, the clank of pots, clack of plastic slippers on tile floor, the slam of a screen door, and the voices of women doing housework. Blaine Ramsey sat sweating on an extruded-plastic garden chair of Israeli manufacture under the waxy green leaves of lemon trees, in a niche of shade where the blue-whitewashed stucco of his rented house came within two meters of the garden wall. It was the coolest place in the garden, though still prickly with June heat. Beyond the tiny house, where the flagstone walk ran between rows of okra bushes, cucumber vines, thyme, and lavender, the sunlight was almost too bright to look at, though still fresh with a dusty morning paleness. At the bottom of the garden were orange and fig trees, and by the concrete garden wall a tall jacaranda with blossoms like crimson birds perching on its fernlike leaves. The gardener had left the hose running since early morning, and Blaine could hear its faint ripple, smell the hot dampness drawn out of the earth by the sun.

It would have been a relief to go indoors to the frigid blast of the air conditioner, but that would have defeated the purpose of his presence in Kraima. His job during the day was to absorb local atmosphere—in this case the burgeoning peasant megavillage stretching along the highway between the desert mountains and the Jordan River plantations. It was a hot, dusty, monotonous atmosphere.

Footsteps shuffled on the flagstone walk, and Abu Saleh came around the corner of the house. He was wiry, short, and mustached, skin burned almost black by the sun like most of the local people's, work clothes and forearms dusty from his slow, methodical weeding. He carried a tiny tumbler of tea brewed on his kerosene primus.

"God give you strength, Abu Saleh," said Blaine, using the proper Arabic salutation for people at their work.

"May He strengthen you," Abu Saleh replied reflexively. He squatted against the wall in the shade and sipped his tea, studying Blaine. Blaine knew he looked like an American— tall, rangy, and clean-shaven, wearing jeans and a cotton shirt—but he didn't carry a translator palmtop, and he spoke Arabic with almost native skill, the result of a university major and the fact that his father had been an ethnic Arab. His mixed ethnicity was also why Icon used him for Middle East postings: local genetic affinity was supposed to increase the nervous system's sensitivity to local atmosphere, while his foreign roots improved the chances that any Images he dug would have cross-cultural appeal. Though neither his local nor his foreign affinity seemed to have helped much on this job.

"The water has been turned off," reported Abu Saleh, sipping his tea.

"Again?" The quiet ripple of the hose was no longer audible, Blaine realized. Though the Jordan River was only a kilometer away, the dispositions of the local pumping stations and the authorities who ran them were unpredictable. "Everything is in the hands of God." Blaine sighed piously. The fact that he could buy plastic bottles of drinking water at the tiny shop down by the highway made it easy for him to exhibit the resigned surrender to the divine will prescribed in such situations. He would probably be gone in a week or two anyway, whether the water came on or not. And without having pulled down a single Image after two months in this supposedly fertile area.

"Everything is in the hands of God," agreed Abu Saleh, sipping his tea and squinting at the sun-washed garden.

Despite the heat it was a relief at lunchtime to have an excuse to go out. Blaine put on his straw hat—which he knew made him look even more like a foreigner, but without which he would get sunstroke—unlatched the green metal garden door, and stepped into the sun-blinded dirt street. At the corner of his seven-foot-high garden wall he turned right onto a wider dirt street that ran down the gradual slope toward the Shuna-Tiberias highway five hundred meters away. He could see a wide swatch of the local village area from here: dirt streets, one- and two-story houses of bare cinder block or prefab concrete with clotheslines, dusty solar panels, and satellite dishes on their flat roofs, everything washed pale by the intense sunlight except for an occasional palm or jacaranda arching out of a walled garden. An aboveground water main ran up the rocky shoulder of the street, leaky joints feeding tiny, riotous oases of mint, pigweed, and nettles.

Blaine trudged down the street, the sun like molten iron

on his shoulders, the noon call to prayer, amplified from the three-story minaret of the local mosque, echoing somberly over the shimmering landscape. Down close to the highway the houses were tiny, without window-glass or screens, low walls of cinder block or piled stones enclosing yards of dust and camel-thorn where donkeys were hobbled and chickens pecked.

The highway was four lanes of potholed asphalt divided by a concrete median painted with faded black and orange stripes. The river was an invisible presence beyond the lush citrus and banana groves across the highway, palpable in the smell of irrigation and a hint of humidity, oppressive in this heat. Villages like Kraima had burgeoned along this strip of asphalt in the past twenty-five years, growing together at their edges so that now the road was flanked for most of its ninety kilometers by a profusion of unplanned, unzoned construction: houses, shops with roll-down garage-type doors and wares hung from their awnings, small coffeehouses, the walled gardens the Arabs called "villas," tiny official buildings faced with cut stone, an occasional small mosque or church, an occasional cinema strung with colored christmas tree lights. The fruit groves limited expansion west in the direction of the river, and the desert mountains rose abruptly to the east, so most of the population of the Eastern Jordan Valley Semi-Autonomous Region lived in view of the highway.

Blaine turned left along its shoulder. Occasional cars and trucks rattled and swayed past at perilous velocities, raising dust, while tiny children played close by among the rocks and thorns. A couple of robed peasants sat on the median, calmly watching the traffic. A local teenage scion with an American-style brush cut cruised by in a vast Buick, booming illegal Euro gut-thump that momentarily disarranged Blaine's internal organs.

The roll-down door of the local shop was pulled a third of the way closed to keep out the sun. Blaine stooped to enter. The windowless dimness within smelled strongly of cumin and allspice. Behind a plywood counter the walls were covered with rough shelving reaching to the ceiling, stacked with everything from canned vegetables and jars of local olives to Palestinian-made radios to soap and faded boxes of Dutch cookies. On the floor open canvas sacks displayed beans, lentils, rice. An electronic fly trap next to the door crackled almost constantly. Perched on a stool behind the counter was a dark girl who looked about eight years old, wearing a clean, frilly pink dress. She shyly brought Blaine bread, a can of sardines, and two local eggs, and accepted the scrip he printed from his wallet bank terminal.

"God bless you," Blaine said to her, and trudged back up to his villa.

It was a day like any other in the two months since he had come here.

—

That evening the scent of jasmine and a nightingale's song came softly on cooling air through the barred window of Blaine's small, whitewashed bedroom. He sat on the narrow bed and drank the bitter decoction of herbs that helped bring on the Image dreams, murmuring the archaic invocations to Hindu deities that the Icon neurosociologists had found somehow magnified the herbs' potency. He did it distractedly, with the automatic poise of five years' practice, wondering meanwhile where his next assignment would be.

Probably not Morocco, which had already been hot for a year. He had seen some of the commercials based on Images dreamed in the ancient cities of Meknes and Fez: they were beautiful, primitive, and powerful, but that vein had to be just about exhausted by now. Images from any particular series only stayed hot for a short time; after that they lost their power to grab attention, inspire fantasies, and compel people to buy the products associated with them by the admen, exposure to the mass consciousness of the consuming public draining away their numen. That was how they worked. While psychoanalysis sought to dissipate disturbing unconscious material by bringing it into consciousness, psychologically active advertising employed the same dynamic to sell products, using mesmerizing Images from the collective unconscious. Each one had to be discarded as soon as it lost its potency, which was why Icon and the other big multinational advertising firms had huge R&D budgets supporting hundreds of Image-diggers all over the world dreaming for new material that tapped powerfully into the human psyche.

Maybe it would be Cairo next, Blaine thought, putting his empty teacup on the wobbly rattan night table. There had been Company rumors of recent strikes there—and other rumors, some of them strange. He hoped it wouldn't be Cairo—even the Jordan Valley with all its heat and monotony was better than a collapsed Third World city of 35 million people jittering with earthquake tremors.

But it was time to move on somewhere. In two months here he had turned up only personal dreams and fantasies, not even one lucid Image dream. Either he was having tie-in problems or the Icon scouts who had marked the Jordan Valley as a potentially rich source of unconscious material had misread their tea leaves.

He turned off the ceiling light and climbed between the rough, sun-dried sheets, then flicked another switch, this one on a console attached to a frame of wires stretched over his bed like the skeleton of a mosquito net. A tiny green light showed that the electroneural anchoring device—wired to trees, rocks, and earth in the garden outside—was activated.

In a few minutes, the song of the nightingale trickling over him, Blaine fell asleep.

He woke gradually in the early dawn, the nightingale still singing. The deep blue twilight was cool as he slipped out of bed, the floor tiles chilly on his feet. He put on clothes and went outside, the kitchen screen door slapping quietly behind him. The air was just a little damp, perfectly still. A vague pinkish glow dimmed the stars above the eastern mountains. Other than the pausing, meditative song of the nightingale, the world was silent.

Blaine went down the flagstone walk past the fig and orange trees, stretching and yawning in the deep blue, faintly purplish light that filled the garden like cool water. At the bottom of the garden a seven-foot concrete wall separated his villa from the next. He had stood for a minute rubbing his eyes and breathing deeply of the delicious air when there was a sound beyond that wall.

It was a quiet, slapping shuffle, the sound of the cheap, brightly colored plastic sandals worn by peasant women in this part of the world.

The sound struck Blaine with a strange excitement. He knew there were women in the next villa: he had heard their laughter and housework conversation many mornings. He had once seen three of them coming out of their garden door carrying plastic shopping baskets; by their long dresses and headscarves he had perceived that they were fundamentalist Muslims.

He said in the direction of the wall: "*Sabah el khair. Good morning.*"

He said it quietly, but in the perfect stillness it could not have been mistaken in the next garden.

The sound of sandals stopped. He had scared her, Blaine thought, at the same time wondering at himself for risking the wrath of his conservative neighbors by talking to their women, even over a wall.

There was a scraping, as of something being dragged, and then a couple of thumps and a light exhalation, and two hands appeared at the top of the wall. A girl pulled herself up and straddled the wall easily, so that her long black robe was pulled up to the knee of a smooth white leg.

Her robe covered her to the wrists and throat, but her head was uncovered. She was breathtakingly beautiful—so beautiful that with an electric jolt of shock and exhilaration Blaine realized that this was an *Image,* that he was dreaming—dreaming at last the lucid dream, the deep astral fantasy of the collective unconscious that the Icon scouts had sensed buried somewhere in the Jordan Valley.

He tried to relax, to release the aesthetic rush of the Image so it wouldn't wake him, so he could scan the dream, memorize every detail: the beautiful Muslim girl smiling down at him, twilight the color of violet smoke etching clearly each exotic leaf in the garden, its stillness holding the liquid song of the nightingale.

"*Sabah el noor,*" said the girl softly, using the proper response to his greeting. "Morning of light."

She was slender and erect, with dark eyes and thick, dusky hair. Her smile was a child's, though she herself looked in her late teens—delighted but tentative, shy, as if unsure whether she should be smiling at him at all. The small, bare foot thrust over the wall was high-arched and perfect.

"Who are you?"

Her voice—soft, guileless, inquisitive—gave him chills. He couldn't tell whether she was mentally undeveloped or simply innocent with the wide-eyed innocence of a cloistered village woman.

"I am your neighbor, my sister. Who are you?"

"My name is Buthaina. Oh! Your garden is so beautiful!" The breath caught softly in her beautiful throat, her tresses falling over her shoulders as she gazed back and forth, the dark eyebrows below her broad, high forehead raised.

This was good, Blaine realized, trying to keep his excitement in check—this dawn scene in the Jordan Valley with a Muslim child-princess was as good as anything they had pulled down in Morocco.

"I have a gardener who tends it," he said to keep her talking.

"A gardener?" she gasped, fixing her wide eyes on him. "Oh Peace! How lovely that must be!"

Blaine's eyes were tracking back and forth now, his trained dream-senses registering every detail: the smell of damp earth and jasmine, the nightingale's song, dawn highlighting the girl's stray tresses pink, the sky still dark blue behind her. And vaguely, from the garden behind the wall, the slam of a screen door.

On an impulse he took a step forward and caught the girl's foot in his hand. It was cool and smooth as silk.

"What are you doing now?" she said, laughing. Blaine laughed too, the touch of her bringing a full, happy feeling into him.

Through her foot he felt a sudden jerk, as if something had yanked at her from the other side of the wall.

She looked around so violently that she almost lost her balance.

Then another terrific yank jerked her foot out of his hand and she fell backward.

He heard her fall heavily to the ground behind the wall, and then mingled with her gasps and the sound of desperate struggling in dirt and gravel was the thick, bubbling hiss of someone else's breath.

Then a heavy, sickening blow.

The girl screamed.

Blaine stood rooted to his spot, head swimming with horror. *It was a dream,* he reminded himself—not real, just a lucid dream; yet an Image dream, and never before had anything like this happened to him in the programmed euphoria of an Image dream. The girl was screaming incomprehensibly and there were more blows, the bone-breaking thud of fists and boots on a living body, the sounds receding as if she was being dragged away.

Blaine tried to call out but the words choked in his throat. Was it an intruder, a rapist? One of her fundamentalist relatives punishing her for immodesty? But it was a dream! There was nothing to fear. Yet something was wrong; Image dreams didn't do this, didn't turn suddenly into nightmares—

A man's voice screamed with insane rage from inside the house beyond the wall, and there was the thick, sharp lash of a whip, then again, and again. The girl's cries had broken into animal shrieks of unutterable agony interspersed with great gasping sobs and something like laughter, as if she had lost her mind.

And suddenly he was standing no longer at the bottom of his garden in Kraima, but in a filthy, rubble-strewn yard in a hazy, dark gray, acrid atmosphere that went up between canyons of decrepit high-rise tenements; and as he watched, the tenements with a booming started to shake, started to crumble and fall, tumbling down in slow motion, raining down thousands of tons of concrete—

Blaine's scream woke him, shot him bolt upright in bed trembling and slick with sweat, heart pounding, yellow light of dawn coming in the window, a few birds singing and a rooster crowing somewhere nearby.

—

Blaine had never had an Image nightmare before; though it was common knowledge that disturbing Images surfaced sometimes, he reflected as he stood by the high wall at the bottom of his garden that morning. Except for the bright sunlight already hot on his shoulders, the wall and garden were exactly as they had been in his dream. He listened with relief to the clank of morning pots and pans, the sound of a radio, voices raised in talk and laughter from the house in the next garden. In fact, it dawned on him, Image nightmares probably happened all the time, but for obvious reasons— like the fact that Icon dropped Image-diggers cold at any sign of mental instability—people weren't eager to talk about them. Another cool wave of relief washed over him.

The best thing to do would be to salvage the numinous part of the dream and forget the rest. He had already spent an hour talking into his palmtop, recording every detail of the Image in response to the AI prompts. And it was gorgeous, he realized with a rush, powerful and compelling, just as he had thought when he was having it, before the nightmare part.

He went indoors to work on a package he could upload to Icon.

—

By late afternoon, sitting in his tiny front room in the hum and cool airstream of the air conditioner, wearing his retinal display spectacles and palpating his palmtop's touchpad, Blaine had finished documenting the Image and had begun working up audiovisuals. He had skipped lunch and had been interrupted only once, at mid-morning, by Abu Saleh inquiring if he was all right, since he wasn't sitting in the garden as he had every day since arriving in Kraima. The fascination of the work and the realization that he had tapped something hot had dispersed his upset at the dream—and, of course, he wasn't including the nightmare part in the upload package.

His telephone link rang; the stats showed the caller as Chan Ju Yen, his Regional Manager.

He tapped the Answer icon and took off his specs, picked up the palmtop so he could look into its tiny camera, and opened its nanotube screen, which unfolded around it like a Chinese fan. Jenny appeared in a window overlapping his Image visuals, lank blonde hair elegantly coifed, silver buttons in her ears, delicately slanted almond eyes looking into his face appraisingly from some skyscraper in Los Angeles. He wondered if the look was intended to remind him of her invitation to spend a couple of weeks with her later in the summer.

"You pulling down any truth out there?" she demanded. "Or are you dry?" She smiled, dimpled. "Ready to move on?"

"You should have called yesterday, Jenny. I got a strike last night. Now I've got to stick around and polish it." Often an initial big dream was followed by "aftershocks," which could illuminate unclear areas, supply missing details, add depth to the Image.

"No shit. And I was telling them we sent you to that dung-heap for nothing. And we got a nice little spot for you in Yemen: UFO sightings, tourist suicides, guaranteed hot."

"I can wrap it in a week, Jenny. Got a big dose last night. Hold Yemen for me."

Blaine shared workspace and showed her a couple of stills from the Image; she seemed suitably impressed. He promised to put audiovisuals on the satellite in a week, and she said she would hold Yemen. There were advantages to having a supervisor with a crush on you, Blaine reflected as he hung up.

He worked with the audiovisuals for a couple more hours, and by the time it was dark and cool enough outside to turn off the air conditioner he had roughed out a likeness of Buthaina. It wasn't great: there had been something about her he was having trouble catching. But his head was hurting from using the specs all day and he was restless; wanting to dive dream, he realized, hoping he could see her again. That wasn't unusual: he'd fallen in love with Images dozens of times; it was part of the business. One side effect was that it made you maybe just a little cynical about real flesh-and-blood love. Maybe that was what a decadent, postmodern girl like Jenny Chan saw in him: a decadent, postmodern cynicism that fascinated her.

He ate a dinner of leftover sardines and fresh vegetables from his garden, then went for a walk through the local village area in cooling darkness smudged here and there by dim solar-battery lightbulbs. When he got home he carefully boiled and drank his herbs, chanted his chant, switched on his electroneural anchor, and went to sleep.

—

He wasn't surprised when he woke again at the very edge of dawn, but this time he knew he was dreaming. This time he was scanning as soon as he came out of the house, closing the screen door quietly behind him and walking down the flagstone path. The blue-violet twilight seemed again to hold the garden in a crystalline, almost hallucinatory clarity; Blaine, rushing again with the beauty of it, seemed to see it all at once, godlike: a spider working on a web in the lemon tree, a mole disturbing dirt near the carport, the slow drip of the spigot at the corner of the house—

And through the cool air smelling slightly of damp earth he heard the shuffle and clack of plastic sandals.

The sound made his heart pound suddenly with fear. He wasn't ready for this, he realized, wasn't ready to hear the beautiful girl beaten again like an animal, if that was what was going to happen. Yet why should it happen? Last time had been a freak, some personal nightmare grafting onto the Image, obscuring it. That made it more important than ever to see the dream through now, since without the nightmare overlay he should be able to get more of it, get material that might enrich it.

"*Sabah el khair,*" he said quietly, shakily. He hoped he wouldn't wake himself up with his nervousness.

There was the scraping and noise of climbing, and then the beautiful girl was straddling the wall again, looking down at him with her brilliant, childlike smile.

"Who are you?" she asked softly, with just a hint of the flirting child.

"Blaine. Your neighbor."

"Bleen," she made of his non-Arab name. "I am Buthaina. Oh! What a beautiful garden you have!"

A screen door slammed faintly in the garden behind the wall.

Blaine stared at her, fear rising in his stomach.

A yank made her start around violently, dislodging a couple of pebbles from the wall.

Then the second yank pulled her down, and she screamed in pain and terror.

This time the yard in the smoggy urban nightmare–landscape was clearer, and smells came to him of garbage, excrement, and the stench of something dead, and this time he felt the ground shaking and bucking as the buildings fell.

—

As soon as the sun had peeked above the eastern mountains, strewing the valley with yellow light and long shadows, Blaine walked out to get breakfast. Even at its almost horizontal angle the sun cut the cool air with heat, and there was already the smell of dust from the passage of cars and trucks. A pickup jounced by, elaborately painted with flowers, hearts, and eyes, its bed full of sun-browned men in dusty clothes—laborers or agricultural hands on their way to work, some holding bulky ultraviolet eye shields. Some of them smiled at him. He, the mysterious, reclusive foreigner, had become a fixture in Kraima, and so was now inclined in the reflexive sense of community that enfolds Arab villages.

He nodded politely as the truck receded, raising dust along the street, tried to smile back through the cold foreboding in his stomach. He had heard of Image-diggers cracking up, of course, but he had never had problems himself. If Icon found out and made him retire it meant the loss of a handsome income, the loss of his prestige as a Senior Field Neurosocial Prospector, but more important than anything else it meant the loss of the rapture of digging, the exhilaration of the astral dreams, the rush of numinous delight when you hit a vein of truth. Though none of the crack-up stories he had heard sounded like what was happening to him. Usually they were stress-related: sleeplessness, travel fatigue, drug dependency—not Image dreams linked to recurring nightmares.

A boy rode a donkey out of an alley between the cinder block houses and walled gardens. *"Ka'ek!"* he called, his voice echoing down the village streets. *"Ka'ek!"*

Blaine gestured him over and bought one of the large donut-shaped, sesame-sprinkled loaves, still crisp from the oven, and a small, greasy bag of falafel.

———

For the rest of the day Blaine worked intensely on his Image audiovisuals, painstakingly redrawing, recoloring, detailing, animating the garden sequence that hung around him in his specs and gave him the illusion after a while, and despite the hum of the air conditioner, that he actually sat in his garden in an interminable, still dawn. Whatever happened he was a professional, he told himself; he would deliver this Image to the Company, come what might. For a while this resolution bucked him up, the ease with which his software manipulated the scenes and sounds of the dream giving him a feeling of control, dominion over the visions that had flowed into him from the collective unconscious of this obscure corner of the earth. He was the psychoformer here, after all, the manipulator and seducer, coolly molding the hot emotions and primordial scenes that would end up compelling hundreds of thousands or millions of people to buy the goods and services of Icon's clients.

But as the afternoon wore on his feelings of control started to slip. For one thing, he still couldn't seem to pin down a good likeness of the girl Buthaina. Perhaps his knowledge of what had happened to her afterward in the dream interfered with his attempts to capture her innocent, happy look, his own unconscious sabotaging the picture. To his mounting frustration, every likeness he constructed seemed to express in its face, subtly but unmistakably, a foreboding or anguish he felt sure would interfere with the ability of the Image to attract buyers to whatever product the admen chose to attach to it.

And his frustration kept trying to turn into fear in his stomach. What if he couldn't deliver the Image to Jenny Chan in a week, or ever? What if he had lost his Imaging talent? Or his mind?

Finally, in disgust, he stowed the palmtop, specs, and touchpad in compartments in their small leather case, stretched, and went out for a walk.

2

The sun had gone behind the western plantations an hour before, leaving a blue glow on the horizon. The air was mild but the dust of the road still radiated the heat of day. The distant barking of dogs seemed scarcely to touch the vast stillness below the dry mountains. Occasionally a car passed on the highway half a kilometer away. The dim yellow of low-wattage electric bulbs illuminated the windows of cinder block houses; here and there was the blue flicker of television. Blaine passed a tiny, garagelike shop in front of which a few robed men sat silently on rickety chairs, smoking and looking at the night. Farther up the gentle slope of the lower mountain foothills the houses ended. There was a field surrounded by barbed wire where rows of big solar panels stood dusty black and gray in the rising moonlight, storage batteries humming faintly; beyond that empty, rocky hills stretched all around. Fifty meters farther on, where the road stopped at a couple of whitewashed boulders, the silence was so complete that Blaine's ears hissed. He stood there for a few minutes, feeling himself relax, his frustration and worry slowly draining into the silence, into the rocks of these immovable, ancient hills, until his mind was nearly as still as the air.

Finally he turned and strolled back down toward the dim lights of the village. He didn't hear the sobbing until he had closed and locked his garden door and was a few steps from the house.

He had left the bulb above the kitchen screen door burning. Lying against the house wall half in shadow was a dark figure.

Blaine froze, hair prickling on his head. The figure didn't move, made no sound but the muffled sobbing.

He crept slowly toward it.

He recognized her mostly by the hair, the thick, dark hair, now matted and tangled. Her face was a swollen mass of bruises, and blood had run out of her broken mouth and dried. Her arms were clasped tightly around her body.

"Oh, neighbor," she gasped when he knelt next to her. "Oh, neighbor."

"Buthaina?" He was trembling. It wasn't possible. "Buthaina?"

"Buthaina?" she gasped, and coughing racked her body with agony. "There is no Buthaina. There is no such person as Buthaina. She is dead, don't you know? Don't you know that, oh neighbor?"

Her beautiful long hands were sticky with blood. He took them in his own shaking hands and pulled them toward him.

Her arms must have been broken; she shrieked deafeningly, her eyes black pools of agony and confusion.

Then she was gone.

Blaine stood up fast. The ground heaved under him and his heart was pounding. Her scream seemed still to be echoing among the houses of the village, among the rocks of the dark fields and mountains, but she was gone. Where she had been were nothing but gray flagstones and the pale concrete of the house. He looked quickly, desperately around, though he knew she couldn't have moved.

The night was still, silent except for a few crickets and the distant barking of dogs. Two moths fluttered around the bulb above the kitchen door.

Blaine's legs were trembling so he could barely stand. He went inside and locked the door, turned on every light in the tiny house, fanned the palmtop's screen, put in a high bid for telephone bandwidth, and dialed a number in Karachi, Pakistan.

It rang eight times, then a face appeared on the screen, brown-skinned, goateed, with flashing black eyes and shoulder-length black hair. It began to speak Urdu.

Blaine's heart sank. He touched a key and the greeting started again in Urdu-accented English: "This is the expert system of Haseeb Al Rahman. Haseeb is unavailable right now, but—"

Blaine said a password and the face stopped speaking and broke into a natural-looking smile. The smile had undoubtedly come from one of the live Haseeb's telephone conversations, to be spliced into the AI when appropriate. Haseeb had upgraded his expert system again; apparently he was following Icon's directive to senior personnel to encode themselves in case of death, retirement, or employment by a competitor; Blaine guessed also that the AI was running at least partly on the new bioanalog network circuits that Haseeb claimed would replace digital within five years.

"Where's Haseeb? Can you wake him up?"

"He's not home," answered the AI.

"Where is he?"

"I don't know. Can you leave a fucking message?"

"Has Haseeb," said Blaine, his voice shaking, "indexed anything about diggers seeing Images when they're awake?"

Haseeb System looked thoughtful for two seconds, then

with the slightest jerk got more expression on its face and asked: "Have you seen Image material during daylight hours at a time when you are certain you were really awake?"

"Yeah. Just now."

"I have an indexed segment." It suddenly got animated and humanlike again with Haseeb's spliced expressions. "What it means is you need R&R. What it means is you've been drinking too much yogi devil-sperm and you need to lay off it for a while." Haseeb was a devout Muslim, but one of Icon's original Image-diggers; he had probably drunk more of the herbal decoction in his time than three average diggers. "It means you need to go off and live like a normal human for a few weeks, before you go as crazy as the yogis and start worshiping their devils.

"So what you're going to do, my friend, is not touch the herbs for a few weeks, until this clears up. You're going to get on niacin and ignore whatever aftershock you get. You're going to call management and tell them you're taking R&R, and if they give you any shit, tell them to expect a call from me. And then you go to the beach for a couple of weeks. Exo-area, you understand? Divide the thighs of some white girls in the Great Satan. Eat at McDonald's."

Blaine didn't trust AI to get anything right, but the recorded segment was Haseeb himself, obviously answering for someone else the same question Blaine had asked. Which meant that this kind of thing had happened to other diggers. Which meant that maybe Blaine wasn't crazy, he realized with a lifting feeling.

It wasn't until after he hung up that he noticed smears of what looked like dried blood on his hands.

They were rust smudges, he told himself as he scrubbed them shakily in the tiny, green-whitewashed bathroom, the flaking mirror above the sink showing a tall, wild-eyed man. There was a rusty water pipe that ran along the outside wall of the house just where he had hallucinated the figure of Buthaina. He refused to let himself think any further than that. As soon as he calmed down enough to present a casual front to Jenny Chan—say tomorrow morning—he would call her and request R&R. He wouldn't crack up; it would just be a short vacation. He probably wouldn't be able to do Yemen, but as soon as he was rested and detoxed he would get back in the groove, start again mining Images worth millions to the Company.

—

That night, with his doors locked, on a handful of niacin pills instead of the herb decoction, and with the neural anchor switched off, the lucid dream of Buthaina came to him again.

"Buthaina, get down off the wall," he begged her. He tried desperately to wake up but he couldn't. The screen door slammed in the next garden. *"Get down, Buthaina."*

She stared at him in puzzlement. "How do you know my name?"

Then she was yanked down screaming and the nightmare city earthquaked around him, and he squeezed his eyes shut and prayed desperately, Muslim children's prayers he had learned from his grandmother, and which were the only ones he knew.

—

It took a few days to get the herbs out of your system, Blaine told himself as he went out the next morning haggardly into the warming air and bright sunlight of his garden. He was itching to call Jenny Chan but after looking at himself in the mirror he had put it off. If you were going to ask for unscheduled R&R, especially in the middle of work on an audiovisual package, you'd better be prepared to make it sound pretty casual, or risk getting psychological testing.

Yet the morning bustle and sunlight of the village lifted his spirits, and after a late breakfast it occurred to him that, other than some unpleasant dreams and a momentary hallucination, the past few days had actually been a successful dig. If he were to take a day or two before calling Chan, avoiding the herbs and electronics, of course, and dosing himself with neuron-cleansing niacin, but working on his audiovisuals, he should be able to load his package to her on schedule and make his R&R look that much more innocent. He might have some more dreams, but he was an expert in dreams; he could stand up to them.

He worked on the Image far into the afternoon, sitting in the shade of the house under the lemon trees, his specs banishing the heat and the sound of radios, the smell of bougainvillea and sunlight on dust and leaves, banishing everything except the cool purplish blue of dawn, the dream-woman's face and body, her voice, her gestures. As a time-saving measure he didn't try to fight the haunted look that kept trying to creep into her, and by the time he was ready to stop, his neck aching, eyes burning, and a healthy hunger rumbling in his belly, he had polished a three-minute sequence that wasn't bad, and that he could probably upload without further work if need be.

The door of the little garagelike shop by the highway was rolled partway down against the lengthening afternoon light. The grizzled, unshaven old man who owned it now sat behind the counter in his gray robes and keffiyeh, smoking a hand-rolled cigarette with one gnarled hand and moving prayer beads slowly in the other.

"*Mesa' el khair,*" he said hoarsely to Blaine, eyes blinking and rolling to try to see past his cataracts.

Blaine started to reply, but found himself gaping instead. For a confused second he thought he was hallucinating again, then realized he was looking at a picture, a movie poster taped to some shelves behind the old man, partly obscuring rows of plastic water bottles. It showed a woman's face. Her hair was long and dark brown, her eyes large and dark.

Blaine realized that the old man was ogling him, worry beads still moving in his hand.

"Who—who is this?" Blaine asked breathlessly, gesturing at the picture. Though he could see the name for himself, emblazoned under her picture in jagged Arabic script: Aida!

"Who, father?" said the old man. "That picture? I don't know. Me, I don't watch films." He laughed hoarsely. "It's a new Egyptian film they have sent me."

The film was called *Madame Taya*, Blaine found out when he downloaded it from the net site suggested on the poster, and it was in the same vein as other Egyptian melodramas he had seen: overheated, garish, thinly plotted, made to give the masses of Arab urban and rural peasants delicious glimpses of a glamorous upper-class world that they would never have occasion to discover was unreal. It was a cheaply made DAS—digital actor simulation—barely interactive at all, with only a couple of alternate story lines, and no "offstage" function where you could undress the stars and program them yourself, as you could with Western DAS. The actress "Aida" played a poor but virtuous girl seduced and then deserted by a rich man's son—still the stuff of tragic poetry to peasant audiences. But to Blaine Ramsey, sitting breathless in his tiny front room in the blast of the air conditioner and watching on his specs, the sensational plot and overblown dialogue meant nothing. Clearly—so clearly that it was beyond doubt—the actress Aida was the girl he had dreamed about three nights in a row, his Image girl. Her eyes and hair, her face and voice, even her beautiful, slender hands, were Buthaina's and no one's but Buthaina's. It was impossible to tell if she was a decent actress, since DAS presented only digitally animated photomaps of the cast, but Blaine found himself sweating at the end of the film when predictably, after her seduction had paved the way for a descent into a life of prostitution, the Aida character put the capstone on a bad life by jumping out the fourth-floor window of a police station. From there the camera focused down on her dead body lying in the nighttime street, eyes glittering in death until they were hidden by sheets of newspaper placed over her by a grieving citizen. A gust of wind blew, once more uncovering the eyes, which gazed inquisitively and sightlessly upward.

As evening came on, windless, warm, and dry, Blaine set his chair on the flagstone walk by the corner of the house, the stones and concrete around him still radiating the heat of the day, okra bushes near his feet in the hose-dampened earth giving off their warm, vegetable smell. He had tried to call Haseeb again but again had only gotten the AI system. He was trying to think, to set everything straight in his mind. It wasn't easy, because what had happened to him was supposed to be impossible.

For centuries psychoforming had relied on the *conscious* mind's ideas of how to manipulate the unconscious, but then advertising industry R&D had discovered psychologically active advertising, a way to sell products using mesmerizing Images from the collective unconscious. Yet for that very reason it was supposed to be impossible for Images to involve famous people. Images could be seen in dreams precisely because *unconscious* psychic energy had built up in them—the same energy that gave them their powerful hold on consumers when they were turned into commercials. But an Image thus made public stayed powerful only a short time, the conscious attention of the multitude quickly draining away its pent-up energy. By that straightforward Jungian reasoning, the likeness of an Aida—whom a quick net search had told him was one of Egypt's biggest stars—should long ago have been drained of the unconscious psychic energy needed to make her appear in an Image.

So how had she come into the lucid dream state of an otherwise competent Image-digger? And why had the lucid dreams been nightmares? And, most strangely of all, how had she appeared to him in a waking hallucination?

He walked to the bottom of the garden in the deepening blue light, to the wall Buthaina had climbed three dawns in a row. A muted Quran recitation came from the radio in the next house, and the kitchen noises were limited to an occasional monosyllable or rattle of dishes. He caught a whiff of garlic and *leban kishik,* the dried sheep's-milk yogurt used in Arabic sauces. He put his hand on the wall, the pebbles in the concrete still warm from the day. It was all very quiet and ordinary, reassuring. The dream-girl Buthaina wasn't real, he reasoned with himself. No real assailant had broken her and left her to die. His yearning to see her again, to touch her, to bring her to life, all had to be seen for what they were: hazards of his peculiar occupation. And the psych scientists weren't always right about the kinds of Image dreams you could or couldn't have, or the people that could appear in them. Their theories were just theories, and were based on only a few years of data; the field of archetypal neurosociology, as they liked to call it, was after all only a decade old.

Blaine went indoors, turned off the air conditioner, unlatched the windows, and folded them back against the walls. He switched on his palmtop and put in a bid for long-distance telephone bandwidth, dialed Jenny Chan's office number. She wouldn't be there: it was 10 A.M. in Los Angeles, and Jenny's shift was midnight to eight—business hours in the Near East Region she managed—but that made it a good time to upload his Image and request unscheduled leave. With any luck she would leave him a message back approving it and he would avoid having to answer any awkward questions.

But Jenny answered after two rings, and even on the tiny

pixel-grained palmtop screen he could see that she looked upset.

"Blaine," she said in surprise. "What's the matter? You all right?"

"Yeah, I'm all right. I have an Image to 'load to you. I didn't think you'd be in so late.

"Oh, of course, your Image." She seemed to sigh with relief. "Business, baby, you know." She gave him a worried, harried smile. "You can 'load it to me."

"Oh, and I had one other thing," he said, deciding to push his luck while she was distracted with whatever corporate emergency. "Request a couple weeks' leave time. Beginning immediately, if the Image is satisfactory—"

"Blaine, I really don't have time to consider it right now, I'm—oh, look—yes, yes, go ahead. Go ahead, all right? I'll authorize it tomorrow. But I have to get off now."

And she did, leaving an encrypted upload screen behind her. And without even raising the issue of Yemen, he reflected with satisfaction as he clicked the upload icon.

———

The evening call to prayer had echoed over the houses and streets of Kraima, over the rocky plains and hills and against the barren mountains, its vast, serene cadences briefly seeming to still time, to draw down onto the land a fragrance of sacredness. Afterward the dusk was very deep, a few stars beginning to glimmer above the minaret of the village mosque, and as Blaine walked restlessly through the deserted streets and lanes the moon, white as milk and nearly full, rose above the eastern mountains to gaze down into the river valley.

The thought had come to him that the hallucinatory Buthaina might be in his garden again when he returned from his walk, and that half-hope, half-fear kept him walking nervously beyond his normal time, until he found himself at the whitewashed boulders at the end of the dirt street farthest from the highway, where the ground began to tilt upward more steeply toward the mountains. The moon cast its silvery light on the slope beyond the boulders, making the night seem somehow more silent, as if the crunch of his feet among the rocks were the only sound in the world. The air was neutral in temperature and without humidity. Blaine climbed to the top of the slope beyond the boulders, to where the land fell away again in a low rock cliff, and stood gazing at the surreal landscape of the mountains that reared beyond another range of foothills, wondering how far away they really were.

At the bottom of the cliff on which he stood was something white and squarish, lying half in shadow. It didn't fit into the ancient, wind-worn, sun-scoured landscape.

He climbed down the cliff, the warm, worn rock like rough, ancient hands on his hands. At the bottom he saw that the pale shape was a human body lying in the dirt, covered with sheets of newspaper.

And when he lifted one of the sheets, heart pounding, he saw that it was she, Buthaina, her beautiful dark eyes staring inquisitively, sightlessly at the moon, her nostrils wide, as if sniffing the air. She made no resistance this time when he took her cold, delicate hand in his, knelt by her and took long, shaking breaths, the earth tilting around him.

Then, as before, she was gone.

3

That night he slept dreamlessly in the cool air perfumed with jasmine and the nightingale's song, or if he had dreams they were not of the lucid variety; maybe he heard Buthaina's voice from around the corner of a village street, but she didn't wake him with her torment. The niacin had finally kicked in, or maybe there was another reason: maybe it was because he had heard her call, had already, in some deep part of himself, decided to go to her.

It was ridiculous, of course, he realized when he woke up with the fresh breeze of early morning gently lifting his curtains in the pale sunlight, the plan fully formed in his mind. While Cairo was technically exo-area, he was sure it wasn't what Haseeb Al Rahman would have had in mind had he been mentationally present to deliver his recommendation for R&R leave. Cairo contained little of either rest or relaxation these days, between economic collapse, political instability, and impending earthquakes. And it was the direction exactly opposite the one he should go to leave his obsessive dreams behind, he knew, since in that city lived the actress Aida, the alter ego of the dream-girl Buthaina.

If he had wanted to kid himself, he could have told himself he was going to Cairo as part of his dig, to follow a lead given by his subconscious about the source and meaning of his Image. Or he could have pretended he was on a spiritual quest in search of himself, to find out why he had dreamed and hallucinated the movie star. He could even have pretended he was going for pure science, to investigate a phenomenon in apparent contradiction to established neuro-sociological theory. But he was too old to play games; he knew that the real reason he was going wouldn't stand up under logical scrutiny, and it was this: he had heard the dream-girl Buthaina beaten to agony, had seen her broken, bloodied body, held her cold, delicate hands, and he had fallen in love with her like any bumpkin first-year digger falling for his Image. Yet by some incredible stroke of luck or misfortune, this Image lived, in the person of an Egyptian movie star; and since she had a physical existence somewhere in the world, Blaine would go to her.

An exhilaration went through him as he padded on cool floor tiles into the tiny whitewashed kitchen to put on the teapot, the kind of feeling he remembered from his childhood when, waking early in the morning, he had realized it was the first day of summer vacation. He hadn't had that feeling in a very long time.

—

Blaine could have taken an EgyptAir or Royal Jordanian flight from Amman to Cairo, but the Image-digger imperative for local atmosphere had accustomed him to sharing the *serveese* taxis that middle-class Arab travelers used. He caught one in an oil-stained parking lot in Jericho between a low-rent hotel and an orange grove, where dozens of taxis parked in the early morning, drivers calling out the names of the cities for which they were bound, the fresh, cool air holding the

fragrance of the trees, the smells of motor oil and roasting
peanuts sold by hawkers.

———

The heat of the Sinai Peninsula made the remembered temperature of the Jordan Valley seem mild by comparison. The
venerable supercharged Mercedes taxi Blaine had caught
flew rattling along the flat, heat-rippled Suez road with all its
windows open, and the air that blasted in on the riders was
broiling. At intervals they halted at rest stop lean-tos built of
palm fronds or corrugated iron. As he pissed on the sand behind the lean-tos the sun was like knife blades on Blaine's
head and shoulders, the air almost unbreathable, and the
vast stillness of the endless yellow plain seemed also an arti-
fact of the heat, as if the sun held all life, all movement in an
iron grip. After relieving themselves, travelers drank cold
Pepsis from solar-powered coolers inside the rest stops, and
then, after paying the nearly motionless proprietor, were on
their way again, the rush of wind through the windows drying their sweat.

     Transit at the Palestinian, Israeli, and Egyptian borders
had been slow and suspicious, and Blaine's Icon corporate
immunity identification—protecting his palmtop from con-
traband data searches—had been painstakingly scrutinized
half a dozen times. The regimes in the area had never fully recovered from the prodemocracy *intifadah*s of '02 and '03,
which had left a jumble of autonomous and semiautonomous
regions in their wake, creating fertile ground for smuggling,
gunrunning, and money-laundering, which the governments
tried to combat by strict border control. By late afternoon
Blaine's *serveese* was still in the desert beyond Suez, and heading south now: the northern and eastern approaches to Cairo
went through shantytowns not under the firm authority of
government, and were sometimes dangerous. The driver was
pushing the car now to speeds at which it seemed to Blaine
to be barely under control, its heavy, dented frame rattling,

jumping, and rocking, though the other riders, swaying passively in their seats, seemed unaware of it. Outside, flanked by electric transmission towers, the patched road dwindled to a sand-hazed horizon over a wide, exhausted beige land of rippled sand and rocks and intense heat. Um Kalthoum, the Middle East's most revered singer in the 40 years since her death as well as in the 40 years before it, blared from the taxi's radio, and above her sinuous cries and the labor of the engine, two of the passengers had managed to get into a political argument.

"The earthquakes, the unrest, are a judgment from God," the man in the front passenger seat, directly in front of Blaine, was saying. He was thin and dark, with a narrow face, black hair that curled close to his head, and bright black eyes. While he wore Western clothes, the neat, trimmed beard on his hollow cheeks had excited the suspicion of the police at each of the borders they had crossed: Islamists often wore beards, after the fashion of the Prophet Mohammed. He was turned in his seat to see the man sitting directly behind the driver. "And now the West says it will not give aid to help with the earthquakes. The plans and devices of men have come undone, brother, and no one can save Egypt but God."

The man in the back seat, dressed in the plain gray clothes of a low-level Egyptian bureaucrat, clicked his tongue impatiently. "Brother, the earthquakes come from a feature of geology, a crack in the rocks of the earth. The political unrest is because the people are poorer and poorer, due to the population problem. And the aid—the West will give it in the end. Egypt is their ally in the Middle East. Think of the outrage it would cause if the rich nations let earthquakes destroy a country of a hundred million people. They'll give the aid, brother."

"They will cut it off," said the bearded man. "The Arabs cannot rely on foreign charity anymore. They have to stand on their own feet. Where are the Gulf countries in this crisis, with their billions? Where are the Palestinian scientists and engineers, the Sudanese with their crop surpluses? I tell you, the Arabs have stood on their own feet only once in history: when the whole Arab nation was united under the flag of Islam."

The man riding in the back seat between Blaine and the bureaucrat, a laborer by the look of his rough clothes and hands, sun-darkened skin, and thick forearms, spoke up, to the bureaucrat: "Your presence says the earthquakes are caused by something—biology, or whatever your presence called it—forgive me, I'm not an educated man. But what causes this biology itself? It is God, I say, who has sent this biology."

The driver and the bearded man murmured their agreement.

Um Kalthoum had finished her hour-long song, and the radio began playing Quranic recitations. The riders fell silent, each withdrawing into his own thoughts, the resonant, nasal chanting filling the car with a cathedral-like serenity despite the rush of speed, wind, and rattling. The driver sat relaxed, one hand negligently holding the wheel, the other hanging out the window; the bearded man fondled his prayer beads, lips moving silently; the laborer sat with his rough hands folded patiently in his lap.

They rushed past a bedouin shepherd in ragged black robes and turban, face nearly blackened with sun, tending a group of skinny goats foraging on nearly invisible desert scrub. In that instant the chanting from the radio and the lengthening rays of the still-fierce sun seemed to interpenetrate in Blaine's mind, as if the sunlight was some visible aspect of God's grace, giving the tall, straight bedouin man, as it poured upon him, a dignity and noble individuality worthy of a child of Adam.

Late afternoon came, the vast, cooling blue of the sky a relief after the fierce heat and glare of midday. They were going

west again, and Um Kalthoum was singing again. There was
a haze in the sky ahead that turned the sunset a violent purple and orange, as if there were a dust storm, and it seemed
to Blaine that the cooling air blowing on him from the window had a faint smell now, like smoke. There was no sign of
habitation yet except a two-story concrete checkpoint at the
side of the road jutting out of the bare desert, and a couple
of machine gun–toting soldiers who motioned them to pull
over and went through the usual check of the riders, with
special interest in Blaine and the bearded man. Soon after
they were on their way again another sign of civilization appeared in the dusk: the desert became strewn with trash—
trash stretching to the horizon, as if every plastic wrapper,
cigarette butt, and scrap of paper that had ever been thrown
away in the world had finally blown to this forsaken spot
and struck against a rock or ripple in the sand. Then, as
darkness fell Blaine noticed that the land along the road had
assumed the shape of regular mounds, and, squinting his
eyes, he saw that they were indeed mounds—heaps of
garbage and rubble, as if the desert had become a vast dump.
Along the sides of the road too someone had planted tiny fir
saplings, looking impossibly fragile against the massive desert.
Blaine guessed they were sustained by some kind of drip irrigation system, embryonic windbreaks against the day when
this land would be reclaimed for agriculture in accordance
with some grand Five Year Plan—which ignored the fact that
nothing would be able to grow on the mounds of garbage: a
typical collision between government bureaucracy and private sector anarchy that seemed to define Egypt. The smell
coming on the west wind was stronger now; it smelled like
burning garbage.

The dark sky above them was murky. A sudden spatter-
ing of drops hit the car in the dark.

The laborer, who had begun to doze in his seat, woke
up. "What is that?"

"Rain," said the bureaucrat, looking out the window.

"Rain?" asked the laborer incredulously. "But the month is June!"

"Yes," said the bureaucrat. "Don't you watch television, brother? They flooded the Qattara Depression nine years ago through a trench to the Mediterranean, and made an inland sea right in the middle of the Western Desert. Now the weather is changing, just as they planned. It has begun to rain in Egypt even in the summer." His hands excitedly illustrated his words. "I am a planner at the Ministry of Agriculture, and we have studied this effect. In a few years this soil will be rich enough to start light agriculture, and someday, with the help of God, the desert may be a beautiful garden, and Egypt may be able to feed herself again."

The other riders murmured their approbation and invoked the Creator.

After this excitement Blaine dozed uncomfortably in his seat like the laborer, noticing in his waking moments that the humidity and smell of smoke were increasing. A dirty orange glow grew on the western horizon as if dawn was coming, though the sun had set there only two hours ago. He roused himself. There was a light in the darkness ahead, and they rushed past a tiny cinder block structure with a palm-thatched awning under which a dim solar bulb burned. Under the bulb a group of robed and skullcapped men sat on low stools around a backgammon board, smoking *argilas*. Above the awning a flickering Arabic sign said "Pepsi-Cola."

"Welcome to Cairo," said the driver.

More buildings appeared, a sudden clot of tiny huts made of mud brick, all built against each other in the peculiar urban style of Egyptian villages, with narrow dirt alleys between. But this village didn't end; the huts went on and on, stretching away from the road in ramshackle chaos. Dusty, rocky open spaces and dirt streets appeared here and there, seemingly at random. Giant electric transmission towers rose amid the sprawl, carrying high-tension cables above it. There were more lights now, tiny shops and shallow, tiled coffeehouses illuminated by solar bulbs or kerosene lanterns, with what looked like robed villagers sitting on the ubiquitous low stools outside them.

"This is Cairo?" muttered the laborer, puzzled. "What has happened to it?"

"We are still in the outskirts," said the driver. "And the outskirts expand a kilometer every year."

The desert road had now become the main street of this squatter metropolis, and the taxi's rushing passage was slowed to a walking pace by pedestrians, crammed mini-buses, tiny battered cars, donkey-carts, and motorcycles carrying three and four riders, all jostling for position on the narrow pavement. The night air was full of exhaust fumes and alive with the sound of engines, the blare of radio music, laughter and catcalls from groups of ragged youths. The cars used their horns liberally, giving constant little beeps like warning sonar. An occasional helicopter or VTOL limousine passed overhead with a roar, navigation lights flashing.

They crawled on. After an hour the main road had four lanes, but traffic was heavy and often came to a stop. The air was nearly unbreathable with raw exhaust. Now they were in an older squatter neighborhood where the walls were grimy and marked with graffiti, people sleeping against them here and there on the dirt shoulder. There were a few two- and three-story buildings of concrete or cinder block. They passed a tiny mosque with a tiny, fake minaret deco-rated with molded cement gingerbread. The shops had metal shutters and roll-down doors, many of them closed, but the streets were still crowded with pedestrians, hawkers with pushcarts calling their wares, children playing soccer under streetlights, people walking in the night air.

"Is there an occasion?" Blaine asked timidly. "A feast?"

The driver smiled. "The occasion of nighttime," he said.

Blaine barely had time to take this in when their taxi swooped in front of oncoming traffic, the driver holding his hand out slightly to signal the left turn, and they pulled into a dirt lot where twenty or so other taxis were parked, some of the drivers leaning against their cars talking and smoking, though it was after midnight. At the other end of the lot big, smoke-blackened buses idled, filling the air with the smell of hot diesel.

"*El hamdulillah 'a salameh,*" said the driver, stopping his taxi behind the others. "Praise God for your safe arrival."

After such a long period of motion the taxi felt strange stopped, and when Blaine stepped out of it the stillness and solidity of the ground were almost dizzying.

A group of boys were around them suddenly, skinny and ragged, their faces pinched with hope and hunger. "*'Hamdulillah 'a salameh! 'Hamdulillah 'a salameh!*" they shouted, crowding around Blaine and the other travelers, foreigners rich enough to ride in a car from another town.

"Go! Go!" yelled the driver angrily, waving his hands vigorously to protect his customers. The boys ran away, some in bare feet, one loping behind clumsily in a pair of ruined men's shoes.

The driver opened the taxi's trunk and handed each of them his bags, the riders murmuring blessings upon him. A ragged man came forward from the darkness and put his hands on the bags, pretending to help the driver lift them out, but he was ignored. He slunk away a few steps with a sickly, ashamed look, but not able to tear himself away from the possibility that someone might give him a tip.

The Arabs' bags were huge and heavy, tied around with cords that they had retied after every border checkpoint; Blaine had only one small suitcase. And standing there holding it, looking after the others lugging their bags toward the buses, he suddenly realized that he was in Cairo and had no idea what to do next.

The driver, who had emptied his ashtray onto the ground and was now vigorously brushing crumbs out of the open door of the taxi, noticed him.

"Where are you going, brother?" he asked.

"Well—I need to find a hotel."

"Which hotel?"

"I don't know Cairo. Can you recommend one?"

"Cairo is full of hotels. The ones foreigners usually stay in are near the Nile downtown. The Meridien, the Nile Hilton, Nile Marriott. That first bus goes to Tahrir Square, from which you can walk to the Hilton."

"Perhaps I should stay somewhere nearby tonight and go tomorrow—"

The driver held up a warning finger. "No. Night is the time to travel; the traffic is light. You had better go now if you want to get there."

The bus the driver had pointed out seemed completely full when Blaine approached it, but the men standing in the aisle squeezed backward until there was just room for him to stand on the steps by the door, his suitcase between his feet. A few more men got on, squeezing Blaine up the steps so that they rather than he would be in danger of falling out onto the road. The passengers were mostly men, though a few women wearing the local Muslim garb—long dresses and head coverings, like nuns' habits made of cheerful, patterned fabric—were crammed into some of the seats, some holding plastic shopping baskets on their laps despite the lateness of the hour. As soon as it was clear that the bus could hold absolutely no one else, the sweaty, unshaven driver put it shudderingly into gear and rammed it, rocking dangerously under its excessive load, out of the lot into traffic, drawing angry honking from the cars he had nearly hit.

They lumbered along, the powerful engine vibrating the floor, the inside close with breath and the smell of diesel oil though all the windows were wide open. Thankful as he was not to be sitting anymore, Blaine was dog tired, longing for a soft bed in a quiet room and local atmosphere be damned. He wondered how far it was to Tahrir Square. Cairo's population growth had played hell with city planning and the government's ability to keep track of the new suburbs, streets, and neighborhoods that sprouted up as 150,000 new residents arrived every month from the countryside and the womb. Perhaps there was actually no one alive who knew exactly how far Tahrir Square was, or how long it took to get there, he thought groggily.

A smoke-blackened steel and resin superstructure carrying elevated utilities now arched above the street, its girders whirring slowly by the bus windows. They crawled in a crush of taxis, cars, motorcycles, trucks, and minibuses traveling three and four abreast in the two lanes on their side of the crumbling concrete median, horns echoing against dark four- and five-story buildings mixing with blaring music from the tiny, bright shops. The bus driver joked with a couple of the men standing over him, their hands braced against the wall and bars to keep from falling on him. Finally traffic stopped once and for all, the taillights ahead of them winking at the smoky, fume-choked air that haloed the streetlights.

Through the open windows Blaine thought he heard distant machine-gun fire.

He could feel the crowd stiffen around him, hear the intakes of breath and low exclamations. The distant gunfire sounded again.

"Oh, Lord," the driver groaned. He rammed the gears into neutral and the bus idled. "We'll be here all night now."

There was low, excited talk from the crowded interior of the bus, and someone pushed against Blaine's back, softly at first, but with increasing insistence, until Blaine in turn pushed the person in front of him, making enough room for whomever it was to pass.

It was a dark, bearded man with anxious eyes. "Excuse me. Excuse me," he said softly.

The bus driver opened the door and the man climbed down and hurried away between the idling cars, got lost among the people on the sidewalk, most of whom were standing and listening, staring down the street toward where the shooting had come from.

"God be with you," said the bus driver neutrally. It was hard to tell whether he was being ironic.

Three more bearded men and one without a beard struggled off the bus and quickly got lost in the night.

"If the security police find them here, they'll interrogate them," the driver said to no one in particular.

Many hushed, intense discussions were going on in the bus now. Blaine listened anxiously to the men crushed around him; they seemed more excited than worried.

"It's not an Islamist attack," one was saying. "They don't attack in a *baladi* neighborhood in the middle of the night. The Socialists, perhaps, or the Southern separatists."

Another of the men saw Blaine listening.

"*Il dit que c'est un embouteillage,*" he said in Arabic-accented French, grinning.

"God increase your substance," Blaine said to him in Arabic, and the men laughed.

In the distance they could hear the crackling bellow of a public address system. The booming of a helicopter came into hearing, and soon they could see its flashing lights and finally the dark body of it, a big double-rotor police gunship floating slowly along the street above the buildings.

"Do not panic," its bullhorn blared deafeningly. "This is the police. The situation is under control. We regret the inconvenience. Do not panic."

It passed directly overhead and on behind them, the sound of its rotors and its announcement Dopplering slightly.

"God panic you and who begot you!" said the bus driver, and a number of people laughed.

The discussions got louder and there was laughter from the back of the bus. The driver sighed, opened the door, turned off the ignition, and struggled into a more comfortable position in his cramped seat.

"May you wake to happiness," he said at large, and closed his eyes.

"And you to happiness," said a man standing next to Blaine reflexively.

The bus got gradually quieter. A few more people got off, and others seemed to be going to sleep, some in their seats and a few standing up. The remaining conversation was sporadic and quiet. Ahead of them the street was a vast parking lot, some riders leaning on their cars and smoking, others listening to their radios, many sleeping, two men arguing and waving their arms. A few motorcycles with four and five riders puttered along the sidewalks, shrill horns beeping to clear pedestrians out of their way. Blaine was stupefied with fatigue. He scrutinized the street as best he could between the people standing around him.

Half a block up, a small, lighted sign said "Hotel" in Arabic, English, French, and pre/postliteracy iconography, and an arrow pointed into an alley.

It took Blaine a surprisingly long time to excuse himself the one meter to the bus door past five or six half-sleeping men, and then about the same amount of time to jostle through the people on the sidewalk to the alley. While he was doing it another helicopter boomed along the street, its sweeping searchlight hazed by smog.

The alley opened next to a tiny, bright booth selling bootleg CDs, its wares covering every inch of wall space as well as the insides of metal shutters swung open against the wall of the street. It blared sinuous Arabic rock & roll into the murky darkness. On the other side of the alley an old man sat on a stool in front of a square wooden tray piled with bread and *ta'amiyeh,* the Egyptian version of *falafel.* Next to him, in a shadowy corner, a beggar girl of perhaps ten or eleven in a filthy headscarf and long dress held a sleeping baby.

As Blaine approached, two young women in tight jeans, the latest style of optical-rejection jackets, and slick, boy-short hair came out of the alley; they were followed by a robed peasant leading a bleating goat by its ear. The alley floor was dirt, mounded here and there with filth that had been swept away from the doors of the shops on either side. There was a coffeehouse, a shallow, tiled alcove with tiny aluminum tables where men in *gelabiyah*s and Western clothes drank from tiny cups and smoked *argila*s; its lights made a faint radiance around it in the smog. Beyond that the alley was full of smoky darkness, quiet, and not too crowded, partly roofed by awnings and washing hanging between the buildings. Blaine almost missed the "Riyadh Hotel" sign above a narrow metal double door, one half of which was open. Within was a dim, whitewashed stairwell where an old man in a skullcap and dirty *gelabiyah* slept on his side on some sheets of cardboard, using his hand as a pillow. The stairs led to a narrow second-story hall illuminated by bare ceiling bulbs a little hazed by smog. They dimmed momentarily as he went down the hall. The stairs continued upward at the end of the hall, and next to them was a small wooden table where two men were playing cards.

Blaine stopped at the table. "Peace be upon you."

"And upon you peace," the two men said. "Welcome, welcome," one of them added, a wheezy, bespectacled fat man whose shirt was unbuttoned at the bottom over his hairy stomach. "Welcome, welcome."

"Is this the Hotel Riyadh? I would like a room."

The fat man murmured polite, pious expressions. "One hundred dollars for the night," he added.

Blaine had lived in the Middle East long enough to manage outraged protestations and expostulations bordering on the rude even in his fatigued condition. Among other things, if he didn't bargain, the proprietor—whom the other man called Abu Yusef—would feel uncomfortable, as if Blaine had cheated him in some way. As it turned out, payment in U.S. dollars required a black market premium, since use of national currencies other than the worthless Egyptian pound was illegal; he could save money by paying in private currency. His cause was also helped by the fact that the hallway bulbs dimmed all the way out halfway through the negotiation, leaving them in pitch darkness and allowing Blaine to rail against hotels that provided no backup power for their guests. In the end the lights went back on and Blaine had a room for 20 American Express Value Units, which his wallet bank terminal printed out in scrip on a square of bond paper Abu Yusef handed him.

Abu Yusef led him up two flights of whitewashed stairwell, wheezing and puffing and smelling of sweat and garlic. In the narrow fourth-floor hall an old man and a young man squatted against the wall and smoked hand-rolled cigarettes outside a slightly open door through which could be heard the sounds of babies, women, and children.

"Please come in," the old man said, gesturing at his door. "We're honored."

Blaine and Abu Yusef declined politely, as was proper, and Abu Yusef unlocked a room two doors down.

It was small, the walls whitewashed, the floor worn linoleum. A shower curtain stretched across one end hid a toilet, washbowl, and shower nozzle over a floor drain. The room had a window, the upper half of which opened on the alley, the lower half fitted with an Indian-manufactured hand-cranked smog filter. Under the window was a bed with a smog-yellowed spread. A vintage electric fan, which Abu Yusef turned on with a flourish, stood on a tiny, much-painted bureau, next to an empty plastic bottle standing on its mouth in the hollow of a dented hubcap.

"This is what?" Blaine asked, gesturing at the bottle and hubcap.

"May evil stay far from your presence, but in Cairo we sometimes have small earthquake tremors, God forfend. Not often," Abu Yusef reassured him. "But if, God forfend, your presence should hear this bottle fall down and make a noise, if you would please run out into the street without even bothering to put on your clothes, if you are sleeping or in the shower. You will find many others in the street wearing nothing more than what God gave them should such a thing happen, God forfend."

After he had left, through the closed door Blaine heard him gently scolding the old man. "Father, haven't I asked you not to smoke in the hall? This is a hotel, not a street."

The sounds of music, voices, and traffic were loud even on the fourth floor, but the room was too stuffy with the window closed, especially after another brownout killed the fan, so Blaine lay and listened, and fell asleep not long after 2 A.M.

Despite his exhaustion, or perhaps because of it, he had uneasy dreams. In one the beggar girl he had seen on the alley corner seemed to watch him intently from her shadows, while in his ears, echoing down the dark, endless, but now strangely deserted streets of Cairo, came a whispering voice, speaking words he was unable to understand.

4

A rooster crowing woke him early next morning, and for a second he thought he was back in the house in the Jordan Valley, but when he opened his eyes he saw hazy light at the hotel window and the sound of the city came to him.

The crow came again. Blaine sat up and looked out the window, smelling the burning-rubber tang of smog. As much of the sky as he could see between the cracked and dirty buildings rising around him was filled with a thick, bright haze.

On the roof of the dilapidated three-story brick building four meters across the alley from him, a few chickens pecked in trash and rubble next to a leaning shack cobbled of scrap wood, flattened metal cans, and cut plastic containers. Two goats bleated nearby, tethered to rusty reinforcing bars that thrust out of the roof; a small child sat near them pouring handfuls of dirt onto its bare legs. On the roof of the building beyond was another shack, with a vegetable garden, two lean-tos and two tents, chickens, dogs, a few bales of hay, and some dilapidated chairs set among the detritus of decayed construction; an old woman in a black *gelabiyah* was hanging up washing. Aged five- and six-story buildings rose beyond these, the fault line cracks running through their weathered, discolored brick making them look like natural rock cliffs pierced by glassless windows, hung with laundry, and plastered with commercial signs and posters. There were other traces of earthquake damage too: a rough scaffolding of telephone pole–sized timbers was lashed across the alley at second-story height nearby, bracing the cracked and leaning walls of two opposite buildings.

A big, black VTOL limousine passed 50 meters overhead with a hooting roar. A young woman in a ragged dress came out of the shack on the nearest roof and swept up the child in her arms, scolding, sending chickens flapping and scurrying out of her way. Blaine withdrew from the window lest the woman or her relatives think he was watching her.

The fan was going again. Blaine stretched and went around the shower curtain, turned on the shower. Only a distant gurgling came out. After waiting a few minutes in vain he put on some clothes and went downstairs.

Abu Yusef was still at the table in the hall, wearing the same clothes and looking no more or less sleepy than he had at 1 A.M. After they had exchanged pleasantries, Blaine told him there was no water in his room.

"The pressure is low," said Abu Yusef sagaciously. "I will bring you some."

"If you please, God keep you. I'm going out for breakfast."

The old man Blaine had seen sleeping in the stairwell the night before was now very slowly and methodically sweeping it out, leaning over his worn broom as if watching shortsightedly for dirt. A shower of flowery morning greetings came from his toothless mouth as Blaine passed. Two dark, ragged men sat in the street doorway of the hotel; they jumped up and apologized when Blaine spoke to them. The alley was crowded; Blaine had to let a man riding a donkey and a vendor wrestling a pushcart go by before he stepped out. Then he was moving at the slow speed of the crowd, receiving the close, unself-conscious jostling he had gotten used to in Middle Eastern cities, trying to keep his feet out of piles of trash and the water the shopkeepers sprayed to keep down the dust. He got a few curious glances, but his body language was Arab, and few people stared.

It was still early and the acrid air of the alley was pleasantly cool and a little damp. The oceanic voice of the city was pierced by hawkers calling their wares and the distant, constant honking of cars. Arabic music undulated from a loudspeaker. A man and his son sat on chairs outside a shop, its awning hung with plastic tubs of all sizes and colors; in the next shop ducks and chickens clucked crowded in stacked wooden cages; nearby, a vendor had stopped his pushcart piled with tiny green lemons; a man passed carrying on his head a rattan basket piled with loaves of bread; an old woman in black robes lay asleep in the doorway of a shop that had not yet opened, her head on a plastic bag full of odds and ends, her grimy face puckered as if she dreamed of her hard life. There were fruit-sellers, tiny shops selling canned goods and every kind of household item, beggars in rags sitting exhaustedly against the walls, their lips moving in mumbled blessings and entreatries, women in robes and headscarves, peasants in *gelabiyahs*, people wearing Western clothes. A robed man on a sputtering motorcycle with a front cart five times its size hollered out as he rode at walking speed through the crowd: "Move aside, sir! Move aside, grandfather! Move aside, mister! Move aside, boss!"

At the main street Blaine emerged into an even greater crowd of people, and beyond the sidewalk a laneless glut of traffic moved at a stop-and-go pace under the superstructure from which bundled resin-plastic water pipes and electric cables branched off overhead to feed the cracked, dirty, sign-plastered buildings. Clouds of blue exhaust rose in the sun-blinded smog, making Blaine's lungs labor, scraping his throat raw. A sooty bus labored by, full to bursting and listing heavily from the mass of people holding on to the outside by windows and doors. A helicopter chopped by above.

Blaine jostled his way to the alley corner where the grizzled old man was still sitting behind his tray of bread and *ta'amiyeh*. His shaking, three-fingered hands—mutations of some ecological disaster lost in the sea of disasters that was Cairo—wrapped Blaine's food in newspaper and accepted one of the fractional AmExVUs Blaine had printed before leaving his room. The beggar girl still sat in a recess of the wall behind him, face hidden by her dirty scarf, but in the daylight looking older, perhaps fifteen or sixteen, and so conceivably the mother of the skinny, dirty baby that cried on her knee.

Something made him want to look at her—maybe the dream he had had last night. Perhaps to have an excuse to study her, Blaine held out a small scrip.

She took it slowly and very carefully, as if to be sure she didn't touch his hand with her small, dirty one. She said nothing; underneath the scarf dark eyes and a twisted mouth were quickly hidden. Her baby cried and she bounced it mechanically on her knee.

———

Back at the Riyadh Hotel Abu Yusef said: "I brought you some water. It is in your room."

"Thank you. Abu Yusef, is there a video store nearby?"

"Not so nearby. I will get a boy to go for you. There is a shop with all the latest American films."

"I'm looking for Egyptian films. Not animated films, but real ones. Featuring an actress name Aida."

Abu Yusef's fat, nearsighted face split in a wide grin that showed a lower front tooth missing. "Do they know Aida in America?"

"No. But I am interested in her. I have come to Cairo to meet her," he added, surprising himself.

Abu Yusef grinned even more widely. "Americans are no different from Egyptians, it seems. No one can meet such actresses, darling. Can you meet movie actresses in America? Neither can you meet them in Egypt. Every man in the Arab world wants to meet Aida. Not one of them can do so. People like that are surrounded by guards, police, officials, authorities, every kind of assistant, secretary, servant, and attendant. They live in great villas in neighborhoods where only rich people are permitted. Millionaires and billionaires vie to sit at the same table with such actresses, darling. So if you came to Egypt to meet Aida, you have wasted your time. But I can get you all the films of her you want. And I will send you to see the Pyramids. Please consider this hotel your home in Egypt. Anything you want, tell me. God send his contentment upon you."

Two buckets of water sat inside the door of Blaine's room. Bathing with two buckets of water requires concentration. But sitting on his bed afterward and drying his hair with the room's small, thin towel Blaine felt a little foolish, as if Abu Yusef's lecture had knocked some sense into him. Here he was in Cairo, but he had given no thought to what would happen next. He had come to find Aida but instead had found 35 million other people whose city was about to collapse under their weight, and of course, as Abu Yusef had said, his chances of meeting the actress were just about exactly zero.

It struck him again that the trouble he had had in Kraima, which seemed so far away now in the real city of Cairo, could have been just plain and simple nightmares and hallucinations with no particular meaning, though the memory of Buthaina lying in his garden still made his palms sweat and his heart speed up. Yet he had had no lucid dreams last night or the night before. Perhaps now that he had knocked off the herbs and taken a change of scenery the whole thing would clear up on its own. Perhaps he had unwittingly taken Haseeb Al Rahman's advice after all.

He was eating his bread and *ta'amiyeh* along with a prophylactic antibiotic pill when there was knock at the door. It was a thin, polite, hook-nosed young man with oiled black hair, a large Adam's apple, and the shaved beginnings of a beard: Yusef, the son of the hotel proprietor. He held out to Blaine a ROM chip.

Blaine printed scrip for him, including a tip, which Yusef protested that he couldn't accept, but then accepted, and left. There were a dozen features on the chip, none of them digital simulations: seven movies, three plays, and two Ramadan song-and-dance presentations, all dating from the past five years.

An ashen stink that had been growing at the edge of Blaine's attention made him look up at the window. The bright haze outside had turned dull gray, as if with an impending storm. But it wasn't a storm, he saw when he got up and looked out; instead, the pale morning smog had been thickened with a dense cloud of atmospheric filth. The alley and all the air between the buildings was hazed with soot, and the shirtsleeve he leaned on the windowsill was suddenly powdered with tiny black dots. Most everyone in the alley seemed to have gone indoors; the few stragglers wore grimy filter masks or rags over their mouths; a few wore long smog cloaks with full-face breathing apparatuses. The stinking air was hot and close, seeming to muffle the faraway sounds of cars and music like a shower of hot black snow, and a lungful of it made him cough violently.

Blaine shut the window and turned the crank on the Indian smog filter to wind a ratcheted spring. He poured half a liter of water he hadn't used for his bath into a reservoir at the top, replaced the gauzy paper filter, and turned the spring-driven fan to High. The air the fan drew in through the damp filter still smelled a little of rotten eggs, but it was breathable. As the noon call to prayer echoed outside, muffled by the closed window and the whir of the filter, he leaned against his bed pillow, plugged the specs into his palmtop, and slipped in the Aida chip.

—•—

He was still watching when the call to prayer came again; he took off his specs disorientedly. The room was nearly dark. He got up and opened the window. The air outside was smoky, haloing the bright light from the coffee shop down the alley, but breathable. He left the window open on the sounds of traffic and music, and put on the specs again.

He had watched four of the movies in a row. They were all cheap, thinly plotted, and sensational, but the actress Aida had held him spellbound. It wasn't only that she seemed at times nearly supernaturally beautiful; there was something compelling about her, a desperation that ran far deeper than the sordid scenes she played, an intensity and vulnerability that made him watch her almost fearfully, as if she might go mad right on-screen. And she was so clearly Buthaina that his doubts had left him again in an avalanche of exhilaration and fear before the first film was half over, so that without taking time to puzzle it out he had sat riveted to the specs in the intense hope that he could divine something about Buthaina, understand how and why she could have appeared to him in dream and waking, by watching the actress Aida as a young village girl married off to a mentally unbalanced wife-beater; as a dancer in a down-and-out Cairo street carnival, undulating and leaping in a tattered red dress worn over a pair of striped pants; as a teenage mother sinking into the desperate, chaotic poverty of Cairo, begging near the *ta'amiyeh* stand of an old man who occasionally fed her—

The call to prayer was spreading its cool, vast serenity in the darkness outside the window, fading in waves of echoes from the dozens of minaret loudspeakers scattered over Cairo's miles of concrete canyons. Blaine sat up suddenly.

He ran the film he was watching backward, ran it forward again, then again.

In the film—*The Stain of Blood*—the beggar girl sat in the recess of a wall on a traffic-choked street, holding her skinny, crying baby. The old man with the *ta'amiyeh* stand had a patchy, dirty-white beard and three fingers on each hand—

Blaine took off his specs and stood up. Of course there must be such scenes of misery on every street corner in Cairo, he told himself, and Aida's face was a common Egyptian type—

He went down the stairs, resisting the urge to run, past a dozing Abu Yusef and out of the hotel, along the alley among the pedestrians and a few evening hawkers selling broiled corn, peanuts, and hot tea.

The girl and her baby and the old *ta'amiyeh* man were gone. Blaine stared at the stained, dirty wall and pavement where they had been, then up and down the main street. He walked a hundred meters in either direction through the crowds, through shadows and the bright lights of the shops. The girl and the old man and the baby were nowhere to be seen.

He walked uneasily back to the Riyadh Hotel and watched the rest of *The Stain of Blood*.

The winter rains came and the beggar girl had no place to sleep but on the streets. The owner of a local restaurant began pestering her, offering her money for sexual favors. She refused, but soon her baby got sick, and in desperation she went to the man's house. Her baby died in the next room while he was having his way with her. The girl went mad and, screaming, ran out into the street, where she was hit by a speeding truck, her beautiful corpse rolling into a heap of refuse in the gutter.

The high melodrama completed and the credits rolling over a freeze frame of the beggar girl's dead face to overblown music, Blaine found himself shaking. For a moment he had been back in his garden in Kraima, listening to Buthaina's screams—

He shook off that memory, but he couldn't shake off the conviction, creeping over him now, that the beggar girl on the street corner who had disturbed him with her familiarity was the same as the girl in the film, the same as Aida, the same as Buthaina. He tried to recall every detail of the beggar—her eyes, her face under the scarf and layers of filth, her figure in the shapeless, greasy dress, her hands holding the baby on her knee, reaching out to take his alms. . . .

He skipped through *The Stain of Blood* twice more, playing some parts over and over, watching intensely as the beggar girl made her descent into misery and madness, as if trying to unlock a secret hidden in the tawdry melodrama. He went down to the alley corner again. It was still empty. He fell asleep exhausted sometime after midnight.

That night he dreamed he was lying in his bed in the hotel, the thin window curtain lifting in a cool night breeze to let the silver, silent light of a half-moon puddle on the floor, when there was a scream from the street insane with pain and terror. Blaine leapt out of bed, rubbing his eyes to get them open. The night was quiet, with no more than the distant sounds of car horns, the distant laughter of pedestrians, music from a shop. Yet he knew that scream, knew the throat that had made it.

He struggled into his clothes, ran downstairs again past the dozing Abu Yusef, out into the alley. Only a few people walked there. There were no more screams. Blaine ran to the corner, toward the noise and smell of cars, still rubbing sleep out of his eyes. In the passing headlights the corner was empty, dirty, exhausted.

Blaine felt drained next morning when he woke up to the bright haze and early noises of the city. Abu Yusef had left two buckets of water outside his door; he washed and dressed, then went down the alley to the corner. Against the wall where the *ta'amiyeh* man and beggar girl had been a peasant woman now sat behind a wooden tray of stunted and spotted zucchini, which she was rearranging, putting the best ones on top.

"Forty piasters for a kilo,"she said, giving Blaine a gap-toothed grin.

When Blaine came back in from a breakfast of fava beans, olives, tomatoes, and flat bread, Abu Yusef was sitting at his table with a tiny disposable radio pressed to his ear. They exchanged polite morning greetings, but as Blaine was about to climb the stairs, Abu Yusef said: "Mr. Ramsey."

"Yes?"

Abu Yusef was holding the radio in his fat hand now. "Have you listened to the news, Mr. Ramsey?"

"No."

"The Western countries say they will not give aid to Egypt to repair the damage from the *zilzal*, the earthquake tremors."

"Impossible! Why not?"

"They say we have too many children. And as you can see"—he spread his hands to take in the city—"they are right. But . . ."

"Perhaps it's a bluff. Perhaps they are using it to bargain with Egypt over birth control measures."

"That is what some people are saying."

"I hope it is true, God willing."

He climbed the stairs to his room. The experts were predicting a major quake in the Cairo area, he knew. Though what kind of aid could keep the clapboard and tottering rubble of Cairo from collapsing on itself in such an event, he couldn't imagine.

All the more reason to hurry up and do what he had come to Egypt to do.

He clipped his palmtop's playing card–sized antenna onto the frame of his room's open window, where it whirred, adjusting to the narrow slice of sky visible from the alley. The net was technically illegal here, since it couldn't be censored, but the black market was so near the surface in Egypt it was often hard to tell it from the legal market. He climbed a satellite to his server in Beirut and got into virtual Cairo within two minutes.

The local net—servers physically in Cairo and those elsewhere with Cairo topics—was extensive, and full of psychologically hot liquor commercials. Alcoholic beverages were now virtually illegal in Europe and the U.S., so the liquor companies targeted most of their advertising at the Third World. The Images hit Blaine with their yearning and mystery: a black, horned skyscraper piercing a stormy urban skyline; a man swimming in a river that wound down miles of flat delta to a distant city under vast, blowing art-deco clouds; a beautiful naked woman with penis, horns, and hooves. When he looked up from those vast, cool Western fantasies his peasant surroundings were left seeming dirty, narrow, and sordid. He had a momentary urge to buy a drink.

He pulled a search agent out of his palmtop and filled out its form with a request for information on Aida. When he was satisfied with his description and had specified the net tolls the agent was authorized to pay, he uploaded it.

Hot, smoky mid-morning air wafted into his window along with the clucking of chickens and the more distant sounds of car horns and music, the calls of hawkers four floors down. Blaine squinted out over the baking housetops and roof dwellings, the alley a slash of relative coolness below him. For some reason he felt uneasy, unable to shake off the sense of heavy weather marching toward the sun's patch of dazzling brightness in the smog; to his Image-digger's inward senses there seemed a watchfulness in the nearly windless air, like the vague pressure before a storm. Perhaps it was just a sensation of disturbance from the city around him, where 35 million people perched precariously on the lip of chaos. The animals on the nearby rooftops seemed to feel it too; the goats were bleating and pulling desperately on their tethers, the chickens screeching, scurrying frantically in all directions, treading on each other and beating their useless wings.

Blaine's netphone link rang. The stats showed a Cairo address.

He knew no one in Cairo. He fanned the tiny screen and answered.

A pixeled face filled the screen in fish-eye perspective, ogling blindly, not seeing him; Blaine's camera function was turned off. It was the face of a dark young Egyptian man, dirty and sweat-streaked. A baby was crying in the background.

"*Salamu 'aleikum,*" the young man said hesitantly.

"*'Aleikum es salam,*" said Blaine. There was the second's lag bespeaking satellite net link; the call was going through Blaine's server in Beirut. There seemed to be an infrastructure glitch or bottleneck somewhere: though he was just across town, the young man's voice was garbled, his face freezing and jerking as digitized speech packages got lost or delayed over the link.

"I hope your presence does not mind my calling. I found your agent searching my files. What a beautiful piece of software! It must be a new American invention, yes? It erased itself when I tried to copy it. May I ask your presence's name?" The young man licked his lips and passed a work-gnarled hand over his face half-dazedly. Blaine saw now that he was thin, his cheeks sunken.

Blaine hesitated, then turned on his camera. The young man's weak eyes focused on him. "I'm Blaine Ramsey." If the agent had searched the young man's files long enough to be detected, they must have something to do with Aida.

"Dr. Ramsey, welcome, welcome," said the young man excitedly. "You are American, yes? Your Arabic is very good. Are you speaking from America?"

"I'm in Cairo."

"In Cairo! Welcome, welcome, Dr. Ramsey! I am 'Abdeen

Mohendis. I have my Ph.D. in computer engineering from Cairo University. I am very much in love with the new agents coming from America. Your agent is a new product from America, is it not?"

"It is."

"Is it Yava- or Intelagent-based?" asked the young man with breathless excitement.

"I'm sorry, I'm afraid I don't know."

Above the sound of the baby a faint cry came from behind the young man on Blaine's screen; it sounded like a woman's voice.

The young man looked off-camera. "Excuse me," he said, and the palmtop got put down. Blaine found himself looking at a bare concrete ceiling streaked with water damage. He could hear the young man's voice and someone else's off-camera.

The young man came back. His eyes looked haunted. "I'm sorry to take up your presence's time," he said. "But if you need a computer expert, I am available for employment. I myself wrote the code that detected your agent! This server"—he waved toward the screen—"is a disposable IBM palmtop I found in a Dumpster behind the Ibis Hotel in Tahrir Square: I opened its case without triggering the security system; I myself built a solar power source to replace its battery. I make a small income providing access to the local net through this machine, but—"

"Your accomplishments are very impressive, God give you increase," said Blaine. "But my immediate interest— what my agent was searching for was information on the Egyptian actress Aida."

"I know everything about her!" said the young man with almost frenzied excitement. "She is a subject of interest to my subscribers, and so I have constructed a site devoted to her on this server, based on enormous research, many discussions with her intimates. Her real name is Mona Ghali. She is a magnificent Egyptian treasure!"

"What do you know about her?"

"I know everything about her, Dr. Ramsey! Her mother was Laila Sharifa, a well-known dancer of twenty or thirty years back. She worked in the Cairo theater and she caught the eye of a visiting Saudi billionaire, who married her. She was still pregnant with their first child when the Saudi divorced her. She came back to Cairo and gave birth to Mona Ghali. She raised Mona in the theater business. But Laila Sharifa died in her late thirties—amid rumors of scandal—when Mona was only twelve years old, and Mona was taken into the home of Abdullah Ghais, the famous film producer. He began using her in his films. This was fifteen years ago; he gave her the stage name Aida, and she has used it ever since."

"And this producer, this Abdullah Ghais, is still her mentor?"

"No, he died many years ago, not long after he took her in. She has her agents, of course, and her lawyers and accountants and cronies." In the background there was another weak cry, and the crying of the baby intensified. "But Dr. Ramsey," the young man burst out desperately, "if you need assistance in this or any other matter, or if you need computer assistance, or inexpensive access to the net, or any other of a hundred services—"

A clatter next to Blaine made him jump, and he looked around to see what it was. He was still trying to figure it out when something uncanny happened. The young man's fisheye face on the screen got a look of panic, and Blaine's room began to rattle. The plastic bottle that had fallen from the hubcap on the bureau jittered on the floor. Distant thunder echoed outside his window.

Then it was over. For a single second the city of Cairo was silent, its silence otherworldly, as if the thick, hot daylight was an amber into which it had fallen, stilling all movement.

But then there were screams, shouts from the people in the alley below, a cacophonous swell of honking from the street, and the crying of babies and children. People were pouring into the alley from all the buildings, and it seemed to Blaine that they were both crying out with fear and shouting with joy that this time the earthquake had just been a tremor. He looked at his palmtop screen, but it showed only a still of 'Abdeen Mohendis's panicked face and a text message about remote server failure.

Down in the alley people were swirling, talking excitedly, shouting; two men embraced each other; others plastered cell phones to their ears; a vendor was standing in an attitude of prayer behind his pushcart in the shade of the alley wall, hands and eyes lifted, lips moving; a stout woman in a black robe and headscarf had put down her shopping bags and was shouting blessings over the crowd and praising God.

There was a hammering at Blaine's door.

"Are you well?" asked the old man from the room next door. His son stood next to him and they both eyed Blaine anxiously and curiously. "Not hurt, God forbid?" Three or four round-eyed, curly-haired children hung on their father's and grandfather's legs, and seemed not at all affected by the nearness of disaster: they giggled and looked with saucy curiosity up at Blaine.

"Praise be to God—," Blaine started.

Abu Yusef came huffing heavily around the corner of the stairs, sweat dripping from his panicked face. "May evil stay far from all of you!" he shouted wheezingly. "Father! Brother! What's wrong with you? Is anyone hurt, God forbid? Not thus, children, not thus!" he shouted angrily as they ran from him, giggling. "Don't play at such a time!"

It took them a few minutes of loud expostulation to convince him that no one was hurt and that all was well, and then he puffed back downstairs to see to his other guests, muttering protective blessings upon everyone and upon his "destroyed hotel."

5

Blaine stayed in the hall a few more minutes exchanging polite words with his neighbors, then went back into his room. There were distant sirens. An excited group of men, a few pressing tiny radios to their ears, others talking and gesturing loudly, stood outside the coffee house; the pedestrians in the alley seemed to be hurrying this way and that nervously.

His heart galloping in what seemed to be a delayed reaction to the tremor, he pulled up a search agent on his palmtop, programmed it to prepare a report on the likelihood of major earthquakes in Cairo. Ridiculous to trust your life to these senseless AI things, he thought as he uploaded it to the net; but nowadays it was the only way you could find out anything, search through the massive information overload on the net and everywhere else.

An icon on his palmtop screen showed that his previous agent had assembled a report on the results of its Aida search. When he had calmed down a little, looking out his window into the alley and breathing deeply, he put on his specs and opened the report.

The source list showed a thousand hits: ads, fan sites, publicity sites, pay movies, home videos featuring Aida simulations, fundamentalist diatribes against the pandering of sin in modern films, chat topics. The report itself was lengthy, marginally grammatical, and uninformative—or rather, overinformative. It listed no fewer than 31 reported home addresses, 49 Cairo places of entertainment she reportedly frequented, 104 reputed associates, and went on in that vein until Blaine realized that he was no closer to figuring out who she was or how to find her than he had been before.

He telephoned Karachi, Pakistan. Haseeb System answered.

"Where's Haseeb?"

"He's not home; can I take a message?"

"You've been taking messages for a week." And when the machine paused, trying to compute the significance of this true statement: "Have you given Haseeb my messages?"

"I've cued them, but he hasn't picked them up yet."

"Great. Look, I have to talk to him. You have search protocols, right? For when you have to find him in emergencies?"

Below the simulated face text appeared: "Please say, in the following order: 'political,' 'protocol,' 'portable.' "

"Political, protocol, portable," Blaine said impatiently, to let the machine benchmark his voice.

"Haseeb has disabled the search protocols," it answered his question.

"I've got to talk to him."

"Cool off your jets, party-boy," the AI said with sudden animation, then lapsed back into woodenness. "He hasn't picked up his messages in twenty-two days."

"Twenty-two—But where is he?"

"I don't know. Can I help you with something, eh?"

"Not unless you can find an Egyptian movie star named Aida," said Blaine in frustration.

Haseeb System paused for a second. "She's making a film called *Days of Sunlight and Rain* at Nile Studios in Cairo, Egypt."

"What? How do you know that?"

"Haseeb indexed it."

"But what—how would he know that? Where would he—?"

Haseeb System got the thoughtful look bespeaking heavy language processing.

After a round of fruitless questions and language comprehension snafus Blaine disconnected and sat back on his bed, baffled. Where could Haseeb have gone without telling his System, and why had he disabled its search protocols? Even more puzzling, how would he know about an Egyptian movie actress named Aida? Could he have dreamed her all the way out in Karachi? he wondered with just a little chill of fear. No, that was impossible; but it *was* possible that one of Haseeb's other protégés, someone working in the Middle East, had dreamed her and told Haseeb about her. Yes, that had to be it. Who was it? Blaine wondered. He would give a lot to talk to that person right about now.

❧

"I'm scouting local talent to use in psychologically active commercials," Blaine said to the jerky AI system that answered Nile Studios' telephone. He tried to make his accent broad and casual, obviously American. He was probably violating Icon regulations about misrepresenting his position; he had to hope Nile Studios wouldn't do an active check with Los Angeles.

"I'm sorry," said the AI in Arabic, unable to process his voice. Below her face a form appeared. He clicked the items that would let him make an appointment with someone in the Talent Department, leaving the box labeled "Confirmation Code" blank.

"Please specify your confirmation code," said the AI, which was having trouble lip-synching her words.

Blaine maintained radio silence, and after a minute found himself looking at Nile Studios' logo of sunset on the Pyramids.

He stared at it blankly. His only possible source of an Icon confirmation code was Jenny Chan, but he had no real excuse to request one. On the other hand, last time he had called she had done what he wanted without asking questions. And maybe he could come up with an innocent, touristy cover story—like that he wanted to see the inside of Egypt's famous, "Hollywood of the Orient" Third World film industry.

There was a diffident knock on the door. It was Yusef, carrying a tray with a steaming plate of *koshary*—layered macaroni noodles, tomato sauce, lentils, and fried onions—with bread and yogurt, a dinner made by Im Yusef, his mother. Blaine looked at the window and saw with surprise that it was dark.

Yusef firmly refused all payment for the dinner, which he explained was sent with the blessings of Abu Yusef and an apology that Mr. Ramsey's visit to Egypt should have been ruined by the unfortunate events of this afternoon. After this speech, he asked how Blaine had liked the Aida chip he had brought him.

"Are you interested in Aida?" Blaine asked him, starting to eat.

"Of course; everyone is," said Yusef. "A friend of mine at school, Marwan, his father is a journalist—Latif Nezam, have you heard of him? He wrote some articles about Aida for *Al Dustour*, so he had to learn all about her. The real stuff, not the stuff the studios put out. He told Marwan and me all about her."

"Really? What did he say?"

"Well, she's from a village in Upper Egypt, along the Nile. Her parents were peasant farmers, fellahin. They both died of bilharzia by the time she was twelve, and she came to Cairo to stay with an aunt, her only relative. But she was so beautiful that the aunt's husband began taking an interest in her, and the aunt threw her into the street without a piaster. She almost died on the street, but then she found a job as a dancer in a *mulid* carnival, and when she was in her early teens the famous film producer Abdullah Ghais chanced to see her dancing when he was passing in his limousine. He made his chauffeur stop and pick her up right then and there, and he put her in his next film. He died a year after that—suicide, they say, though the newspapers said it was an accidental overdose of sleeping medicine—but by that time she was already a star. She has always been a little crazy, but she has started to go really unstable recently, Marwan's father told us: in the last few months she has become so addicted to drugs that the studios can hardly handle her, and she can hardly act."

Blaine finished Im Yusef's excellent dinner, then called Los Angeles. Jenny Chan's secretary said she had gone home for the day. He dialed her home priority number. It took six rings for her to answer, blinking sleep out of her eyes and holding a robe at her throat, pale hair tumbled over her shoulders. Fresh from the womb of sleep she looked slight and vulnerable. Her voice was husky. "Hello?"

"Jenny."

"Blaine. Damn it." She sighed heavily, squinting at the screen. "How you, baby? Your R&R going OK?"

"Yeah. I'm in Cairo."

He didn't know what reaction he had expected; still, it was odd. Shock came slowly into her eyes and the knuckles of the hand at her throat seemed to whiten. "What?"

"I'm in Cairo."

"Oh, God, Blaine," she whispered, and he thought for a moment she was going to faint.

"Jenny? What's the matter? Jenny, you OK?"

"What—what're you doing in Cairo?" He could see her trying to compose herself. "I thought you said—"

"R&R, Jenny, like I told you. Always wanted to see the dump. Why? What's the matter?"

She was studying him hard, as if trying to gauge something through the digital connection, her face almost black and white in the dimness of her bedroom. "Are you OK? You look OK. Haven't been digging in Cairo, have you, baby? Just R&R, right?"

"Yeah, just R&R. Right." He was watching her, trying to figure out what was wrong.

Her eyes were abstracted, as if she was thinking fast. "You been in touch with any of the Cairo diggers?"

"No, I haven't seen anyone. Where are they?"

"At the Nile Meridien. Where you staying?"

"Nowhere you'd recognize." He paused. This wasn't going the way he had anticipated. "Jenny, I need some help out here."

"Maybe we can help each other."

He studied her, confused. She didn't seem to mean romance; the look on her face was business now, as if she had thought her way through something in a hurry.

"What do you need?" she asked.

He told her, staying vague on exactly what he wanted with Nile Studios.

When he was done she nodded. She didn't ask any of the questions he'd been afraid she would ask. Instead she said: "You got your dream kit with you?"

"Yeah, I got it." After years in the business he never traveled without it.

"Then technically you're digging, could we say?"

He took a breath. "We could. Jenny, what's going on?"

"Don't ask me, Blaine." She looked him straight in the eyes finally, and it was a strange look; whether guilt, anxiety, or the same old crush, he couldn't tell, but somehow an *anguished* look. "I'll give you confirmation into this Nile Studios. But listen to me. In exchange, you have to do something for me. Right?"

"Right."

"Get into the Nile Meridien; we have an account there, and security arrangements in case of politico problems, which you may see if this earthquake aid thing blows sour. Got that?"

"OK."

"Number two: if anybody asks, you're on assignment digging for Icon. OK?"

"OK."

"Number three, and this is important. This is important." He thought her voice shook a little, or maybe it was just a warble on the long-distance feed. Her face was business-hard and a little flushed, a stray strand of hair hanging along her cheek. "*Under no circumstances are you to dig dream in Cairo.* That's a priority directive, got it?"

"Yeah, I guess. But—"

"Listen to me, Blaine. I can't explain right now, baby, but it's important. You have to promise me that you'll say you're digging but that *you won't dig.* Don't even ask what it's about. You just have to take my word."

"OK."

"You won't dig?"

"I won't dig." The AI-organized recording of Haseeb had already ordered him off the herbs; and anyway, his main interest now was getting into Nile Studios.

"And this is just between you and me? Nobody hears about it?"

"Scout's honor."

Jenny studied him tensely for a minute and then seemed to relax. "OK. You do this for me and I'll give you— whatever you want." She grinned. "Hopefully I'll be able to explain later. Open a download window and I'll feed you a conf code right now."

When she had hung up and he had the code, Blaine sat staring at the long-distance carrier's logo. Whatever was up had the sophisticated, world-weary, business-hard Ms. Chan spooked, and that Blaine thought, was not an easy thing to do. What could it be? Had some Cairo diggers seen the things Blaine had seen, dreamed the things he had dreamed? But he had cognized Aida in the Jordan Valley, five hundred kilometers away, in a completely different neurosocial region. No Image he had ever heard of had a geographical reach like that. And yet why would Jenny order him not to dig dream in Cairo? And at the same time why did she want him to give out that he *was* digging?

With the Icon confirmation code it took about two minutes for Nile Studios' clunky AI to make him an appointment with a Mouhsin 'Abdel Halim of the Talent Department, for eight o'clock the next morning.

—

There was a knock on the door. It was Yusef, returning to take away his dinner tray.

"Yusef, do you know where Nile Studios is?" asked Blaine.

"Of course; on the Avenue of the Pyramids in Giza, at the New City of the Arts."

"God's contentment upon you, could you ask your father to arrange a car to take me there early tomorrow morning?" asked Blaine.

"Of course," murmured Yusef, turning to go. "Good health," he said, referring to the dinner.

"Upon your heart," Blaine replied properly.

When he was gone, Blaine got on the net and clicked the addresses of a couple of Icon diggers he had heard through the grapevine were assigned to Cairo. None of them answered; he left messages.

Yusef knocked and stuck his head in to tell Blaine that his car would be waiting at the bottom of the alley at two o'clock.

"But I want to go in the morning," said Blaine.

"I'm sorry, I meant two o'clock A.M.," said Yusef. "It's impractical to travel by car during the day—the traffic won't permit it. The only time to go is in the very early morning, when the traffic is light."

"But will Nile Studios be open at that hour?" asked Blaine.

"I don't know," said Yusef, embarrassed. "Does your presence wish me to ask my father?"

"No, that's all right. I'll wait until they open."

"The driver's name is Shukri," said Yusef. "He's from the neighborhood, so he can be trusted. My father says you should go to bed now if you are going to get up at two in the morning to go to Nile Studios."

Blaine lay in bed listening to the night call to prayer echoing in the city's concrete canyons, vast and serene and sober. Despite the music, voices, and car horns outside, the night air's soft stirring of the window curtain brought to his mind the solitary stillness of the desert under a moon invisible in the murky city air. Though he had turned off the Aida movie he had been watching, the radiance of her presence still seemed to glow on him somehow. The room felt full of her, as if she had been here in the flesh just a moment ago; he could almost catch the smell of her, the rustle of her clothes, the glitter of an eye in the dim light from the window. The sensation was so strong that he got up several times and prowled around the tiny room, the linoleum cool and gritty on his feet, and looked out the window. It must be the kind of impression the Icon advance scouts worked from, he thought, this almost-seeing, almost-hearing, this *feeling* that something was about to appear before you from thin air, this yearning so intense it was a physical ache.

His herbs and anchoring hardware were in his suitcase. If he used them he would dream her, he was sure of it; he only needed to get Abu Yusef to send up some hot water for the herbs and then he could see her, talk to her, touch her. The niacin he had been taking for days had washed the herbs out of his nervous system, yet he could feel the pressure of dreams building up below the surface of his mind, his own unconscious impregnated by the hunger of the collective unconscious beneath it.

But he had promised Jenny Chan he wouldn't dig dream; and he had to admit she had spooked him with her insistence of it. He hadn't been afraid of the herbs in years, not since he had gotten used to the vague intoxication at bedtime, the subtle sharpening of the senses, the intense lucid dreams. Yet Jenny seemed to be trying to protect him from something. From what?

He rolled over with his face to the wall, prepared to forget the herbs and go to sleep.

There was an intake of breath in the room.

Blaine sat up, eyes wide. The sound had been unmistakable, and as unmistakable the source of it: he knew that beautiful throat—he had just been listening to its voice on his laptop.

He got up and looked behind the shower curtain. The tiny, dark cubicle was empty.

Automatically Blaine recited the Quran *sura* that was supposed by Arab superstition to protect the reciter from jinni, spirits. He hadn't been a Muslim in a long time—he had abandoned traditional religion, like most other Westerners of his generation who hadn't become fundamentalists— but he had learned the *sura* long ago from his grandmother, and had used it as a child to protect himself from the dark.

He is God,
The One and Only;

God, the Eternal, Absolute:

He begetteth not,
Nor is He begotten;

And there is none
Like unto Him.

He listened. The room was silent now. He got back into bed.

Could she be a jinn? some childish part of his mind wondered, and he fantasized briefly about being wrapped in the arms of such a creature. Then suddenly, because it seemed important, he tried to recall the sound of the breath exactly, to listen to it again in his mind. Had it been passionate? Fearful? Sobbing? Languid?

"Buthaina?" he said softly, aloud.

He fell asleep soon after, and in his dreams he seemed to be still lying in his bed in the Hotel Riyadh. Across the tiny room, her face half in darkness, half in the dim light from the street, sat the woman he had come here to find, dressed in a gown of white lace and ruffles like a wedding gown. She was staring at him. As he watched, a thick ooze of blood came from the streetlight side of her motionless mouth and ran slowly down her cheek.

6

He woke in terror, his watch alarm sounding. It was twenty minutes to two. The glow from the window was dimmer now, and the acrid air had become still and heavy, damp. The city murmured restlessly and distant outside. Blaine dressed and went downstairs carrying his suitcase. Abu Yusef wasn't at his table in the hall, though the light was on. Blaine hadn't told him he was changing hotels. He left a note now and scrip for what he owed on his room.

The old toothless man was sleeping on his cardboard in the stairwell, and the hotel's heavy single-sheet metal street door was on the latch. Blaine went out quietly and pushed it shut behind him.

He passed only a couple of late pedestrians in the alley, though men still smoked and read newspapers under the bare bulbs of the coffee house. Someone was asleep in a bundle of rags against the alley wall. There were the noises of tires and engines and an occasional honk from the street, but most sounds seemed to have been absorbed by the silence of the stones and concrete, and most of the shops were closed up tight behind metal shutters and doors.

At the street corner a tiny, dented Peugeot taxi waited, its lights and engine off. Blaine looked in the open passenger window at a large, bearded young man in a white *gelabiyah*. "Are you Shukri?"

"Yes," said the young man. "Welcome."

Blaine climbed in the back seat and shook a broad, strong hand.

"You are Abu Yusef's guest," said Shukri. His face was dark and round, his beard emphasizing its broadness. A cell phone and hypertext Quran in an ersatz leather case sat on the car's dusty dashboard.

"Yes. My name is Blaine Ramsey."

"Welcome, Mr. Ramsey. What do you think of Abu Yusef's hotel? It is very clean, is it not? As clean as anything in Europe, I guess?"

"Very clean, certainly."

"And you want to go to Nile Studios, according to Abu Yusef."

"Yes, if possible."

"God willing," said Shukri, starting the cab rattlingly and pulling away from the curb. Traffic was still crowded at this hour, but the vehicles were moving quickly, and the utility superstructure uprights swished by rapidly. "Why do you want to go there?"

Blaine sometimes wished he lived in a culture where everything wasn't everybody's business. It was especially awkward when your interlocutor was an Islamic fundamentalist who wasn't likely to understand the subtleties of looking for a beautiful movie star to quench a strange yearning.

"I work for a company that produces films," Blaine started.

"Your Arabic is good. Are you a Muslim?" Shukri asked, accelerating the taxi flat out and swerving to pass a bus.

Blaine held on to the door handle until they were out of danger. "My father's family was Muslim."

"Then you are a Muslim," said Shukri. "Thanks be to God. Do you practice your religion?"

"I'm afraid not."

"It's good you are honest about it. Self-deception is a great cause of sin. There are many in Egypt who claim to be good Muslims but instead are idolaters, serving those who have set themselves up as gods for the worship of the ignorant. A real Muslim would never have anything to do with Nile Studios, of course, but many who call themselves Muslims work there."

"But the religious authorities preview and approve their films, don't they?" asked Blaine. "How then—?"

"*Religious authorities,*" Shukri sneered loudly and excitedly. "They are appointed by the government to legitimize whatever the government and the rich want to do, so they can go on pretending to the people that we live in an Islamic society. If we live in an Islamic society, why don't they implement the *shari'a,* the religious law? Then they would close down all the film studios, as well as the cinemas, video stores, and cabarets."

They came to a traffic circle and Shukri grasped the steering wheel with both hands and added his aggressive honking to that of the other five hundred cars swirling chaotically around it.

"Do you really think the *shari'a* is relevant for modern times, Shukri?" Blaine asked when they had gotten off the circle and he could breathe again.

"It is indispensable for modern times!" shouted Shukri, waving one hand. "Look around you! Look at the modern world!" He narrowly missed an oncoming truck that had swerved into their lane.

The smell of ancient human grime came though the windows of the taxi. They were jouncing along a street now that seemed to be nothing but rocks and dirt, the wheels of the cars churning up white dust. There was no elevated utility superstructure here, and the smoky sky was open above them. By the wall of a building a very old, ragged man was bent almost double in the glare of passing headlights, picking through a heap of trash; Blaine watched him put a scrap into his toothless mouth and chew it quickly and with great concentration. Skinny children lolled dully from a tenement window lit by the flicker of a cooking fire. They passed a miserable household consisting of a bare mattress and broken-down bureau pushed against a building wall; what looked like a whole family slept on the mattress, covered with sheets of dirty cardboard. "This is what the extirpation of Islam from society has wrought! Do you think that in the time of the Prophet Mohammed, prayers and peace be upon him, or in the time of the first Caliphs, you would have seen anything like this? Anything like this hell for men, women, and children? Is this not shameful? Is it not shameful?"

"It is shameful, Shukri. But the population explosion—"

"The population explosion! People are having children just as they have since the beginning of time, but the government blames all problems on 'the population explosion' to hide its own corruption and incompetence."

As they drove between tottering brick tenements a deep rumble from the murky darkness made Blaine jump with a visceral fear bred by the afternoon's quake tremor. "What's that?"

"Thunder. But you do well to be afraid. What if it were the Day of Judgment?"

A wind gusted, blowing dust and papers up, and then a bolt of lighting forked down, glaring on low clouds and illuminating the city, and Blaine was transfixed by a strange sight. Standing massive, dark, and ancient a couple of miles from him, and framed by distant high-rises, two enormous Pyramids rose above the vistas of low, ramshackle buildings. Shukri was murmuring a *sura* from the Quran:

Perish the hands
Of the Father of Flame!
Perish he!

No profit to him
From all his wealth,
And all his gains!

Burnt soon will he be
In a Fire
Of blazing Flame!

The New City of the Arts was a block-long walled compound fronting on a run-down six-lane road rumbling with traffic even at two-thirty in the morning. The modernistic sculpture of a woman representing Art stood on the wide, uneven sidewalk outside it, but her breasts had been hammered off by vandals, or maybe by fundamentalists protecting public morals. A flock of goats was trotting by her as Blaine and Shukri pulled up to the curb, herded by two teenage boys in ragged clothes and flip-flops, carrying switches. A wet wind gusted with a smell of rain, blowing up a small sandstorm of dust and debris that got in Blaine's eyes through the taxi's open windows.

It was impossible to see anything inside the compound except the tops of a few buildings. In spite of himself, Blaine was taken aback. This dirty street and dirty wall with its cracked and peeling stucco, surrounded by leaning tenements—this was Hollywood on the Nile, where all those glossy Egyptian movies about the rich and glamorous were made, where Aida herself came and worked her romantic magic for audiences numbering in the millions. Well, he should have expected it. He was beginning to wonder if there was anything or anyplace in Egypt that wasn't old, shabby, and dirty.

A cracked stucco guardhouse was set into the compound wall next to a gated, one-car-wide entrance, its window brightly lit. "It is closed at this hour," announced Shukri. He didn't seem to want to pull up too close. Blaine remembered that Islamic extremists were blamed for attacks—polemical, legal, and physical—on Egypt's film industry.

Large, dirty raindrops hit the windshield.

"Where shall we go now?" asked Shukri. "You have brought your luggage, but the only hotels in this part of town are near the Pyramids."

"Drive around," said Blaine. "Let's find someplace where I can wait until they open."

The rain brought the smell of wet dust and the acid tang of dissolved smog. Blaine rolled up the back windows of the taxi, disoriented. He had never been anywhere in the Middle East where it rained in summer, and he found it disconcerting, as if he had been transported suddenly to Europe, or even America, except that here the unlighted streets were flanked with tiny, shuttered shops, low, poorly made concrete buildings, and destitute people huddling under awnings and scraps of plastic or cardboard.

Behind the New City of the Arts were run-down four- and five-story colonial-era apartment houses, black with soot and streaked with rust from their antique wrought-iron balconies. The rain was slackening already, rills of it running down the greasy sidewalk and flowing in the gutter. Up ahead, in an empty lot, bright lights shone. As they came closer Blaine saw awnings and people strolling, and heard what sounded like live music, the brisk, sinuous strains of a small Arab orchestra.

"It's a *mulid,* a saint's day celebration," said Shukri. "What tomb are we near? Oh, of course, the tomb of *Shaykha Sukkariyya*. It must be her feast day."

The street carnival was lit by strings of painted lightbulbs and christmas lights hung between booth awnings and poles stuck in the ground. Hawkers pushed handcarts with sizzling spiced meat or garish sweets piled on trays. There were jugglers, sword-swallowers, and fire-breathers wearing embroidered *gelabiya*s and skullcaps damp from the recent rain. A fortune-teller with his mouse and box of tiny scrolls called nasally for the uncertain and troubled to flock to him. Tiny Ferris wheels barely higher than a man's head and carrying only four sets of seats lifted squealing children, and there were similarly small-scale versions of other circus rides playing scratchy carnival music above the roar of their gasoline-driven motors. A sign on a curtained booth announced in Arabic and atrocious English that tattoos and circumcisions were performed within.

"Will it last all night, Shukri?" asked Blaine.

"A few more hours," said Shukri. "As long as there are people to pay. This is a mockery of Islam."

"Drop me off here," said Blaine. "I can walk to the studio easily from here in the morning."

"Impossible," said Shukri. "You are a guest of Abu Yusef. I'll wait for you until eight o'clock, and until eight at night, as well, if need be. You just tell me—"

"Nonsense, Shukri. You need to get home before the traffic gets heavy. Can I leave my suitcase in your car?"

"Impossible! Impossible!"

After a decent interval of polite expostulation the one working taillight of Shukri's taxi disappeared around the corner, and Blaine was left in cool, damp air washed clean of the smells of smog, filth, and heat.

Now that the rain had stopped people were crowding the *mulid* again; hawkers and beggars; fellahin—peasants fresh from the countryside—and *baladi*—urban peasants; noisy groups of dark teenage boys with sparse hair on their faces, dancing and laughing; young married couples holding the hands of their children. As usual, Blaine's height, clothes, and complexion drew curious looks, but his body language and speech were Arab, and after a while people assumed he was some Palestinian or Lebanese expatriate from Europe or America, and lost interest.

He strolled through the carnival. The music he had heard came from near the middle of the lot, where a crowd of people were standing; as he listened to it a strange feeling came over him, like a premonition, like the intoxication from his Image herbs, like the smell of Buthaina.

People were gathered in a large circle. At one end a small, ragtag orchestra with fiddles, accordion, lute, flute, and tambourine played energetically, and in the middle of the muddy space a girl danced, and when Blaine saw her he stood gaping.

She did a vigorous version of the belly dance, with much leaping and twirling, as if she sought to make up in energy the erotic interest lost because of her outfit. She wore a red dress over striped pants and tattered high-top tennis shoes, all spattered with mud. She had dark, thick hair, and in the torchlight her skin was pale, large eyes dark—

The movie star Aida, seemingly identical with the dream-girl Buthaina and the beggar girl from Abu Yusef's alley, danced before him in a scene from *Dancing Girl*, which he had been watching on his palmtop just two nights before. He looked around dizzily for the cameras, arc lights, and microphones, vaguely realizing when he failed to see them that the movie had been made several years ago.

His heart pounded as he grasped at theories. This was some young Aida wannabe who was using the clothes and hairstyle as part of her act. But the resemblance was too perfect, down to the dimpled, bittersweet smile, the arching white arms, the eyes that fluttered sometimes as if she was about to swoon, down to the members of the orchestra, the old accordion player he knew was her father, the blind flutist—

Then it had to be Aida herself, who had for some reason decided to come down here from her dressing room in Nile Studios and dance for the workmen and hawkers and street people. But why didn't they recognize her, why weren't they mobbing her? And how had she gotten together a band that looked exactly like the one from the movie?

As he continued to watch, dumbfounded, these theories evaporated, and he knew he was watching a scene from *Dancing Girl,* was *in* the scene, participating in some fashion he didn't understand.

He tried to think through his confusion. Here was the woman he was seeking, the woman he had come to Cairo to find. He pushed to the front of the crowd, the palms of his hands tingling, wet. She was sweating too, he saw as she danced past, her hair twirling as she spun, sweat plastering a few strands to the sides of her neck, and he thought he caught her smell, sweet, musky, and intoxicating.

He would catch her the next time she came around; he wouldn't let her escape this time. He would make her explain who she was, what she had done to him, what this was all about—

But, he realized with a sudden sobering as she shook her hips in the middle of the circle of mud, raising her arms graceful as a swan above her head and closing her eyes with the passion of the dance, it wouldn't do to just grab her. *Zina',* illicit sexuality, was strictly prohibited by Islam even when committed only "by the eye" or "by the ear," as was being done by his fellow spectators right now. But if committed "by the hand" in front of a hundred witnesses it could earn him a prison sentence, especially if the girl acted as though she were being assaulted.

The music had stopped, Blaine realized suddenly, and the girl had stopped dancing. There was applause, whistles. She was going around the circle now with a saucy smile and a tin can into which the onlookers were enthusiastically dropping coins. Blaine, gaping, didn't have the presence of mind to get out his money, but didn't her smile deepen as she went past him, dimpling her cheeks, her eyes rolling flirtatiously?

The circle was breaking up now, the audience wandering away. The girl slipped in among the musicians with her canful of coins. Blaine, pushing through the merrymakers, saw her milling among them and then beyond, heading toward a less well-lit part of the lot.

Following her as quickly as he could through the crowd, he was soon at the edge of the *mulid*'s lights and music, near the street. The sound of passing cars came to him, and the smell of wet earth. There was no sign of her. He looked at his watch—a little past four-thirty. The crowd was thinning. Blaine searched the lot, but the dancer in the red dress and the musicians that had been with her were now nowhere to be seen.

The proprietors of some of the carnival rides were dismantling them with large wrenches and hammers, grease covering their hands and forearms.

"The musicians that were over there," Blaine asked one of them, pointing. "Do you know where they have gone?"

"Gone home," said the stocky, large-mustached man, tying a bunch of rusty metal struts together with a greasy cord. "The *mulid* is over now."

"Where is their home?"

"Are you looking for musicians? I can find you much better musicians than those. I am a talent agent as well as a carnival promoter." He wiped his hands on his dirty work apron. "What kind of musicians are you looking for? For what kind of occasion?"

"Well, actually—I was wondering about the dancer that was with them."

"The dancer?" The man looked at Blaine suspiciously. "Cairo is full of dancers. If you go to the cabarets on the Avenue of the Pyramids you can see belly dancers in plenty. Why do you come to a place like this to see a dancer? You are a foreigner, are you not?"

"I am, God keep you." Blaine put his hand on his pocket. "But any information you could give me regarding the musicians and the dancer—"

The man shrugged. "That is the Turki family. They are

very poor musicians; I could find you an orchestra a hundred times smoother. They live in Darb Al Ahmar. I happen to have one of their business cards, I believe. The old man is always handing out business cards, though he doesn't know how to read. . . ."

—

Blaine wandered the streets for a couple of hours in the chill of dawn, then dozed in a doorway, but roused himself in time to get to Nile Studios by quarter to eight. Bright yellow sunlight angled over the tops of the buildings, still only slightly hazed by the rain-washed smog, making Cairo look for the moment almost like a normal city, far from the fogs and smokes that hang around the mouth of Gehenem. But Blaine, still thinking feverishly about his encounter with Aida, wasn't in the mood to enjoy it. You could be sure that if the actress Aida had danced in a neighborhood street carnival it would have caused a sensation. But no one had noticed. What did it mean? Psychological illness seemed again the easiest explanation: he had projected on a carnival dancer the looks of a famous movie star with whom he was obsessed.

On the other hand he had seen the beggar girl with her baby near the Hotel Riyadh *before* he had watched *The Stain of Blood; that* had not been a projection, at least. On the contrary, that episode smacked of introjection of an Image *from* the collective unconscious into his own mind. Perhaps the other *mulid* spectators hadn't seen Aida because they didn't have an Image-digger's sensitivity to the fantasies of the collective unconscious. But if that was so, it meant that the collective unconscious was fantasizing Aida so intensely that an Image-digger could see her even while wide awake, without the herbs or electronics. And he didn't see how that could be.

He passed a man cooking *ta'amiyeh* on a pushcart set

against the grimy, graffitied compound wall—which daylight showed had been painted an unlikely peach color long ago—frying his wares in a big metal can over a kerosene primus, the crisp, spicy smell making Blaine's mouth water. But it wouldn't do to go into Nile Studios smelling of *ta'amiyeh*: he was supposed to be the emissary of an American film production company, who would probably have breakfasted on waffles or cold cereal, or whatever abominations they ate in the morning back in his native country.

In the compound's guardhouse half a dozen middle-aged men in street clothes sat on shabby plastic chairs and counted worry beads or sipped tiny tumblers of tea. They were surprised to see him walk into the driveway entrance, but once they had called his name into some central office they gave him courteous greetings and one of them came out of the guardhouse and called "Abu Malik!" through the rusty metal compound gate. An old grizzled man wearing bedroom slippers, his rumpled security guard uniform unbuttoned over a dirty undershirt, shuffled over and unlocked the gate, and invited Blaine to follow him.

Inside, the compound was bigger than Blaine had imagined, and quiet once they got away from the street. It looked like someone's unambitious idea of a park or pleasure garden, everything run-down and gone to seed. Patches of bare dirt alternated with knee-high crabgrass, aloe, and weeds that overgrew little dirt walks edged with bricks leading to small, dirty ornamental fountains through which no water flowed now. Blaine followed Abu Malik along a narrow, crumbling asphalt road between palms and ficus trees whose leaves were limp and streaked with brown from last night's acid rain. There were several large three-story buildings in the middle of the compound, their ornamental facings and stucco cracked and dirt-streaked, blackened by soot and smog. A few dented cars were parked where the road ran past the buildings. In the nearly clear morning sun-

light, and compared with the rest of Cairo, it all looked luxu-
riant and serene.

A heavy, hooting roar came into hearing above them. A
late-model VTOL limousine was descending onto the roof of
one of the buildings, its mirrored windows glinting in the
bright sunlight.

Abu Malik chuckled. "Just like Europe, isn't it?" he
wheezed. "They come like that all the time. Movie stars and
important people. You see them all the time here."

"You see the movie stars, Abu Malik?"

"Of course, father. I see all of them. They are my friends."

"Have you ever seen the actress Aida? No, I suppose
not, of course."

"Of course I have seen her, darling! She is like my
daughter."

"Where does she live, Abu Malik?

"Ah, that would be telling," wheezed Abu Malik, wagging his finger with a gap-toothed smile. "Every man in
Egypt, as well as in the whole world, wants to know where
she lives. 'Where does Aida live?' the Prime Minister asked
me once. 'Your Highness, I cannot tell you, I am sworn to secrecy,' I told him. 'If I were to tell you, she wouldn't invite
me anymore. I am like her father,' I said to him. 'If I were not
able to look after her, what would she do?' She is a wild girl,
you know."

"Is her father dead, then, Abu Malik?"

"Of course he is dead, darling. She is a Copt, didn't you
know that? Both her parents were killed in the riots twenty
years ago, by the Muslim Brotherhood. I could mention
your name to her, if I remember."

Blaine handed him a small scrip.

"God keep you, and keep your children. God's contentment be upon you. May God return it to you," Abu Malik
blessed him effusively.

They entered a building on whose dirty ornamental portico was lettered in Arabic: "Nile Company for Studios and

Film Production." Inside was a small lobby with white-washed walls and a dirty tiled floor, a stone staircase in back. A dozen functionaries loafed in plastic chairs against one wall. They resembled the men in the guardhouse: middle-aged petty bureaucrats and college professors who had enough connections to supplement their penurious salaries by running errands and bringing coffee at the exclusive Nile Studios.

Abu Malik shook hands with a few of the men. "The effendi is here to see Mr. 'Abdel Halim," he told them.

There was a shuffling of feet, and the men looked at Blaine curiously, murmuring greetings. A smiling, pock-marked man with a large paunch led him up the stairs and down a dim, damp hallway whose peeling walls were flanked by miniature columns holding dusty ornamental urns, and reverently opened a door near the end.

"Blease," he said in English, extending his hand.

Inside was a dim, cool office. Behind a massive, cheap-looking varnished desk an air conditioner hummed in a white-washed pebbled-glass window. A purple velvet-upholstered couch and set of armchairs smelled strongly of mildew. Spider-plant shoots trailed from water-filled soda bottles set on side tables and on the windowsill. A nameplate on the desk announced "President of Talent."

"Blease," said the pockmarked man again, indicating the sofa. His eyes were sparkling, as if he knew that Blaine would feel right at home in this luxurious Western setting.

"Thank you," said Blaine in English, and smiled.

The man grinned widely in delight, then withdrew, closing the door very quietly behind him.

In a few minutes the door opened again and a large, grave, worried-looking man in the gray civilian uniform of a career civil servant came in and shook Blaine's hand. He was trying out his English when Blaine interrupted him in Arabic, and they did the prescribed round of greetings and inquiries. Then Mr. 'Abdel Halim sat behind his desk and listened politely as Blaine expressed pleased surprise at the modern facilities and praised the wonderful output of films of Nile Studios. This done, and another round of pleasantries exchanged, Blaine got to the point of his visit. He was looking for local actresses for possible use in high-profile international advertising campaigns based on Egyptian themes and images, just as a recent campaign with which Mr. 'Abdel Halim might be familiar had been based on Moroccan themes. This recent campaign, as Mr. 'Abdel Halim might know, had coincided with a significant increase in tourism to Morocco.

"One of the actresses who has caught the interest of people in my organization," said Blaine, "is a property named 'Aida.' I suppose you are very familiar with her."

"Aida; of course. She is one of Egypt's leading actresses," said Abdel Halim judiciously. "She is making a film on our lot right now, as it happens. But the studio has only a one-film contract with her. You must understand that most of the films today are animated, produced completely within computers at Media Production City in the suburbs. We do only live-action films, and so we have little market power today, and our facilities are nearly unused. Though this particular actress's live-action films are widely popular, thanks be to God. But, of course, we would have no say in whether she would be able to become involved in the project you are describing. However, you are in luck, because her agent, Mr. Munir Helwan, happens to be on the lot today. Shall I ask Mr. Helwan to speak with you?"

Mr. Munir Helwan, when he was conducted in with much murmured obeisance by one of the middle-aged functionaries, turned out to be as elegantly Western as Nile Studios was squarely Third World. He was in his early middle age, clean-shaven, stocky, and handsome in a blunt, almost Western way, his dark, long hair pulled into a neat ponytail. His suit was of sophisticated cut and expensive material, and he wore tasteful but expensive-looking rings. The only traditional Arab touch was the set of polished stone prayer beads he ran through his manicured fingers.

They shook hands and Helwan sat with obvious distaste on the mildewed armchair across from Blaine's. After a round of polite remarks, Mouhsin 'Abdel Halim, President of Talent, sat with his hands clasped on his desk and watched with grave solicitude as Munir Helwan said in excellent English: "What can I do for you, Mr. Ramsey?" The smile that made lines around his nut-brown eyes was polite and rather weary.

"I'm looking for local talent," Blaine started. "I'm with Icon, the—"

"Permit me," said Helwan, holding up one hand and jiggling his beads idly in the others. "You're looking for local talent to appear in some psychoform commercials. You've seen an actress named Aida and you think she would work in the commercials you have in mind. You want to set up a meeting with her to discuss it, maybe give her a screen test. You simply *must* see her."

Helwan jiggled his beads some more, and glanced at 'Abdel Halim. Blaine watched him mutely.

"Yet you're in the Research & Development Department. If I talk to my Icon production contacts in Los Angeles they'll say they don't know you. Forgive me, but I've heard all this before."

Blaine was suddenly aware that he could get himself fired, and probably Jenny Chan too, if he said the wrong things to this man. At the same time he realized that he didn't really care. "Heard it from whom?"

Helwan's expression was weary, with a flicker of disgust, a flicker of glum humor.

"Mr. Ramsey, let me give you some advice," he said gently. "Go back to America or wherever you come from. Go back to your wife or girlfriend. Forget about Aida. *She has the same effect on everyone,* Mr. Ramsey." He held up his hand to cut off Blaine's protest. "We have to deal with this all the time, most recently from several foreigners in your line of business. But she's our 'hottest property,' as you would say in America, and for various reasons there is no way—*no way*—we could even let you near her, much less let her work for you. And for another thing"—he looked at Blaine sadly and shook his head—"she's nothing at all like what you think she is. I hope that will make you feel better about going away without meeting her. I said that to the last Icon Research & Development person that came asking to see her, and he burst into tears. Isn't that strange? He begged me, told me he must see her or he would die." Helwan rubbed his forehead momentarily as if the memory disturbed him. "So perhaps she affects you dream surveyors, or whatever you call yourself, more intensely than others. On the other hand, we get hundreds of fan letters a week saying essentially the same thing, so perhaps there's no difference after all." He stood up, his face brightening to a false, professional smile, and he held out his hand. "I'm sorry."

Blaine stood up more slowly. "Who was the other Icon digger that was looking for her? What was the name?"

"His name was Mr. Boyle, or Doyle."

7

A couple of blocks from the New City of the Arts Blaine found an ancient church standing morosely between two apartment buildings, its gray, carved stone giving off a musty, bitter smell, like the cynicism brought on by old age. The apartment buildings were probably a millennium younger but still darkened by dust and smoke, with the remains of ornamental cornices and stonework, antique balconies of rusting rococo ironwork, and kludgy outdoor wiring that threatened mass electrocution at the next shower of rain. Smog was accumulating in a white haze above the buildings again like a storm gathering from the gasoline and diesel smoke rising in bluish-gray clouds above the streets. Blaine wolfed a *shawirma* sandwich at a stand-up booth nearby, the thickening air pinching his lungs, washed an antibiotic pill down with a brass cup of cool licorice-root tea from a strolling vendor, then went into the church. Its low, claustrophobic stone arches were dimly lit by tiny stained-glass windows and decorated with twelfth-century wall hangings; its stone floor was worn smooth as water. Blaine, dozing on a worn wooden pew in the primitive, spiritual smell of frankincense, was roused once by the melancholy, ecstatic chanting of an Orthodox Mass.

He was exhausted but not unhappy. Paradoxically, his unsuccessful talk with Helwan had left him feeling exhilarated. He had gotten close: he had spoken to her agent! The heady feeling had something to do with love, he knew, like the feeling a twelve-year-old gets from walking by the house of a girl he has a crush on. That the same feeling could be produced onanistically by a postmodern advertising fantasy perhaps should have disillusioned him, but it didn't. Maybe that kind of love was the best a person like him, in an age like this, could hope for: a sort of Romeo and Juliet on LSD and Prozac. Even though Helwan had refused him Aida, this had simply strengthened his resolve to see her, against all logic, better judgment, and experience. Very romantic; but the thought came to him that he had been living on an overdose of control for a long time now. Losing it was an antidote a person like him would never seek; but when it came by itself it was hard to refuse.

And, almost as exciting, Helwan's talk about other Image-diggers chasing Aida had given Blaine his first hard evidence that he wasn't crazy. Helwan had mentioned Mark Boyle, who was one of the Icon diggers Blaine had heard was assigned to Cairo. Boyle bursting into tears because he couldn't meet a movie star seemed impossible based on what Blaine knew of the man; yet if the Aida Image had hit him the way it had hit Blaine, maybe Boyle's extraordinary psychological balance had cracked, as it had not in many high-pressure Middle East assignments. Well, if Boyle was in Cairo he was probably at the Meridien, so Blaine would talk to him tonight, and then he would see.

Addresses in Cairo were often useless, Blaine knew, indefinite and ever-changing because of the endless pressure of people, people who changed the shapes and names of streets and neighborhoods, built their unpermitted, unzoned, unregulated houses, shacks, hovels, booths, tenements, and shops around and between and on top of existing structures so that a street today might look nothing like it had a year ago. Blaine was afraid, as he handed Shukri the *mulid* musicians' business card at 2 A.M. the next morning in front of the New City of the Arts, that it would be futile, an address that meant nothing, a grain of dust blowing in the wind.

But Shukri frowned seriously as he squinted in the streetlight coming through the windshield of his cab. "This is a Darb Al Ahmar address, almost at the edge of Shafa'i," he said, turning in his seat to stare at Blaine. "Foreigners don't go to Darb Al Ahmar."

"I'm not a foreigner."

"No one of any kind goes to Darb Al Ahmar."

"I must go, Shukri."

"Why?"

"Is it dangerous?"

"It is controlled by the militias, yes. But the greater danger is to the soul. I told you, it is near Shafa'i."

"God keep you, Shukri, I must go. If you can't take me, I will find another driver, but—"

Shukri started the engine and pulled away from the curb, nearly ramming a speeding car, which swerved to miss him, horn wailing as it receded ahead. "In the name of God, the Compassionate, the Merciful." He sighed. "You are Abu Yusef's guest, and he has put you in my care."

＿＿

Blaine had heard of Darb Al Ahmar, of course. It was one of those world-famous slums, like Lahore's Katchi Abadi or Bombay's Khar, that fashionable philosophers and economists used as examples of this or that trend in world development, a name cocktail-party intellectuals dropped to show they were aware of the very latest catastrophes. It had started out as a *baladi* quarter to which had flocked millions of the immigrants from the countryside who were pouring into the city, squeezed by population pressure out of the narrow strip of green along the Nile that was Egypt's only arable land; but soon the flood of people had become unmanageable: infrastructure and services had been overwhelmed, and during the prodemocracy *intifadahs* civil order had broken down to such an extent that the government had withdrawn from the area and left it to the militias, along with the neighboring horror of Shafa'i, the City of the Dead. It was not now known how many people lived in Darb Al Ahmar, or how many new ones were born every day, or how many died of starvation or disease, or how those who went on living managed to survive.

As they drove toward Darb Al Ahmar the streets became dirt-paved and flanked by ramshackle apartment houses of bare concrete or uneven brick with shuttered, glassless windows, hung with washing; a few had collapsed into heaps of brick, concrete, and rebar. Trash lay in desiccated piles along the building walls. The neighborhood was dark and nearly deserted at 3 A.M. At a corner, gasoline-powered arc lights threw stark shadows around a military checkpoint where machine gun–toting, black-uniformed internal security police wanted to know where Blaine was going. Shukri told them he was late for a flight and they were taking the short way to the airport. Blaine's luggage in the trunk bolstered the story, and the police let them through with warnings not to leave the main road or stop along the way. Once they were out of sight Shukri turned onto a narrow side street.

Soon they came to another checkpoint, much different from the first. Flames licked up into the darkness from an oil drum in the middle of the street, and around it milled men in *gelabiyahs* and rough, *fallahi* turbans. Some of them carried weapons. As Shukri's taxi jounced toward them, raising dust, several of them raised their hands for him to stop. He pulled over by the oil drum. Blaine could smell kerosene smoke through his open window, feel the heat of the flames. The flickering light showed two thin, dark, dirty militiamen approaching the car, carrying obsolete but still workable-looking machine guns.

"Peace be upon you," said one of the militiamen. "Where are you going?"

"And upon you peace," said Shukri. "I'm taking this gentleman to the airport."

"Gentleman?" said the dark man, looking into the back seat. "Who is this, an Englishman?" He came forward and peered through the window into Blaine's face with his dark, glittering, bloodshot eyes. Then he opened Blaine's door and swung it wide. He stepped back.

"Get out, you son of a dog!" he shouted, and spat on the ground.

Shukri was out of the car before Blaine. "Shame!" he yelled. "Shame! Brother, what is this talk? Shame on you to talk this way to a guest in our town!"

The militiaman pulled his gun from his shoulder, blazing eyes on Blaine. Other men were running up from the darkness.

Blaine knew the game he had to play, and as he leapt from the car he felt his Arab reflexes surging hot into him.

"All right!" he shouted in the face of the militiaman. "Shoot!" He struck himself violently on the chest with open hands. "Go ahead! Shoot!"

The militiaman reared back in surprise. Blaine's Arabic was perfect and he was full of aggrieved Arab fury.

"You want to shoot me? Shoot! You want to call me a dog and son of a dog? What's the matter, why don't you shoot?" He pressed forward, crowding the militiaman. "Why don't you shoot someone who has never done anything to you, who is just riding in a car, trying to pass on the road, before God? Why? Why?"

The militiamen were crowding around them now, and a couple put their hands on the man with the machine gun, pulling him back and soothing him with murmuring words. His glaring eyes on Blaine's face, he was nevertheless not resisting them, allowing them to save his honor by soothing him, dissuading him, asking him for their sake not to attack Blaine. A couple of others were doing the same to Blaine—he felt their soft but insistent hands on him, pulling him backward, away from his adversary.

"Never mind. He thought you were a foreigner. Never mind, brother. His daughter died of cholera," their voices murmured to him.

Shukri was still expostulating loudly, hands splayed dramatically in the air. "He is a Palestinian, brother! He was born in America, but how is that his fault, since his father fled there? Shame, shame on you, citizens—!"

And in another minute they were on their way again, a few of the militiamen waving to them.

"And without paying a toll!" Shukri laughed. "Mr. Blaine, your Arabic is very good!" But Blaine thought that his voice trembled. Blaine was trembling too.

The neighborhood was unlit now, the buildings irregular hulks in the dark outside their headlights, more like beetling and tottering cliffs than buildings, some of them partly or completely collapsed into rubble that yet seemed inhabited, broken windows lit here and there by the flicker of flames. The air smelled of smoke, sewage, and the grime of millions upon millions of human bodies. Some of those bodies lay at the sides of the street, whether dead or sleeping it was impossible to say. Shukri had slowed down now, squinting through the windshield to try to read street names and numbers in the headlights. Despite the lateness of the hour, a dozen ragged, yelling children chased the taxi as it lurched along the potholed dirt, raising a cloud of dust that swirled around them. When they stopped suddenly, the children clambered up onto the trunk and roof, still yelling.

Shukri jumped out, shouting at them, and in the gray dust swirling in the headlights Blaine saw what had made him stop. A misshapen man stood in the middle of the street. He had goggling eyes, twisted, drooling lips, and his head and clawed, useless hands jerked spastically. He was naked, with streaks of shit down his legs; his ribs and the joints of his arms and legs stood out of his starved body so far that it seemed they must burst his skin, and you could see clearly the hunchback deformities of his skeleton. His face worked horribly, as if he couldn't decide whether to scream or show his few broken teeth in a smile.

Shukri was approaching the nightmare figure now in the headlights, approaching him hesitantly and fearfully, though he was easily twice the man's weight and a foot taller, large and handsome in his flowing white robe. "Excuse me, my brother," Blaine heard Shukri say gently above the shouts of the children. "May God keep you and give you substance. Would you be so kind as to—"

The misshapen man began to scream. Though he was to hear it in his nightmares for a long time to come, Blaine couldn't at that moment say why the sound was so horrifying; whether it was the hatred and rage on the twisted face, or the almost-words coming from the bubbling mouth, or whether it was something else, a familiarity, as if he had heard the sound before—

And then the ground jumped. Remembering it later, Blaine could never rid himself of the impression that the very earth had shaken itself in horror at the nightmare man's screams. The taxi rocked crazily on its springs as thunder shook the air, at first distant, but suddenly huge and right on top of them, and two bricks from one of the tottering buildings rammed off the car's hood with shocking bangs.

Shukri slammed into the front seat. He gunned the car and spun the steering wheel, swerving in a cloud of dust to roar back the way they had come. Blaine could smell sour sweat on him. They drove wildly through a blinding haze of dust and pelting rubble like a shower of dirty hail, almost tearing the undercarriage out on potholes and the bricks raining into the street from the shuddering buildings. Shukri was breathing in gasps, as if he was running instead of driving.

In another minute the tremor seemed to have passed. Shukri was mumbling protective prayers. In a few more minutes he seemed calmer. "That was the address you gave me, right back there," he told Blaine. "I told you we should not have come here, Mr. Blaine. I told you."

The going was slow now because the street was crowded with ragged, skinny people, some crying, some screaming, some holding others by the arms and trying to comfort or restrain them, many just staring dully into the window at Blaine as the car jounced by, Shukri honking the horn for passage. In one place torches and kerosene lamps flickered and people climbed over a huge pile of stones, concrete, and timbers that had been a building, trying to pull dead or dying neighbors or relatives out of the rubble.

"In the name of God, the Compassionate, the Merciful," said Shukri, and his trembling lips moved with muttered prayers.

Strangely, the arc-lit government checkpoint was deserted now, as though the policemen had abandoned their post before the onslaught of something beyond their ability to fight. But the streets were milling with people; the scene in Shukri's headlights was a kaleidoscope of bodies moving in every direction, cars, motorcycles, and bicycles weaving among them. Sirens wailed in the middle distance. A helicopter roared overhead.

As soon as they were well out of Darb Al Ahmar, Shukri bumped his car up onto a narrow sidewalk, turned off the engine and lights, and began to pray in a fast, low voice, prayers for the dead.

———

In half an hour the crowds on the streets had cleared somewhat and Shukri started the car again, expostulating on

Blaine's insistence on going to Darb Al Ahmar as they jounced down off the sidewalk, and reminding him that he, Shukri, had told him they should not go.

"I will have to try again, too," Blaine said. "But not tonight," he continued in response to Shukri's horrified look. "Tonight I need to go to the Nile Meridien."

"The *Nile Meridien*," Shukri exclaimed. He turned in his seat and stared at Blaine, nearly hitting a bus that was straddling the center line of the street to make better time through traffic. After he had recovered from that, honking angrily and muttering stern Quran *suras*, he turned to stare at Blaine again. "What do you, or what does any reputable man, have to do with the *Nile Meridien*?"

"Shukri, watch where you're driving! What do you mean? The Nile Meridien is a hotel. I'm going to stay there for a while."

"The Nile Meridien is a hotel of perdition! They have *floor shows* there, a *cabaret*! Every vice and degradation invented by the West! This is worse than your wanting to go to Darb Al Ahmar, which you never explained the reason of to me. Why would you want to go to the *Nile Meridien* when you already have a *reputable* hotel, which is the finest hotel in Cairo? It's not rich enough for you," he concluded gloomily.

Blaine found himself laughing despite everything. "Shukri! Why do you insist on seeing me as a lecher who desires nothing but cabarets and floor shows? Do I really give that impression? The Nile Meridien is a hotel, darling, where my company has an account. I talked to them on the telephone today and they told me to stay there. Of course there is no substitute for Abu Yusef's hospitality and the hospitality of his family, but I'm in Cairo on business, Shukri, and if my company tells me to stay at the Nile Meridien, I have to stay there."

Cajoling and remonstrating like that all the way, Blaine coaxed Shukri across Cairo. As they neared the Nile there were streetlights, and high, modern buildings towered above them and got lost in the smog. The neighborhoods immediately on both sides of the eight-lane expressway they now followed were invisible over tall plywood and corrugated iron fencing plastered with huge, garish movie posters and graffiti. Shukri negotiated a complex tangle of dilapidated, potholed overpasses. In crannies around the overpasses people slept, and households had been set up, reminding Blaine of the homeless in Western cities. Beyond the overpasses were more modern high-rises, and about their feet peasant neighborhoods of muddy lanes and tiny shops, tilting and disheveled buildings of deteriorated brick. They were now on a street Shukri called Cornich El Nil, and on their right hand was a wide, cracked sidewalk out of which huge banyan trees reared into the smoky darkness, their spreading branches and hanging roots making caves in which people slept or hunkered around cooking fires. Beyond a rusty railing the land fell abruptly to the great river looming a stone's throw away, its margin crowded with rowboats and makeshift rafts in which people slept or sat around metal cans in which they had made fires. Shukri turned the taxi abruptly to the right and stopped at a checkpoint under bright arc lights.

Beggars suddenly swarmed around the car, hanging on the windows on both sides with their dirty hands, entreating in broken English and French, trying to catch Blaine's eye, reaching into the car to clutch at him. Many were children or women holding babies. They made room for a security policeman to approach the car but otherwise ignored him. For the first time since coming to Cairo Blaine felt suddenly afraid of them, of the starving, homeless, desperate people in their hordes upon hordes. He rolled up the taxi windows with difficulty, almost catching a few insistent fingers in the glass, feeling guilty, angry, and a little sick, as he guessed visiting foreigners—it was only a courtesy to call them "tourists" anymore—felt.

The policeman took one look at Shukri and gestured, and two others came forward from a guard booth, swinging machine guns down from their shoulders. Shukri produced paper ID and answered the policeman's questions in a subdued voice, while the other two looked in the trunk, under the hood, and into the suspension. Blaine's luggage was opened, and, after one of the policemen with sudden fierce cursing drove the beggars away into the darkness, Blaine and Shukri themselves were taken out of the car and wanded down.

Finally they were waved through, and Shukri drove over a two-hundred-meter causeway onto Al Rodha, one of the two big islands in the Nile in downtown Cairo. The streets were narrow and lined with palm, banyan, and ficus, most of the elderly apartment buildings well kept up, their cracks patched with structural resin, and there were even some palatial detached dwellings in lush villas. A little farther on Blaine saw the cabarets Shukri was worried about, holographic signs sprouting ten meters above their decorative roofs fuzzy in the thick, smoky air. Shukri recited protective verses and honked energetically at the traffic. Just beyond the cabaret district was the Nile Meridien.

It was a massive, dozen-story edifice facing out over the river, scoured clean of grime, and gently floodlit at this hour with peach-colored light. Shukri got into the line of vehicles picking up and discharging passengers under the deep, brightly lit portico amid a swarm of doormen, bellmen, carhops, and flunkies, all wearing crisp, Western-style uniforms. Shukri's dusty and dented taxi, looking like a donkey-cart among the gleaming limousines and touring cars, caught the interest, Blaine saw, of the private police personnel standing unobtrusively with their submachine guns in nooks along the hotel's wall. A flunky approached the taxi gingerly, as if reluctant to soil his white gloves on the handle.

Blaine shook Shukri's broad, strong hand, and then

popped into it a generous fare and an even more generous tip for the rides he had been given over the past two days.

"Hey!" yelled Shukri angrily behind him, but the flunky shut the door, and another uniformed functionary blew a whistle vigorously and pointed for him to take his scabrous taxi out of the way of the important guests waiting to arrive. Blaine saw a last glimpse of his white *gelabiyah* and then turned to the gleaming brass and glass door a doorman held for him.

In the shallow entranceway air blew briskly down from a grating above his head and was sucked into a grating below his feet. An inner door slid back by itself, and he found himself in a large, marble-floored lobby, and he could breathe.

8

Blaine's suite on the eighth floor of the Nile Meridien was the first completely quiet place he had found in Cairo, the flower-patterned carpet silent under his feet, indirect lighting filling two handsomely appointed European rooms with Impressionist prints on the walls and graceful Louis XV furniture. And he could breathe. He hadn't realized it, but panting had become second nature to him in the past three days, a strategy his body had adopted automatically to protect his lungs. He had gotten used to the soreness in his throat and aching in his chest, the instinct that inhaling deeply would injure him. But now he drank delicious, cool lungfuls of air and nearly giggled with the exhilaration of it.

Yet it struck him as strange. Mark Boyle was indeed here, the front desk man had confirmed upon seeing Blaine's Icon ID. But how could a local atmosphere fanatic like Boyle work from a hotel that was a hermetically sealed container of European air and ambience?

He took the elevator to the ninth floor. It was 5 A.M., and

Boyle was an early riser, peasant style, and Blaine's curiosity was eating him.

The door to Room 914 opened almost at once at his knock. Mark Boyle stood staring at him. He was fully dressed, even wearing a suit jacket. But something was wrong with him.

Blaine had worked with Boyle a couple of times, once in Marrakesh and once in a place called Ein Helouh in Yemen. Boyle was a quiet, pale, bald Irishman, his psychoneural compatibility with the Middle East a result of having grown up in Damascus, son of a petty Irish Embassy official. Blaine had always liked Boyle, liked his Irish accent that could change to perfect Arabic in an instant, liked his aversion to Westerners, liked his understated stories about digging in a haunted Crusader castle in the Jordanian desert, where he had been sent because no one else would go. Looking at the man, he realized that he had always assumed Boyle was unshakable.

But now Boyle's face was like a mask, and there was something wrong with his eyes.

"Boyle?" Blaine said, studying him. "Boyle, what the hell—"

Boyle's irises were two flat blue disks, the pupils shrunk to pinpricks. "Boyle, it's Ramsey."

"Ramsey," Boyle repeated distantly. There were deep pouches under his eyes and he had lost weight; his suit hung on him. A row of bulging suitcases stood in the small foyer behind him. "What are you doing here, Ramsey?" His eyes didn't move when he talked; they stayed perfectly still, staring at Blaine, or maybe a little past him. "They didn't tell me you were here."

"Just got here," said Blaine slowly. "Can I come in?"

"Just got here?" Boyle said absently. He moved aside for Blaine, but left the door standing open. "I thought you were the bellman."

The two stood an arm's length apart.

"Boyle, man, you're on diazepam, am I right?" said Blaine. "What's the matter? You take a hit?" Diazepam was a family of neuropharms that blocked dreams and most kinds of waking fantasies; it was used in emergencies to stabilize diggers who had been hit too hard by an Image.

Boyle was getting confused, agitation building up under the tight frost of the drug. He waved his hands. "Just a minute. Just a minute." He cupped them over his face. "Just a minute. Just a minute," he kept repeating softly to himself. Then he put his hands down and smiled at Blaine as if he had figured something out. "I can't talk to you," he said.

"Boyle, I'm not going to shake you. OK? I'm your friend, and I'm not going to shake you, but give me some kind of hint. What hit you?"

One of Boyle's hands went to his face again, cupping the side of it as if to protect it from seeing Blaine. "No one told you anything. No one told you anything," he said over and over. Blaine wasn't sure who he was talking to.

"No one told me anything," Blaine said softly. "So you tell me."

Boyle shrieked. Blaine jumped with fear. Then Boyle was talking in a low fast monotone, not looking at Blaine, his shoulders and head hunched fearfully, drool sputtering at his mouth.

"Tell him they're businessmen; they don't care about us. He can't stay here, understand? He especially can't *dig* here, understand? And if you're a digger, you shouldn't even be here. You should get as far away as you can. I'm in the airport now. I'm on my flight, sitting in my seat, flying away. Tell him Geb, Seb. *Geb, Seb. She* creeps into you if you even think about her—" He shrieked again.

There was a knock on the open door and Blaine looked around. A wide-eyed bellman stood in the doorway.

When Blaine looked back at Boyle he was iced again, hands hanging at his sides, pinprick pupils looking mildly at the bellman. He waved gently at his luggage, and the man started loading it on his cart.

Blaine followed the two of them down the hall. The

elevator pinged unctuously and the doors opened. The bell-man dragged the cart in.

"Boyle—"

The doors closed over Boyle's mild, neutral face, saliva still wet on his chin. He paid no more attention to Blaine.

There was an LDTV telephone in Blaine's suite, just like in a Western hotel. There was no answer at Jenny Chan's apartment, so Blaine tried the office. His hands were shaking a little. After a short search, a secretary put her on the line.

Her face on the big wall screen was lined and tired, and Blaine wondered whether she had slept since his call the previous morning.

"Hi, Blaine," she said, searching his face anxiously. "Are you— How are you?"

"Fine. I got into the Meridien like you told me."

"Good. You following my other directions?"

"Yeah." He paused, studying her. "I saw Mark Boyle a couple minutes ago."

"Mark Boyle." She pretended to think. "Yes. He's out there." Her face was closed, unreadable.

"Was," Blaine said. "He's gone now."

"Ah." She nodded gravely.

" 'The fuck is going on out here, Jenny?"

"Meaning what?"

"Meaning Boyle was wrecked. Diazoed. Started screaming when I asked him his problem. I didn't know you could do that on diazepam. Said I should get out of Cairo."

Jenny seemed to color slightly through her tight control. They watched each other.

"You're holding something on me," Blaine said.

She made a wry face. "Nothing worth mentioning. Couple of unstable diggers panicking about a 'psychic storm' in Cairo. They put a buzz on the net and now my people are getting skittish. And the scouts are scoring the area Priority One. Omnicom and IntraVision have half a dozen diggers out there scooping us right now."

Light was dawning on Blaine. "And the veeps are leaning on you, and you want to report you got a digger on the scene, even if he kind of just wandered into it."

Jenny's face revealed nothing.

"But so why tell me not to dig? What do the research guys say about this 'psychic storm' buzz?"

"They say it's bullshit, Blaine, you know that. And the reason you can't dig is you don't have neural compatibility clearance for the Middle Egypt Region. I want you clear on that point: you don't dig. Understand?"

"So it's just for appearances' sake? You going to tell your bosses I'm here and maybe forget to mention I'm not working, and if Omni and IntraVision scoop us, jeez, that's just how it goes sometimes?" A slow grin came onto his face. "I guess I didn't realize what it takes to be management."

She flushed a little. "You're overstepping, Ramsey," she said coldly. "I've overlooked your credential misreps with this Nile Studios"—so she'd found out about that already—"but don't push me. Don't try to play on some imagined relationship between us." She watched him to see how the double threat had taken. Then she coaxed him. "Look, help me and we'll forget all that. Stay in Cairo 'til I get coverage out there. Then I'll give you Yemen or whatever. OK?"

So the love of postmodern middle management women came down to this in the end. Not that he had deserved better. "Sure."

She nodded. "I got a call coming in I got to take. I'll check with you soon."

———

He had heard the Image-digger folktales, of course: the stories about this or that team of diggers shipped off quietly to private sanitariums in Switzerland or Austria. And there was that benign-looking provision near the end of everyone's employment contract, providing that Icon "agrees to render all psychological care and services needed by Researcher as a result of his work for the Corporation, and Researcher consents to Corporation taking unilateral action in this regard in case of psychological disability on the part of Researcher." He had never given any more credence to the "psychic storm" stories than most of his colleagues did, any more than he did the UFO photos displayed by the garish newspapers at U.S. grocery-store checkout counters.

Yet Jenny Chan's story about "unstable diggers" getting spooked by rumors was bullshit, if she was referring to Boyle. It would take something to shake Boyle, maybe something like Blaine's Image nightmares and hallucinations. Her line about neural compatibility clearance was bunk too: Blaine had dug everywhere in the Middle East without a hint of the depression and disorientation indicating a compatibility problem. And Jenny could get a compatibility clearance in seconds if she wanted one. If she was telling her bosses she had a digger working Cairo, why wouldn't she be willing to go to a little trouble to make sure it was true?

He checked with the front desk, but there were no more Icon personnel in the hotel. He tried again to netphone the diggers he had heard were working in Cairo; again they didn't answer.

His room's silence oppressed him. He opened the door to the semicircular balcony and the roar of Cairo came in, vast and reassuring: a million distant engines and horns across the half-kilometer of river, the roar of barges carrying ore, music from brightly lit pleasure boats with their darkened police-boat escorts, the clatter of helicopters and hoot of rotorcars, and beneath it all the heartbeats and breath and voices and footfalls of 35 million people, swirling into his room on air that smelled like burning garbage and rubber tires, relieving for a moment his anxiety and homesickness. He stepped out into the murky dawn twilight twinkling with the lights of the tin-can cooking fires in the rowboats moored thick along both shores of the river, the glittering chains of headlights on choked streets and bridges that faded into smog. He realized suddenly, with a moment of irrational panic, that he had no idea where in this vast, smoky landscape the Riyadh Hotel and his friends Abu Yusef, Yusef, and Shukri were; he had forgotten to get any addresses or telephone numbers. Now he faced the slow-burning apocalypse of Cairo and whatever had driven Mark Boyle mad without even the warmth of human neighborliness, in the sanitary isolation of this Western jewel box of a hotel.

He did just one more thing before he slept. *Geb, Seb,* Boyle had said in his babblings: *Tell him Geb, Seb,* and then a reference to "she." It sounded like nonsense, but Blaine checked his palmtop's encyclopedia.

Geb and Seb were the same thing: "The ancient Egyptian god of the earth, son of Ra. Worshiped in primordial times by burial of a virgin up to her neck in the earth for several days; if earthquake tremors came, it meant that the god had chosen the virgin as his priestess and sent his spirit into her. She was then disinterred and her words were treated as prophecies."

—

He had just one dream that night, lying in his soft bed in the hush of the Nile Meridien's fuzzy-logic climate control. It was only a sound, a sound that seemed to penetrate a pitch blackness that had closed around him and that he couldn't dispel, much as he tried to open his eyes: a screaming. It was a screaming insane with rage and violence, babbling with sounds that were almost words, and he knew it was the screaming of the shit-covered nightmare man from Darb Al Ahmar. He lay awake in the dark and sweated when he finally woke up, afraid not so much of the sound itself but more of the realization of where he had heard it before: behind his garden wall in the Jordan Valley, the voice from his dreams in Kraima, from the unseen assailant who had beaten the dream-girl Buthaina.

"—as the world's population approaches ten billion, the demands on food supplies and ecological systems are becoming prohibitive and unsustainable," said the United States' Ambassador to the United Nations, a slender, middle-aged woman standing behind the podium in the Great Hall of the General Assembly. "The developed nations' World Food Aid program was based on the premise that zero population growth could be reached without catastrophic resource depletion. We turned a deaf ear to the critics who said that without the natural correctives of resource shortfalls our world would die under continued explosive population growth. Yet we are tormented now by the fear that we were wrong. If we are, we dare not go on. We cannot—we *must* not leave a ruined world to our children; we must not kill our Mother Earth."

Blaine watched her with professional fascination on his room's big HDTV wall screen. Her persona psychoforming extended even to the tremor in her voice, which, together with the large, soft eyes, reminded him vaguely of the twentieth-century movie star Judy Garland, or perhaps Betty Crocker, wholesome and pure, with just a hint of eroticism and good cooking thrown in. Maybe not an accurate personification of a country whose 3 percent of the world's population consumed 25 percent of its resources, but an effective one for projecting an impression of innocence and compassion to the starving hordes of the world. Blaine wondered vaguely which of the big advertising firms had gotten the contract to research her, and whether they had been able to find an actress to project the resulting Image, or whether it had taken plastic surgery, pharmacological implants, or hypnosis.

It was noon, but you wouldn't have known it inside the Nile Meridien. The nearly inaudible hush of the air system and a comfortable 22 degrees centigrade replaced the city's roar and glare of smoggy heat. Blaine sat, bathrobed, in a pink armchair waiting for his laundry. He wondered dully why the Egyptian government hadn't blocked broadcast of the U.N. debate on the WFA's refusal of earthquake aid to Egypt; maybe it wanted anyone who had a television to understand what it was up against—maybe, by the expedient of letting people see uncensored news, it was explaining why it would be unable to repair their collapsed buildings and broken water mains, increase hospital capacity, or provide emergency food after the Big One came.

Watching the U.S. Ambassador's sensitive face and listening to her earnest voice, it was hard to disagree with anything she said—exactly the effect intended by the psychoformers. Yet Blaine felt anger stir in him. Egypt had had a chance to industrialize in the nineteenth century, to get on the First World economic curve where development stayed ahead of population, as the Western countries had done. But the European colonists had stepped in during the 1880s, and with their bombardments and economic manipulations had destroyed the country's budding textile industry; it suited them better to quash competition with their own textiles and keep Egyptian cotton a cheap raw material for the European mills. So by the time Egypt gained independence in the 1950s its economy had already fallen hopelessly behind: by that time there were no longer any fiscal surpluses for development or investment, no chance to do anything but play catch-up, to try to feed the ten thousand new mouths that came into being every day, and long-term development be damned.

But that was only half the story, he reminded himself wearily. What about the government corruption and endless red tape, the heedless economic policies, the lavish lifestyles of graft-taking officials, the bloated bureaucracies, the mismanaged state industries? Surely no victim of colonial plunder had ever participated more enthusiastically in its own rape than Egypt.

Whoever was at fault, Egypt, with its 100 million people,

its high birthrate, and its lack of serious weapons of mass destruction, was a perfect sacrificial lamb, a perfect country of which to make an example, to hold up to other Third World nations whose population growth had remained outside the parameters defined by the WFA as a condition for aid. Watching one of their fellow recipient countries crash and burn would bring the point home. And wasn't that a lesson this desperate, overburdened world needed right now?

Blaine's laundered clothes arrived with a price tag that probably exceeded the annual income of the median Cairo family. He turned off the TV, put on jeans and a cotton shirt, and went out into the roar and thick heat of his balcony to clip his satellite antenna to the railing, then checked his net messages. None of the Cairo diggers he had called had replied, but there was an icon on his screen indicating that his search agent had compiled the earthquake report he had requested back at the Riyadh Hotel.

He glanced through it. North African seismology was apparently almost as chaotic as its politics. Barely 250 kilometers north of Cairo, in the middle of the Mediterranean Sea, the African and Eurasian continental plates were in the process of a slow, cataclysmic collision; 200 kilometers to the east, the African and Arabian plates were tearing away from each other. Egypt had become especially active in the past few years; one theory was that the flooding of the Qattara Depression in the Western Desert had lubricated longdry underground rocks, allowing them to slip against each other and relieve pressure built up over millennia. Swarms of tremors, disturbances in the earth's telluric currents, and a twenty-centimeter uplift of the ground surface had all been reported in the Cairo area in the past months, and scientists were predicting a major quake.

The experts had recommended strengthening and reinforcing buildings, resettling population, and installing elaborate early-warning technology. The Egyptian government couldn't afford these measures, especially without foreign aid. So if the dice rolled sour there could be hell to pay: by comparison, the 1976 Tangshan earthquake in China had killed 750,000 people, and that had been a low-density urban area with semimodern building standards.

One of the Related Topics listed at the end of the report caught his eye: Social Unrest. He clicked it and a summary blurb told him that natural disasters such as earthquakes fed strongly into the destabilization side of predictive models of social unrest the search agent had seen at think tanks and universities around the world. Cairo would be a perfect place for that effect, it occurred to Blaine. He knew Haseeb had dabbled with some social unrest models for Icon; maybe he had indexed some code that could help Blaine decide how dangerous his Cairo movie-star hunting really was.

Haseeb System's black eyes smoldered across 3,400 kilometers of telephone cable as Blaine tried several times to explain what he wanted. Finally it said: "Haseeb has indexed a dynamic simulation model for the Cairo area."

"Wait a minute. What are you telling me? Haseeb has a Cairo disaster model already built?"

"Its existence is to be revealed only to high-password users, and only if Haseeb is out of touch for twenty-one consecutive days. He has now been out of touch for twenty-nine days."

"OK," said Blaine, puzzled. "What was he doing with it?"

The AI paused, looking thoughtful, computing heavily to try to give an appropriate answer to this associative, vernacular question.

" 'Load it to me and I'll look myself," Blaine said, hands tapping nervously on his hotel-room desk. "Wait, before you go— I struck out at Nile Studios. In junk auto parts language that means I went to Nile Studios, but they wouldn't let me see the Egyptian actress Aida. Do you know where else in Cairo I might find her?"

9

Haseeb's software was about a dozen gigabytes compressed, zipped, and encrypted, and took about that many minutes to download from Karachi on a high-bandwidth feed. As soon as it was in, Blaine, eaten with curiosity, expanded it, initialized it, and opened it.

It looked complicated; the interface hanging close around him in his specs resembled an airliner cockpit. It had a name in a decorative panel at the top of the display, and the name brought a little chill into Blaine's stomach. Haseeb had called it "Mindstorm."

Blaine tried to go through the model systematically despite the sweat on his palms. At first the parameters were similar to sociometric models he had seen before: population data, social patterns, economic measures; then came a group of geological parameters like depth to bedrock, overburden type, and seismographic time-series. Here was the linkage between social unrest and seismic simulation models his search agent had mentioned.

Then, deep into the model, Blaine came upon a parameter called "psychic flux."

He took off his specs, squeezed his eyes shut, and wiped a little perspiration from his face in the hush of the hotel's air system. "You know it's bullshit," Jenny Chan had said of the Cairo psychic storm rumors; and it was true, he had known that. Psychic storms were the old wives' tales of a discipline too young to have old wives.

But "psychic flux" was a term in the new, bastard, and still not entirely respectable field of archetypal neurosociology, a term Blaine remembered from his Icon training courses. It was a measure of the "charge" of the collective unconscious at a particular time and place, the "pressure" of unconscious Images welling up toward consciousness. The job of the advance scouts sent out by the advertising companies was to sense areas where psychic flux was high enough to justify the expense of sending Image-diggers.

But why would Haseeb Al Rahman build a simulation model called "Mindstorm" that linked neurosociological parameters to earthquake and political unrest data?

He slipped his specs back on and brought up the next parameter.

It was called "Image focus." Image focus was a measure of how tightly concentrated the collective unconscious was on a particular Image or family of Images.

After that were more neurosociological parameters: "psychic load," "Image depth," "cognition duration."

Blaine dug a flow chart out of the model's documentation. Even at a summary level the model looked complicated, yet somehow elegant, as if the animated diagram of its tortuously swirling feedback loops within loops, dynamically linked variables, counterregulating and equilibrating equations, and converging and diverging values were a work of art, an abstract, highly compact, subtly symmetrical representation of some higher-dimensional object.

The thought kept trying to come into his head that he

was looking at a psychic storm model built by Haseeb Al
Rahman. But there was no way to run it and find out for
sure, because it was unfinished. A handful of initial conditions still had to be specified: "areal homogeneity," "leakage
coefficient," "exhaustion half-life," and "warning variable."
He was vaguely familiar with all of these terms except "warning variable."

———

The Blue Nile Club, which Haseeb System's index said was
an Aida hangout, was on Al Rodha less than half a kilometer
from the Meridien. It was on the water, and its holographic
roof display was simply a rippling column of blue light
standing ten meters in the smoky air above its round, four-
story pillbox of windowless concrete. Blaine arrived by taxi
wearing a rented tuxedo. The entrance was through a river-
side tea garden of the kind so beloved by the Arabs, but used
now just for show, empty tables gleaming with dinner service set up under arbors of plastic jasmine, bougainvillea,
and climbing rose, lights of a passing pleasure boat with its
blaring music rippling on the oily river. There was an ornate
metal railing on which you could lean and listen to the water
slapping and gurgling on the rocks below, smell its wet,
alive, sewery smell.

A round, two-meter-high cowl of concrete made a short
tunnel to the side of the Blue Nile building. At the end of it
was a double metal door without a knob or any other feature, sealing whatever was within from the outside air. No
one else was in the tunnel or at the door. A small glass panel
was set in the wall. Blaine stood in front of it and saw the
tiny flash as a laser read his retina.

Nothing happened.

He tried it again, with the same result.

He pounded on the door with his fist. It was like pounding on a cliff.

"Open the fucking door," he said.

A man materialized like dust falling from a couple of lenses in the ceiling, grainy and translucent. He was grinning.

"Mr. Ramsey," he said in perfect, American-accented English, though he was a dark, good-looking Egyptian. "Go home. You can't crash a place like this, man. There's plenty nice clubs elsewhere."

"Who or what do I have to know to get in?" Blaine asked the hologram. "Or is there a cover?" He brought his wallet terminal out of his jacket pocket.

The man looked at the terminal and laughed. "Who or what *do* you know?" he asked.

Blaine thought about that. "Haseeb Al Rahman."

The holographic man got a faraway look. Sparkling a little with static, he said woodenly: "Distinguishing marks."

"Dark birthmark on his left ear. A thin scar between the second and third fingers of his right hand, where he—"

The man sparkled back up into the ceiling and the two halves of the metal door slid silently apart.

Just as Haseeb always seemed a jump or two ahead of him, it appeared that he had preceded him on his quest to Cairo too, Blaine thought as he stepped into the Blue Nile.

The doors hushed shut and Blaine's bank terminal chirped, indicating it had been charged. A small, distinguished-looking man with a blue rose in the buttonhole of his tuxedo came forward with murmured obsequies.

The circular entrance foyer had a cloakroom on one side, but otherwise looked like a wraparound aquarium: the walls and ceiling were curved glass with dim electric-blue light refracting through it and the water behind it, in which exotic flora and fish undulated. Not glass, actually, but some light-transmitting, transparent plastic, Blaine thought, and not the Nile either: the stuff floating in those murky waters wouldn't be appropriate for an exclusive nightclub.

A passage slanted off from the foyer, following the curve of the building's outer wall. The greeter stretched out his hand, murmuring polite invitations.

The passage continued the foyer's motif, the only light coming through the aquarium walls. In some places they were only a half-meter thick; behind the flowing water at one place he could see people sitting crowded at tiny tables. Elsewhere they were thicker, and through their blue, cloudy, and rippling depths he could catch only the vaguest impression of what was happening beyond.

A chamber opened on Blaine's left, a smoking room to judge by the smell and hazy air, traditional carved wood paneling and *mashrabiya* screens enclosing alcoves, an old-fashioned brass lamp shaped like a star hanging from the ceiling. Beyond it an upward slope was perceptible in the curving passage. A giggling Euro girl ran down the passage past him, dragging a tuxedoed Egyptian boy whose dark, handsome face, frizzy black hair, and low forehead would have looked more natural in a *gelabiyah*. Ten meters farther on was a cybercafe in underwater motifs where flesh-and-blood men and women sat in booths across from telemetered holograms of their friends in other parts of the world. After that was a crowded bar, expensively dressed people holding drinks and cigarettes spilling out into the passage.

He didn't see Aida, but he could have missed her in dozens of dim, blue-lit places.

As he went on, the incline of the passage increased and the air began to gather a deep, intermittent hum that filled him with a vague excitement. He climbed the last steep turn of the passage. There were steps and then thick double doors that opened into a vertiginously steep and alternately dark and blinding blue floor show theater, and the humming blossomed into music.

It was modern music, a clash of African, North American, Arab, and Latin rhythms, sinuous but syncopated, melodramatic but sophisticated, with modern electronics and the wail of peasant ballads. It turned in his chest and belly like the pangs of love, the fire of sex, the ferocity of murder, turned his skin to tingling fire, the center of his body to orgasmic liquid. They were using subsonic reactive harmonics—what Western kids called "gut-thump"—a technology illegal in most of the Arab world: subsonic vibrations modulated to carry messages to the brain stem, bones, and viscera without the intervention of consciousness, a technique originally developed in advertising to take advantage of the unconscious parts of the body that were naive enough to believe anything they were told.

Blaine tried to see through a thick, quivering soup of emotion and sensation. He was at the top of a steep, crowded two-story theater. The 'thump thundered up the acoustic nautilus and back down from the ceiling in exquisitely roiling interference patterns. The floor show was psychoactive. On a bright stage shaved women, hairy men, and dancers in fantastic animal and god costumes gyrated frantically in repetitive, ritualistic motions probably based on material purchased straight from Icon or some other psychoad firm, their shapes projected up at intervals through the smoky air as if giant, primitive archetypes danced there.

A hand touched his arm and an usher—wearing earplugs and a stiff uniform that Blaine guessed contained countersound electronics—conducted him to what was probably the worst seat in the house, high up and at the very back. He sat there forgetting everything. The 'thump tore into him, telling his viscera wordless things, obliterating everything outside the core of orgasm and sheath of fire that was his body.

He pressed his hands over his ears and tore his eyes away from the stylized sex/death/god images on the stage. The aquarium wall was immediately behind him, water crawling with wave patterns from the 'thump, so that he could barely make out a vague figure drawing closer behind it—

He found himself looking at a face through the blue,

distorting water. Its rouged lips were parted erotically, but the rest of the face was slack, as if drugged, the beautiful dark eyes dull and sullen—

It was Aida. Blaine's eyes lost focus, the shock of seeing her combined with the disturbance of the 'thump nearly making him faint. When he could see again she was still there. The 'thump churned forgotten in his body, as if he was dreaming.

A hand reached from the hazy blue behind her and jerked her around so that an exquisite shoulder blade and a mass of brown hair were suddenly pressed against the glass. The 'thump doubled in intensity and an orgasmic unconsciousness nearly swallowed Blaine; he twisted around farther in his seat, drooling. The increased vibration made the water harder to see through but he thought muscles stood out in the white back, and that the woman's body jerked, as if she were struggling or being shaken. Suddenly her face swiveled hard and hit the glass, pain penetrating its dullness. Then it jerked away again, leaving a smudge of blood or lipstick, and in the warped darkness Blaine half-saw tearing hands, a downward confusion of frantic movement, and then a bare, writhing white foot hit the glass over and over, as if its owner was lying on the floor.

Blaine staggered up blindly through an incinerating crescendo of 'thump. He could barely stumble up the stairs toward the exit. An usher helped him. The instant he got outside and the music and somatic pounding dropped away he sagged against the wall with a sudden, agonizing headache, his body heavy as wet clay. The usher held him up, fingers digging painfully into his armpit.

"Are you okay, sir?" he asked in accented English, looking closely into Blaine's face.

"I saw— I saw—," gasped Blaine in English, struggling to get his balance. "Someone's getting crashed in your club, man."

"What?"

Blaine could stand on his own now, with one hand on the wall to steady himself. He switched to Arabic. "Being raped, brother. Behind the wall of the theater, a woman being raped!"

The man looked at him with shocked alarm.

"Behind the wall! The wall of the theater!" Blaine yelled, jabbing his finger.

"No, sir. It's impossible—"

"Are there rooms back there? I saw it through the water, brother!"

The usher was murmuring into a pin on his lapel, and thirty seconds later two tuxedoed men trotted up the passage.

One of them took Blaine's arm. He was shorter than Blaine, impeccably groomed, square-jawed, good-looking. "Relax, Mr. Ramsey," he said in excellent English. "Cigarette?" He offered him a gold-plated case. The usher was talking to the other man in a low, urgent voice.

"There's a rape on in your club, asshole," Blaine spat at him in English, moving to disengage himself, but the man held on to his arm, began conducting him down the passage the way he had come. Blaine, still wobbly from the 'thump, went along. "Where is this rape?" the man asked in the same soothing voice. "On the show floor?"

"Yeah, sure, and it was real pretty. But meanwhile behind the wall somebody was crashing an actress named Aida."

"Aida, you say." The man studied him, smoke from his cigarette curling lazily from a gold-ringed hand. "We sometimes overestimate Westerners here. How familiar are you with 'gut-thump,' Mr. Ramsey?"

"You gonna tell me it was a 'thump-mirage?" Blaine turned roughly and stood in the man's face. He switched to Arabic. "Perhaps you would rather that I called the police."

The man, in Arab fashion, didn't mind standing eye to eye; he smiled. He switched languages too: "You are an

Arabic scholar, God give you strength. This club is off limits to the police," he added absently. He earnestly put a hand on Blaine's arm. "But listen to me, brother. Nobody was raped tonight. We keep surveillance here twenty-four hours a day. The walls gather light as well as diffuse it, and a computer puts it together for us into pictures. If anybody so much as writes graffiti in the bathroom, we know it. The actress you mentioned wasn't even in the house tonight, darling, take it from me."

The man took Blaine's arm again and conducted him politely down the passage. Laughter and the buzz of voices came from the bar and the people outside it as they passed.

"What I saw wasn't a hallucination."

"It was, darling, it was," said the man soothingly. "More and more of our patrons have been hallucinating her during the shows recently. She really is a very beautiful actress, but it's strange: you wouldn't believe the effect she has on people. Perhaps the studios are buying scenes from some of your Western psychological companies to put in her films, and they're driving people mad over her."

They had reached the circular foyer where Blaine had come in.

"I suggest you see your doctor for medication recommendations," said the tuxedoed man politely. "And perhaps he will suggest that you take precautions, such as avoiding stomach music and the like. And if you really want to see this actress, try Ehlam Towers in Giza, where she lives."

The doors of the Blue Nile hushed open discreetly.

Blaine walked past the line of limousines at the curb outside the tea garden, and over to the tree-lined street beyond, where a few hopeful *baladi* taxi drivers had parked their tiny, battered vehicles. He stuck his head in the window of one of these and said: *"Burg el Ehlam."* He had no way of knowing if the Blue Nile bouncer had given him good information, but he was in a feverish mood and going somewhere would give him something to do.

Ehlam Towers was on the Giza side of the Nile, near the river. It stood out like a beacon as they drove, above the smelly shantytowns where donkeys pulled carts and men in *gelabiyahs* sat in lantern-lit coffee shops, above the dilapidated, cracked, and dirty high-rises without window-glass, above the ancient, acid-damaged banyans along the river, its twenty-five-story towers outlined in blue neon hazy in the smog.

As they got closer Blaine saw that it was a vast block ten stories tall with two glass towers rising another fifteen stories at either end. When they were still half a block from it the street ended at a high, dirty corrugated-iron barrier that faded off into murky darkness in both directions. Heaps of rags along the fence were people sleeping; an old, wrinkled woman in black robes and headscarf sat cross-legged by a tiny fire in a tin can.

"You can't get nearer than this, effendim," announced the taxi driver, a small, bony man, very dark, with several silver teeth.

"How do people get in?" asked Blaine.

"By God, they come in through the roof, effendim. They come in sky cars."

"And why didn't you tell me there was no entrance before you brought me here?" Blaine demanded angrily.

"No, effendim, I thought—"

"You wanted to cheat me," snarled Blaine, his Arab market reflexes taking over. He got out of the taxi and slammed the door. "You thought I was a foreigner and you wanted to cheat me, hah?"

"No, no, effendim—"

Blaine took a small scrip from his pocket and threw it in the window of the taxi. The bland face of the Blue Nile bouncer who had sent him on this wild-goose chase was before his eyes, fanning his fury. "OK. Go."

"Effendim, if your presence would let me explain—"

"Go. Hurry, go from here, and may God destroy your house."

Blaine walked along the dirty, graffitied barrier, which was higher than his head, stepping around the sleeping people and breathing exhaust from the steadily passing cars. He ignored the taxi driver, who drove alongside entreating him through the car window. Finally the man gave up and drove away.

The glow of the city made the sky a dirty orange. Ahead, a group of thin young men stood against the barrier smoking cigarettes and talking. One broke away from the group and followed Blaine as he passed.

"Hey, man, you wanna taxi?" he said in accented English idiom above the traffic noises.

Blaine held up his hand in polite refusal, still walking.

The man dogged him. "You looking for girls? Hash? What do you want, man?"

"Your blessing only," said Blaine in Arabic.

"God bless you," the man replied reflexively in Arabic, then stood still in surprise, getting lost in the murk behind as Blaine strode on. Blaine's blood pressure had been scarcely elevated by the encounter. Street crime was as rare as high-level graft, and political repression was common all over the Middle East, as if crime too was one of the luxuries of the rich.

Still, a hiss behind him made him turn quickly.

For a second he thought the young man had come after him, but he was nowhere in sight. Instead, one of the bundles of rags against the corrugated-iron barrier had begun to move. As Blaine watched, it uncoiled twisted limbs, knelt on all fours, then stood up shakily. Blaine could see the dark glitter of eyes in the orange glow from the sky. The hiss was breath coming through a narrow mouth and broken teeth in a labored wheeze. The figure limped forward with deliberate wariness, leaning a hand on the barrier.

As it came closer Blaine saw that it was a man no bigger

than a boy, thin, ragged, and dirty, wearing noisome, split-open boots.

The tiny man stopped a meter away. He smelled of grease and urine and rotten teeth. He wheezed asthmatically.

"You want to see her," he hissed. "You've come to see her too. OK. She's coming. She's coming in the air car."

"What, brother?" asked Blaine softly. "What are you saying?"

The man looked into Blaine's eyes with his orange-glittering ones. "You want to see her."

"See who?"

The stunted man laughed, a wheezing, choking sound. "I know you. I can *smell* the ones who want to see her. I smelled you as you passed." He joined the fingers of one hand together and made a gesture of smelling them as one might smell a flower, with concentrated appreciation. "I see them everywhere, everywhere I go. None of them can resist her, though they don't know why. But me, I know why."

"You mean Aida? The actress Aida?"

The man jumped at him, face contorted. "*Shut up!*" he hissed. "*Shut up! She's here, don't you know? Here, and here, and here, and here.*" He jabbed the air with his finger. "Don't you know? If you say her name she'll *hear* us, she'll *find* us."

Blaine stared at him. "What do you know about her?"

The little man made a secretive, rotten-toothed smile. "I know when she comes and when she goes. I *feel* her. She is coming now, in a few minutes. Everyone dreams about her at night, but I *feel* her. I know when she comes and when she goes. *I know who she is.*"

At the words "dreams about her at night" Blaine had started, and now he leaned forward and put his face down near the little man's, enduring the smell of his teeth and un-clean body.

"You are from Switzerland, eh?" asked the little man as if sharing a secret. "Do you have a cigarette?"

"Why do you say everyone dreams about her?" asked Blaine steadily.

"Do you have imbeciles in Switzerland? The people in the neighborhood take care of me, they give me food, and Mustafa lets me sleep in his stairwell when it's too cold to stay here to watch over her, but I know something they don't know. I know that she is coming back in a few minutes—"

Blaine grabbed the stunted man's shirt, his hand huge against the man's tiny, heaving chest. "Why do you say everyone dreams about her?"

The stunted man looked up into Blaine's eyes without fear, his hand still on the barrier. He whispered: "I saw her in the cinema. She gave us warnings. Have you heard her, brother from Switzerland? She has come to warn us."

"Warn us of what?"

"*Yaum ed din,*" said the little man, but just then a hooting roar came above them. They looked up as a gust of gritty wind blew a sheet of newspaper through the murky air, and Blaine saw the running lights of a VTOL a hundred meters overhead, making for one of the huge blue-edged towers.

A sound next to him made him start.

The little stunted man was shaking violently as with a seizure, eyes goggling out of his head, teeth clenched and cracking.

Blaine put out his hands to try to help the man, then withdrew them, afraid to touch him.

———

He looked fine, Blaine saw, studying himself in the crystal-clear mirror in his tiled and sanitary hotel bathroom back at the Meridien. A little overdressed, perhaps, for an encounter with a tiny, rotten-toothed, stinking prophet, but the flesh of his face was a good disguise, stolid and innocent—a little troubled, perhaps, but no more than the faces of many men that hid who knew what in this troubled world.

Strange that the stunted man had tagged him right away

as looking for Aida, he thought, staring into his eyes, and that he had predicted her return in the VTOL. Though VTOLs probably came and went from Ehlam Towers five hundred times a day, and there was no reason to think Aida had been in that one. Still, the stunted man might have something; if he had managed to stay sane Icon might have been able to use him as an Image scout. As it was, deformed and made mad by his hellish life, he had become what prophets had probably always been: not frauds, for they themselves believed what they had seen, but pitiful creatures, dreaming some salvation from this crushing world in their malfunctioning brains. *Yaum ed din,* the little crazy man, the prophet Aida's John the Baptist, had said: the Day of Religion, the Muslim's term for Judgment Day. *Yaum ed din,* the last consolation of the crazy and the weak.

10

The next morning a special program of Egyptian traditional dance had preempted CNN on Blaine's HDTV wall screen. With a slight chill he clipped his satellite antenna to the balcony railing, climbed NetStar II, and pulled CNN through his server in Beirut. The top Mideast story was that rioting had broken out in neighborhoods in north Cairo heavily damaged by the earthquake tremor of two nights ago. Excited newscasters speculated on how Egypt would deal with the situation in the absence of foreign aid, and how simmering social problems might come to a boil; at the very least, Egypt's radical opposition groups would be sure to take advantage of the situation, etc., etc.

He got room service for breakfast, hardly tasting the dumbed-down Arabic food, made bland and germ-free for the Westerners who could order it here and believe they had consumed a robust taste of local color. His mind was running feverishly over everything that had happened. The rioting was near the Darb Al Ahmar address where the dancer he had seen at the *mulid* was supposed to live. Probably there was no way for him to get back there now; though he had a hunch that all he would find if he *did* go back would be a woman, young or old, upon whom the likeness of Aida had been projected either by his own malfunctioning brain or by the collective unconscious, and a spastic cretin upon whom had likewise been projected some other, awful likeness.

No, one way or another everything came back to the movie actress Aida, who seemed to be exerting such tremendous pressure on the collective unconscious of the Middle Egypt socioneurological region that she had driven Imagediggers mad, that half the population seemed to be obsessed with her, and that Blaine had dreamed her three hundred kilometers away in the Jordan Valley. And the famous Haseeb Al Rahman, who scoffed at digger mysticism but was by all accounts a firm believer in Judgment Day, had built what looked like a psychic storm model of Cairo containing a parameter called "warning variable."

"She has come to warn us," the crazy little man at Ehlam Towers had said.

Haseeb System answered Haseeb's phone, and Blaine asked it: "Has Haseeb indexed any research associated with a computer model parameter called 'warning variable'?"

Text on the screen said: "Please repeat in this order the words: 'bearable,' 'variable,' 'terrible.' "

Blaine did that impatiently.

"Yes."

"Upload it to me."

"That information is classified as 'Confidential.' "

"How could it be confidential? You sent me the computer model it goes into two days ago."

"Haseeb has it classified as confidential."

"Listen, you fucking lawn mower, it's a mistake. It goes in the model. Haseeb just forgot to declassify it along with the model."

The machine looked thoughtful, computing furiously.

"Look," Blaine tried to calm himself, "just give me Haseeb's index headings. He didn't classify the index headings as confidential, did he?"

The AI paused, then said: "Visions of the Virgin Mary, Medugorje, Yugoslavia. Visions of the Virgin Mary, Fátima, Portugal. Motzeyouf, Devils Tower, Wyoming. Chaim Maddox."

He couldn't get anything else out of the machine, but he thought he had the idea. The names in the list were places where religious and mystical apparitions had purportedly warned of impending disasters. The Bosnian genocide in Medugorje, World War I in Fátima, the Cheyenne shaman Motzeyouf's visions of the genocide of the American Indians. Chaim Maddox was vaguely familiar too, but Blaine couldn't place it.

He punched up his names encyclopedia. Chaim Maddox had a small entry:

MADDOX, CHAIM—American, b. 1955, Bangkok, Thailand. Author of texts on the epistemology and ethics of psychoforming.

Blaine remembered now. The Image-digging community considered Chaim Maddox something between an eccentric and a nut. He had been part of the development group that had put together the first experimental Image-digging teams at Young & Rubicam around the turn of the century, one of the most successful R&D efforts ever launched, and which had quickly spawned a whole new industry. But brilliant R&D teams always seemed to contain at least one member who later flakes off into mysticism, and this was no exception. Asked to head up Y&R's Advanced Concepts group, Maddox's ideas had gotten farther and farther out until he was gracefully promoted out of harm's way. He had left Y&R then and started publishing material on the net, making wild claims about Image-digging and psychoforming.

But however crazy he was, maybe this Maddox knew where to find Haseeb.

Blaine climbed NetStar II and did searches. Maddox had half a dozen sites, but no published addresses or phone numbers. Blaine rode hypertext to one of the sites, which was called: "Beneath the Substrate: What Underlies the Collective Unconscious?"

> Geoscientists tell us that Earth's biosphere exhibits the characteristics of a single "superorganism." It is observed, for example, that maintenance over billions of years of the same delicate chemical balance in the oceans and atmosphere closely resembles the homeostasis produced by the coordinated operation of glands and organs within a single biological organism to maintain the conditions necessary for life.

> I will argue in this paper that such a "superorganism," by definition more complex and more cybernetic than any of its parts, must have a consciousness. Further, just as individual human consciousness skates on the surface of the vast ocean that is the individual unconscious, and just as the individual unconscious skates on the surface of the vast ocean of the collective unconscious, so the collective unconscious may be understood to skate on the surface of the superorganic, or "Gaian" consciousness.

The text plunged into a multichapter exegesis, with headings like "The Consciousness of Rocks," and "Who Is the Devil?" Blaine clicked Maddox's other sites too, but none of them seemed to have any relation to psychic storms.

He went out onto his balcony, into the warm, acrid air and vague, vast roar of Cairo. It was nearly dark, the smog over the river a romantic shade of smoke blue-gray twinkling with the fires springing up in hundreds of rowboats. It might have seemed picturesque to someone who didn't know what it meant, who hadn't seen the deformed and stunted children born in those boats.

———

Abu Sheikha's was the second establishment on Haseeb System's Aida list. It was on the Giza side of the river, in a *baladi* neighborhood tucked between the feet of two massive, modern skyscrapers. Blaine's taxi jounced along an absurdly pot-holed street flanked by ramshackle two- and three-story buildings of weathered brick and cracked stucco, glassless windows covered with shutters or canvas curtains, and the usual tiny, unsterile shops, their dirty pull-down doors pad-locked now at midnight.

He didn't need to give passwords to get into this place. A group of large, broad dudes in Western street clothes hanging around an open door—neighborhood strongmen hired to provide security—stepped aside with polite murmurs of greeting as he crossed the sidewalk in his tuxedo. A dark, creaking flight of stairs with a surveillance camera at the top led to the second floor, where aromatic smoke hung thick in the air. In a small, dim foyer with smoke-yellowed plaster walls he stepped through the ring of an undisguised tomography scanner, his retinas catching the split-second flash that meant computer-assisted X rays had gone through him. The machine's operator, a small, blond, dark-skinned man of indeterminate race, creed, and national origin, sat at a rickety table nearby and watched the terminal cabled to it.

"*Spitze Boxer, Man,*" he remarked as Blaine passed through. "Nice underwear."

Abu Sheikha's was a tobacco bar, a dark, crowded, low-ceilinged, arch-doorwayed establishment with a junk-shop atmosphere, blaring with Arabic pop music and the babble of talk, and crammed with musty, old-fashioned Egyptian furniture and run-down antiques: dusty brass charcoal braziers with decorative hoods like mosque domes; antique brass censers shaped like minarets; low wooden tables inlaid with tarnished silver and mother-of-pearl and crowded with crude, long-unused brass pitchers and coffeepots. The plaster walls were hung with obsolete wooden implements, maudlin paintings, and a crazy abundance of shiny brass trays and pitchers. All the brass gave the place a sharp, metallic tang under the sweet, full smell of tobacco smoke. The little light came from old-fashioned lanterns hung from the ceiling, many small holes in their polished brass sides making thin rays through the smoke.

Blaine found an empty place on an uncomfortably upright antique settee next to two women sharing an *argila*. Suddenly and unaccountably, he had begun to feel something unfamiliar. Maybe it was the anonymity of the smoke— or some other property of the smoke, which was making him a little dizzy—or maybe it was the shabby Arab coolness of the place, but he had a sudden feeling of ease of the kind that rarely came to people like him. This place, he saw as his eyes got used to the dimness, was full of half-breeds, multinationals, hybrids, expatriates, speakers of languages with accents, people whose faces were a jumble of racial marks, people who would be at home nowhere, and so, by that very quality, made him feel at home among them. The two women next to him, for example: one was obviously European, pretty in a prematurely party-aged way, blonde and full of ennui; the other was coffee-skinned, with full lips, thin, braided dreadlocks, high cheekbones, a straight nose, and slanting green eyes; the two of them spoke French, then Arabic.

A little bald man with an understanding smile and bloodshot eyes squeezed himself out of the crowd in front of Blaine. "Can I get you something?" he asked kindly.

"What's in yours?" Blaine asked the blonde woman next to him in English; her friend was taking a slow inhalation from the pipe.

"It's tobacco," she said, looking up at him with innocent surprise.

"I believe you."

"But of course," she said as if shocked by his sarcasm. "Narcotics are illegal in Egypt; they carry a death penalty."

The little man watched with smiling patience. *"Numero dix-sept,"* the woman said to him. He nodded and squeezed his way back into the smoke and darkness.

"But of course tobacco can be genetically modified to naturally produce almost any substance. In this way, every one of your desires can be fulfilled legally," said the woman.

The coffee-colored woman handed the pipe to her friend, let out a long, slow breath of smoke like a dragon, and then smiled at Blaine.

"I love tobacco," she said in a voice soft and dusky as her skin. "It's so masculine."

"Don't listen to her," said the blonde woman, her words punctuated with smoke. "She's a lesbian or a transvestite or one of those things."

The coffee woman kept smiling at him.

"And you?" the blonde woman added.

"I'm neither," said Blaine. "But I'm happy to have found this place."

"This place is chic now. All the authentic people have gone," sighed the blonde woman, smoke trickling through her teeth, handing the mouthpiece back to her friend. "I come here only because it's not—how do you say—psychologically shaped—"

"Psychoformed."

"Psychoformed. Most of the clubs are psychoformed now. Yet not-psychoformed places are the only ones you can see clearly, don't you think?"

"All places are psychoformed," said Blaine without thinking; it was the psychoad companies' party line. "People have been psychoforming since they started drawing animals on cave walls. It's just that they didn't have computers and psychological research to help them then."

"Oh, philosophy," purred the coffee woman, as the other looked at him doubtfully. "I love philosophy."

Blaine's Number 17 came, and he watched the little man put the glowing lump of charcoal on the chopped tobacco, then drew on the mouthpiece to start it burning. Smoke bubbled lazily through the water and wreathed indolently toward the hose. He had to inhale again before he got any in his mouth. It tasted of cinnamon and other spices that had been chopped into the tobacco, filling his lungs like hot steam and then his head like cool water. Space took on a different aspect, at once cozier and more expansive. He became aware of the sounds around him as if he had forgotten to listen to them for a while, or as if he was hearing them a second after they occurred. He suddenly felt as if he couldn't talk, as if he would like to spend the night just sitting and listening to the sounds and watching the things in front of him.

"Do you like it?" the blonde woman asked.

"What's in this?" It was as if he had intended the words and they had been emitted effortlessly from some part of his body, like his shoulder. He looked at the woman and good feelings flooded him. He was alive and in this cool place, and he had lots of money and this babe to talk to. Of course, Icon strictly prohibited drug use because of unknown interactions with the herbs, but he was on R&R here, and besides, no one would find out.

"I told you, tobacco. You are in the American foreign service?" the blonde woman asked.

"What makes you think so?"

"All the American civilians are gone because of the political situation. No?"

"No."

"A businessman, then."

"Closer to the truth. A businessman on vacation."

"In Cairo?"

"Why not?"

"Because Westerners don't vacation in places like Cairo. It reminds them of the dirty sides of their own minds. And especially not if it's dangerous."

"Is it dangerous?"

"Talk about the weather with this one," the blonde woman told her friend in English. "He's CIA or something like that."

The blonde woman's name was Chantal and her friend was Monique, and they were "refugees from the European fashion scene," whatever that meant. They had come to Cairo because it didn't cost anything to live here, and weren't afraid of earthquakes or riots. "Because," Chantal said, "Europe is full of worse things every day." She gave him a fashionably anachronistic business card showing a Mohendiseen address.

Abu Sheikha's had gotten even more crowded, more smoky, and louder, though all of these things would have seemed impossible earlier in the evening. At a certain point Blaine's ears began to ring.

Thinking it some effect of the tobacco, he laid off his mouthpiece for a while, but the ringing got worse, so he took a drag to get rid of it, with the same result.

"Does this stuff make your ears ring?" he asked.

"Only when *she* comes in," said Monique, glancing around anxiously. "Do you hear it too? She must be here."

"Excuse my friend. She is—what do you say?—superstitious," said Chantal, and launched some accusatorial French at Monique.

"Who is *she*?" But the thought was already in his head.

"An actress she's in love with, isn't it, Monique, darling? And she listens to some stories the Arabs tell. She got into a party at this actress's house once and now she can't get her out of her mind. Isn't that romantic?"

"You only *wish* you could be in love," said Monique with a bitter sideways glance at Chantal.

"Where does she sit?" Blaine asked.

Monique gestured unhappily toward the back of the establishment.

All taste for engineered tobacco had suddenly left Blaine. His mouth was dry and the ringing in his ears was waxing and waning. The two women were arguing in French. "Excuse me," he said, and got up.

It was a tricky thing to do with the antique bric-a-brac underfoot and the place literally packed with people. He swayed a little, his chest against the broad back of a man who was shouting and gesturing vigorously over the music to half a dozen others. He excused himself very slowly in the direction Monique had waved. It was darker back there. He squeezed past sweating faces flushed with talk, gesturing hands, plumes and mushroom clouds of smoke. Men in peasant *gelabiyah*s and headdresses somehow bustled through the crowd delivering freshly charged *argila*s. Nowhere was any sign of the movie star Aida.

A rear room opened through a wide arch at the back, as crowded as the front room, and behind that was a narrower, curtained arch. Blaine was three meters from the curtained arch when something hard blocked his path.

"Sorry, sir, a private party," said a big, tuxedoed, lantern-jawed man with a heavy five o'clock shadow, in Arabic-accented English, his palms unobtrusively against Blaine's chest. Blaine moved a meter to the side and tried to squeeze past him, but the man got in front of him again. "Sorry, sir."

Behind the big man Blaine could see beautiful people, pure breeds in expensive clothes. Aida wasn't one of them. The curtain kept him from seeing what was behind the back archway.

A smaller, smiling, bald man joined the large one. "Are you looking for something, sir?"

"The bathroom," said Blaine.

"Over there." Both men pointed toward the wall to Blaine's right.

The bathroom was small and dim, the tiles cracked, the trough urinal smelly, and there was a gap-toothed man who pulled paper towels from the dispenser and handed them to you after you washed your hands, for a tip. Outside it was a tiny, dim hallway separated from the smoking rooms by a curtain. The hallway had three worn, dusty doors in it. Two were marked Men and Ladies; the third was flimsily padlocked to a nailed hasp, and opened in the direction of the back room Blaine had been stopped from approaching. On an impulse Blaine yanked this door. The hasp came loose and the nails jingled on the floor.

The room beyond was dark and smelled of corroded metal and sour, ancient dust. Blaine stepped inside and pulled the door shut behind him. It was a storeroom, he guessed from the shapes he had glimpsed in the light. People clattered in the hall behind the door now, men talking in loud, laughing voices, banging into the bathroom.

Blaine waited a little until he could navigate carefully, mostly by feel. The smell of dry decay choked him. The room seemed to be stacked and piled with junk too decrepit even to go in the smoking rooms. At the far end light stained the bare concrete floor.

Blaine's heart sped up. The space- and emotion-bending intoxication of the tobacco seemed to be gone, leaving only a slight headache, but his ears still rang, now sibilantly, now deafeningly. He went toward the light, knocking over some metal object with a dry clank.

The light came from under a door. If his spatial judgment was right the door should open into the back room behind the curtained arch.

He listened at it.

Nothing. Silence with Arabic pop music in the background.

He turned the handle slowly. The door didn't budge.

His fingers felt an old-fashioned round-barreled key, turned it with a slight squeak.

Then the door would open. It scraped a little along the bare concrete floor. Pop music came more loudly to his ears. He looked into Abu Sheikha's back room.

It was perfect. It couldn't have been more perfect if it had been written in a book. The back room was crowded with more junk, piled and stacked on the dusty concrete, some of it covered with sheets, some of the brass objects polished, others corroded. A circle of stools sat in an empty space in the middle of the room, but all were empty except one. On that stool a woman sat facing him. She was Aida. She sat with her legs wide apart, leaning forward with her forearms resting on her thighs, like a man. She was wearing a short, pleated black dress that in her current pose rode up her hips, sheer black stockings, spike heels. Her long legs and bare arms were soft but strong-looking and the curled fingers of one hand held, incongruously, a cigarette. Her head was down so that she looked up from under her eyelashes. Dark hair, tucked behind her ears, fell over her shoulders.

There was no sign in her face or body of the intoxicated gaiety of the crowds outside. She seemed to be looking directly at Blaine but he wasn't sure she saw him. For a split second he thought her eyes were rolled up in her head, then that her face was convulsed with rage, then that fire radiated from her eyes. The ringing in his ears was bursting his head. The blare of it seemed to radiate from her beautiful hard-soft body.

He was suddenly filled with an irrational fear, a panic. He backed into the storeroom, nearly fell over something, turned and scrambled in the dark. In a minute he was shoving through the crowd in the front rooms.

Then something peculiar happened. Through the wail of music and jostling of people something surfaced that was even stronger. He didn't perceive it at first, but then he realized that a rattling and clinking that had grown up all around him was Abu Sheikha's wall hangings and crowded antiques clattering against each other, that a shaking he had thought a movement of the crowd was the floor jerking under his feet. He put his hands out to steady himself; people staggered into him; people screamed; the lights went out and it was pitch dark.

But only for a second; they flickered orangely and went back on, some emergency generator picking up the load. The crowd swayed and shoved with undecided panic, but then there were shouts of *"Khalas! Khalas!"* and Blaine realized that the floor was no longer moving and the decorations were no longer rattling. White, drawn faces of women and men moved before his eyes. The cries and lurches died down.

Except for one voice. It came from the back of Abu Sheikha's. In it was a tone that made faces turn to look, made people catch their breath. It was the wild screaming of utter ruin, the insane screaming of someone who had lost her mind.

There were words in it, words in Arabic. "Oh people, listen! *Don't you know?* It is upon you! Give away all you have! Don't you see the orphans all around you? Give away all you have lest it drag you down—!"

And craning his head above the crowd he saw Aida, arms raised, mouth a gash of desperation, eyes like black holes as she lapsed back into her wordless, crazy screams, tuxedoed men on both sides of her restraining her, murmuring in her ears as they tried to calm her.

Blaine's ears were ringing as if his head would burst.

11

His hotel suite was quiet and still that night, the only sound the faint hush of the air ducts. Perhaps because of the smoke he had taken he slept fitfully, tossing uneasily in his large, soft bed, sometimes half-awake, sometimes mostly asleep, but dimly aware of an uncomfortable feeling that he wasn't alone, that there was someone in his bed. He finally roused himself enough to turn over and open one eye.

Aida lay curled tensely next to him in the black clothes she had worn at Abu Sheikha's, her wide, staring eyes on his face.

He sat up, suppressing a shout of fear. The room was dark, his bed empty. He touched the light on his watch; there were still two hours until dawn.

He lay back down and, when the pounding of his heart had eased, fell back to sleep.

It seemed a long time before he woke again, aware of a faint rumbling, and longer still before he could be sure it wasn't just some harmonic of the air-conditioning system or some other system in the great building. It seemed to be growing, but so slowly that he couldn't be sure; yet now it was certainly louder than a few minutes ago, and he thought he felt a faint vibration through the springs of his bed. He came all the way awake at last, lying soaked in sweat, tensed, listening. It was distinct now: a rushing, rumbling, getting louder, faintly shuddering the building, and now there were little shocks in the shuddering, as if something were hitting the outside walls.

Blaine jumped out of bed imagining in panic a tornado, though he had never heard of such a thing in Egypt, but when he looked out his window he was momentarily relieved. There was no storm: no roiling clouds or debris flying on the night air. Then he looked down.

The Nile had burst its banks and covered the city like a vast, angry sea; huge, foaming whitecaps reached up nearly to Blaine's window; and now the giant hotel building, the last bulwark of the city, was beginning to turn and lean heavily in the onslaught of waters with terrifying shudders, moans, and cracks, and Blaine could only watch in terror as his room tipped with excruciating slowness and his window headed straight down into the crashing gray—

He sat up in bed with a shout, soaked with sweat, heart hammering. Gray dawn lit the window.

The telephone remote was on the bed table. He threw off his covers and dialed Jenny Chan's apartment, using his priority code. After twelve rings the L.A. switch told him no one was answering and he told it to try again, and yet again after the next twelve rings, and on the third pass Jenny answered, looking sleepy and irritated. Her irritation turned to alarm when she saw Blaine.

He could see her control herself. "You OK?" she asked steadily from the big wall screen.

"Where's Haseeb, Jenny?"

"Haseeb? Haseeb Al Rahman, you mean? How do I

know where he is?" But Blaine had seen a flicker in her eyes, and he knew that she knew something about Haseeb.

"I've got to talk to him."

"He's not in my group, remember? Why do you—?"

"Because something's going on out here that I never heard of. Haseeb knows about it. Or maybe you didn't know that Mark Boyle and your other Cairo diggers lost their marbles after dreaming a local movie star? Haseeb was here, in Cairo, you know that? I got into a local hush club by mentioning his name."

"What're you talking about? A hush club? Are you all right?" There seemed to be genuine anxiety behind the words, and also, he thought, a desire to stall so she could think.

"There's an Image that won't stay in the bottle out here, Jen. The city's haunted by a ghost woman who's still alive, who's talking about the end of the world. Haseeb's AI sent me a psychic storm computer model Haseeb was building with a variable in it that has something to do with a warning from the collective unconscious. That enough for you to be straight with me? No? Then I have to go after it myself. But I need to talk to Haseeb."

"You're not going after shit," Jenny rasped. He thought she had gone pale over the link. "Don't you remember what I told you? In fact"—her voice was shaking—"you're out of Cairo. Now. There's no Image there. It was a mistake. We got bad scout. So pack your bags." She looked at her watch. "I'll get you a ticket. Get to the airport and call me."

"Jenny, give me a couple more—"

"I'm giving you a couple more nothing. You're outta there."

"I've got to run this thing down first."

"*You're going to the airport!*" she shrieked in sudden rage. "Get there in two hours or you're terminated! You understand?"

"No can do, Jenny."

"Then you're terminated as of now. I'm doing this to protect myself, Blaine." Her voice broke suddenly. She seemed to struggle with herself. "It's *dangerous*, Blaine. Haseeb—" She paused. Her lips were trembling.

"Haseeb what?"

"In Switzerland. In the *sanitarium*, you understand? Haseeb Al Rahman. The great Haseeb Al Rahman. He crashed and burned. In Cairo. You understand, Blaine? You understand?" She was whispering now, crying. "*You've got to leave.* I shouldn't have let you stay. I needed— But you have to get out."

"What happened to Haseeb, exactly? Have you talked to him? How bad is he? Can I talk to him?"

She shook her head. "I can't tell you any more. I wasn't supposed to tell you what I just told you. Please, Blaine. You've got to get out."

A void had opened up in Blaine's chest, a pit. Haseeb Al Rahman was in Icon's funny farm, had been pulled down into the sea of Images he had always ridden so irreverently and seemingly effortlessly.

Haseeb was down. So that left Blaine.

"Jenny, listen to me. I need a favor. Really bad. I need a—"

"*No!*" she screamed at him. "No more! You're term—" And the connection broke from her side.

A second later a message flashed on the wall screen indicating that a registered document had been received. It was entitled "Notice of Termination."

———

He dialed some of the Icon diggers he knew, chatted them up gregariously while sweat prickled on his body, worked into the conversations the question of the Company's Swiss sanitaria. He got a couple of phone numbers and called them, but none of the places admitted recognizing the name Haseeb Al Rahman or the description of the tall, dark, glowering Punjabi.

So either they had taken him somewhere else—perhaps to keep a hush on the breakdown of such a well-known digger—or the fix was in with the sanitarium staff. Or else Jenny Chan had lied to him.

In any case, Blaine was on his own now. He had forty-eight hours to challenge his termination before it became final, but his Icon line of credit and other privileges were already suspended. The Meridien computer had known that before he had read the termination document: he had had to transfer his room charges to personal credit before making the sanitarium calls.

He fumbled the business card the woman Chantal had given him out of the tuxedo jacket hanging on his desk chair. There was no answer at the phone number on it, but he programmed the hotel phone to give the number ten rings every fifteen minutes.

He paced his room feverishly, tried to eat the breakfast he ordered from room service. Finally, at mid-morning, the number answered.

Chantal's face appeared on his big wall screen. Her eyes were two reddened slits, and she seemed hardly able to stay conscious. Her hair was disarrayed, and without makeup her face was gray and pouchy.

"Chantal, this is Blaine. Blaine Ramsey, the man you met at Abu Sheikha's last night."

"Abu mmm?"

"Chantal, sweetheart, can you—I need to talk to Monique. Monique; is Monique there?"

Chantal dropped the telephone, as if she had passed out. Blaine cursed, waited. After a long time the handset got picked up and Blaine was looking at Monique, in a green dressing gown with embroidered dragons.

She smiled drunkenly when she saw him. "Ah, Philoso-phy," she slurred.

"Monique, I need a favor. Remember you went to a party at a movie star's place here in Cairo?"

Her intoxicated face got troubled.

"Where does she live, Monique? How can I see her? I need—It's important."

It was hard to say exactly what made her help him in the end. At first she was angry, then she cried and tried to explain something in her slurred and blundering voice, but finally Blaine's sheer repetition and insistence seemed to hypnotize her drug-soaked brain. "You can't get in without an invitation. But when I was there, at the party, I—I took her telephone number. I crept into her bedroom and I took it."

She knew it by heart. Sobbing, she gave it to him.

He hung up and dialed it, hands sweating. He was afraid it had been disconnected or changed, or that Monique had lied to him or misremembered it, but after six rings he was looking into the drugged, vulnerable, unreadable, beautiful dark eyes of the actress.

"Yes?" she said coldly in Arabic, and when he didn't answer made a move to break the connection.

He was staring, hypnotized.

"Buthaina," he whispered.

A slow surprise, and then confusion came into her eyes. "What? What did you say?" Her voice was soft, throaty, harsh, as if used to screaming, crooning, whispering, but not talking.

"Buthaina."

She stared, as if trying to see more clearly through the electronic link. "Who are you? Where did you hear that name?"

He was struggling to get enough breath to talk. "I saw you—in a dream—"

A slow expression of fear and astonishment seemed to penetrate the drug-induced dullness.

"Who are you?" she whispered.

This was his chance, his one chance. "My name is Blaine Ramsey. I'm at the Nile Meridien Hotel on Al Rodha. I need to come and talk to you. It's very important."

But she leaned forward and broke the connection.

He tried to call her again several times, but there was no answer. He got up and paced, his mind a jumble. He tried Haseeb System in Karachi but a text message told him the number had been disconnected. So Icon had closed that chink in the hush they had put on the Cairo affair, probably at Jenny Chan's prompting. His phone and net links both rang an hour after that, and the stats showed the caller as Chan. He Declined it, cursing, then listened to her message, a tearful plea for him to leave Cairo, some high Egyptian government official had just been assassinated and there was rioting—he cut it off before the end.

His net link rang again that afternoon with an automated message from the American Embassy advising all citizens who did not have compelling reasons for staying in Egypt to arrange transportation out of the country as soon as possible. Out on his balcony there was no sign of trouble as far as he could see in the thick, hot, acrid air; the vast, distant roar of the city seemed no different than ever.

Evening was beginning to tint the smog blue-gray before a call came down from the hotel's roof landing platform. The sounds of wind and chopping rotors came over the audio, and the face of one of the platform attendants was huge on the wall screen. "Mr. Ramsey, there's a car here for you, sir, and we're so busy I'll have to send him off into the holding pattern unless you can come up right away."

"A car? From where?"

"He didn't say, sir. Shall I tell him to push off?"

When Blaine reached the roof three minutes later he saw that they were indeed busy, so busy that the transit lounge the hotel elevator opened onto was nearly shoulder to shoulder, luggage piled everywhere, as if all the guests had come up at once: Westerners clutching briefcases and overnight bags, sitting crowded together on the deep couches, perched on the arms of chairs, standing restlessly and looking out the

Plexiglas walls that had been meant to give a panoramic view of Cairo but now just showed murky dusk and a few lights on the river. There was a smell of apprehension and cigarettes and aftershave. Blaine wrestled through the crowd, getting nasty looks, as if he was pushing to the front of some line. Outside, half a dozen VTOLs and a helicopter were in various stages of landing, taking off, or taking on passengers, the roar and gusts from their rotors buffeting the smoky evening breeze. Several of them were airport shuttles. Blaine could see the running lights of a dozen more craft circling in the smog, waiting to land. Uniformed attendants directed traffic with light-sticks and headset radios.

"Mr. Ramsey?" One of them ran toward him, hair disarranged, face harried. "If you would please embark at once, sir, God keep you—"

"What's the rush?" Blaine asked as the man escorted him across the tarmac. "What's going on?"

"Everyone is leaving because of the situation. You're the only foreigner I've seen all day that's not going to the airport. Even Egyptians are leaving, if they can afford it."

The craft to which the man led him was the latest-model Mercedes VTOL, gunship black and aerodynamic, poised on the four swiveled cowlings of its ultrahigh-speed rotors: a high-altitude, high-speed hovercraft driven by modern ceramic rotor components and bugfuck turbocharging, and costing probably as much as a yacht.

A slender Egyptian in a black chauffeur's outfit and large mustache shook his hand, murmuring polite greetings and blessings, and closed the hatch of the VTOL's passenger compartment behind him. Inside it was like a plush six-seater Learjet, quiet and comfortable as a salon after the smoggy, rotor-booming air outside. He snapped his seat belt, rotors murmured through the soundproofed cabin, filtered air blew from nozzles above the seats, and they floated buoyantly off the tarmac as if lifted by a balloon. Blaine watched the platform drop away beneath them, watched the

Nile Meridien tilt in the dusky smog as they banked. They headed out across the river, dark water making the smog look like an endless abyss below them. Soon dual towers of glass with rounded corners and roof platform lights floated out of the abyss.

—

They landed. Blaine's palms were wet. The chauffeur opened the hatch and handed him out with the help of a little man in a sky-blue bellhop uniform and tarboosh that looked incongruous on his bald head, his convex Egyptian grandfather's face, his aged hands holding prayer beads. The evening call to prayer was rippling through the sky far below them. The little man led Blaine to the door of the building's empty, luxurious roof lounge asking politely after his health and the health of his family. Blaine could see three other bellhops sitting in their small office kiosk, hands to their ears as if listening to the radio, ridiculous sky-blue tarbooshes all askew on their heads like the Three Stooges.

Murmuring pieties and blessings, the little bellman ushered Blaine into a gilded and mirrored elevator, took him to the twenty-first floor, then led him down a long, hushed hallway with damasked pink wallpaper, soft carpet, and gilded light fixtures.

Blaine could hear music humming faintly through the pearl-lacquered, double-hinged, arched door of Apartment 21C. The bellman stood in front of an inconspicuous panel for a thermogram or iris-scan or whatever they were running, and the door clicked. He opened it for Blaine, letting out an abrupt tumult of thunderous music, and gestured politely, prayer beads hanging from his wrinkled old hand.

Inside it was dark with the luminous darkness of parties and bars and cafes in the West, where deep, midnight blues are focused up into the middle air, tiny visible lights strung here and there high up and low down, and lights just outside the eye's wave band glare from the ceiling, phosphorescing strangely on here a piece of fabric, there an item of someone's makeup, there the petals of a flower. Blaine turned to thank the bellman but the door had already closed, separating him from the name of God and prayers on the little man's lips, sealing him into this compartment of cosmoculture, which lived at the tops of high, hermetic buildings far above the poverty and population in all the cities of the world.

A strapping ebony woman who could have been a model emerged from the general luminescent dimness by virtue of her pale hair, which glowed like plasma in the invisible lights. Blaine was in a two- or three-story foyer through which small, mysteriously illuminated waterfalls tumbled over mossy rocks and between the twining branches and tendrils of potted trees. The deafening, undulating music was Euro cyberclash, the kind rammed out by computer-controlled human musicians on neural interfaces; it had some 'thump in it: not enough to burn your brain, but enough to make you uncomfortable if you resisted its commands to sway, laugh, and be drunken. Screams and shouts went up from denizens of the darkness somewhere beyond the ebony woman, wolf whistles and loud, intoxicated declamations.

All this was a relief to Blaine; a party. It would give him a chance to be anonymous for a while, get his nerve up before he approached the actress. And the very fact that she was throwing this kind of party—which he could look upon with an Image-digger's contempt for common physical pleasures—gave him reason to think she was no more than a human.

Blaine got hold of the ebony woman's arm and said loudly in her ear so as to be heard, in English: "Excuse me."

She turned to him in surprise.

"I'm looking for—"

"Who?"

"Aida."

"Yeah, wha' about her?" She had a British accent.

"She here?"

She gave him a sudden angry look, as if he had slapped her. "Do I look like her keeper?" she said over the music. "Think you can just come in and demand to see her, then? That what you think?"

Through doors at the side of the foyer the music, which had seemed deafening before, was louder, and modulated with a detonating 'thump that tore at Blaine's insides, making them bleed hot ecstatic neurotransmitters. A mob danced close and intense in the strobing darkness. He squeezed between a wall and thrashing people, toward tilting rectangles fifteen meters away.

Beyond these soundproofed doors was a short hall with another door at the end. In the reception room beyond a big chandelier gave tastefully subdued illumination, and along one wall a buffet gleamed under bright lights with polished silver and china, smelly cheeses, smoked fish, exotic salads, and elaborate pastries; a few glamorous people were filling plates while more sat in circular clusters of sofas and chairs. The conversations in the room were quiet and intense, and Blaine wondered if the subject was the political troubles.

He walked past the buffet to look out tall, arched windows. A swiftly fading pink and orange dusk in a clear, cloudless sky lit a jumble of low buildings many stories below, villas with palm and mango trees rising over stone walls, old-fashioned stucco apartment houses with ornate iron balconies and *mashrabiya* latticework in their windows, an antique mosque—the buildings straggled out within half a mile to mud-brick huts and wide, planted fields dotted with clumps of palm, the last rays of daylight gleaming on the water of rice paddies. A few peasants in *gelabiyah*s and turbans walked slowly or rode donkeys along a road that ran out among the fields.

A funny feeling came into his chest. He was looking at Cairo as it had been, or as someone dreamed it had been, a hundred years ago, or maybe only fifty.

"Are you a policeman?" a voice said in English.

He turned. It was the ebony woman from the foyer. She was a Nubian, Blaine guessed: tall, with a shapely chocolate body that looked as strong as his. But she wore a blonde crew cut and had a British accent.

He smiled. "No."

"I'm Frieda."

He shook her strong, elegant hand.

"You're new. I haven't seen you around before."

"Guilty."

"Sorry I was rude. But when you meet someone that doesn't know the rules, you immediately wonder."

"I apologize. No one told me about any rules."

"When you mentioned her name like that, it sounded like you thought you owned her or something."

"Sorry."

"No one mentions her name. People get upset if you do." She looked sheepish. "We're all moths circling a flame here, I guess, and no one wants to admit it."

"Well, I'm circling, too, if I understand what you're saying. In fact, I hope to dive straight in."

"Oh, don't hope for that."

He laughed politely.

"You think I'm joking?" Frieda leaned toward him, eager to talk about her despite the "rules." "Her fifth husband killed himself a year ago. He was found twenty-one floors down." She pointed a long finger at the floor. "Before him they all died badly. One shot himself; one drowned; one took too many skin patches. And her lovers go the same way. She's been seeing a military man for the past few weeks, a fighter pilot, and he's become a patch addict. Have they heard of her even in America?"

"I don't think so. I heard of her in Jordan. I came to find out what she's like."

"She's a suicide. Someone who's trying to drown herself." Blaine made his expression interrogatory.

"She has this party going on twenty-four hours a day. It's quieter now than it's been in a long while: people are starting to sneak away because of the political troubles. She's always full of drugs, especially since the earthquakes started. They scare her, they say." Frieda looked into his face. She was sweating a little, he saw, as if talking about Aida were some kind of drug, perhaps a way of possessing her vicariously. "She devours lover after lover, lives in nightclubs, casinos, parties. She always has to be surrounded by noise, music, followers—"

The low buzz of voices around them had quieted suddenly. People were staring, a few having suddenly risen.

Aida had come into the room. She was standing two meters from the doors opposite where Blaine had come in, smoke from a cigarette in her hand trickling upward, and a retinue of people coming in after her. She wore a plain black dress. Her face was blank, eyes abstracted, as if she had forgotten where she was or had fallen into a reverie.

Every eye in the room was riveted on her. Blaine stared too, though he knew it was rude and uncool. But she was intensely lovely, with a deep, unconscious loveliness, like something of spiritual importance, something that had to do with the real, deep purpose of human life.

The hum of conversation picked up slightly. An old, foolish man in an expensive suit and cravat doddered over to Aida and began mumbling and laughing wheezingly, gnarled, trembling hands illustrating his words, a young, buxom, intoxicated, Scandinavian-looking woman in a dangerously low-cut dress on his arm.

Aida took a drag on her cigarette and smiled faintly, as if amused. Most of the people in the room were standing now in little groups, pretending to talk but keeping one or more eyes on her. Blaine, at the back, could see everything because of his American height.

Aida's cigarette was burning low. She reached out casually and extinguished it on one of the Scandinavian woman's breasts.

After a second of incomprehension the woman screamed and jerked backward. There was confusion, cries. Blaine got a glimpse of the woman's anguished face, Aida's blank profile. There was a flurry of muddled activity. The woman was helped from the room, sobbing. Two men in black tuxedos whom he recognized from Abu Sheikha's, one big and lantern-jawed, the other small and bald, moved forward now, clearing a path among the excited, the aghast, and those who were pushing forward to get a better look, arguing politely with those who protested or tried to ask questions.

"The man behind her is the Deputy Minister of Justice," Frieda breathed in Blaine's ear. "Do you think she'll be prosecuted?" She giggled strangely.

The Deputy Minister of Justice was a dark, bald, stiff-looking man in a conservative suit who stood near Aida with a sober, dignified expression that gave no indication he had seen anything out of the ordinary. As Aida walked forward he passed through the door toward the dance room along with the rest of her entourage.

12

The big apartment was full of wild, almost desperate partying. Some of the more intoxicated guests played computer games, wearing blank goggles, shouting meaningless words to each other, and jostling those who weren't sharing their reality. But Blaine also saw people glancing surreptitiously at their watches, perhaps checking how long it was until they had to be at the airport.

It took him a while to get up his nerve to go to the dance room. In there, mind-burning 'thump drove down like a strobe-lit thunderstorm on a swollen crowd crashing like typhoon waves, a macroorganism of writhing bodies and orgasm-linked minds. Standing against the wall, hands vainly covering his ears, viscera jerking, Blaine squinted watering eyes through the neural haze. Aida thrashed at the center of the crowd, eyes closed, lips parted in ecstasy, sweaty hair clinging to her.

He squinted, stared at her in fascination. Then it was strange. He could feel his attention, his consciousness being drawn toward her like water toward a drain. He realized that the music was gone and the other people were vague blurs in a twilight, but he seemed to see her perfectly. She danced in slow motion. In silence she thrust her hips with utter concentration, as if copulating with an invisible spirit, the slow, lithe movement filling his whole cognition, like a deep, vast swell of the ocean, and he a shipwrecked sailor clinging to a plank.

He went toward her, barely feeling the collisions with the other dancers, their flailing arms. She seemed to give off heat like a bonfire. When he got close he grabbed her wrist. Her skin burned him. Her eyes opened slightly, glittering at him through slitted lids.

Hands grabbed him. Two men flanked him, pulling him away from her. They both wore stiff countersound jackets and headphones. The music crashed around him suddenly again, and the dancers sped up to normal motion.

The two bodyguards pulled him through the sound-proofed doors and out into the hall, where the music was only a loud hum. They didn't seem to recognize him from the night before. He slumped against the wall with the after-effects of the savage 'thump.

Another man came through the doors, letting out a blast of music before they swung shut. Blaine focused on him. It was Munir Helwan, the agent, whom he had met at Nile Studios, his shoulder-length hair loose now and damp with perspiration. He was looking at Blaine with wide eyes. He was shaking, his pupils dilated, perhaps from some 'thump-complementing drug, his breath hissing through dilated nostrils. His neurological arousal and the smell of his sweat made him seem large and frightening.

He looked into Blaine's eyes closely and wildly, as if studying something he had to kill.

"Throw him out," he gritted to the bodyguards.

There was another blast of music and then a light, musical giggle that sent chills up Blaine's spine.

Everyone turned. Aida was coming out of the dance room leaning on the arm of a big, handsome man. She was covered with sweat, and her body was still undulating a little as if she couldn't get the 'thump out of her head. Some of the other dancers were straggling out after her, hooting and laughing drunkenly. Among these the Deputy Minister of Justice walked with oblivious, frowning dignity, wearing a stiff countersound jacket and pulling headphones off his ears, several obvious plainclothes policemen close to him, as well as a fawning PR type who was talking earnestly at his elbow.

"Where is everyone going?" Aida cried. "I told you I want to dance, Munir! What are you doing, darling? Who is that?"

"No one, darling," Helwan said. "A madman. We are just throwing him out."

"Is he the one who touched me?" She giggled again and tossed her hair, pulling at the strands sweat-plastered to her face and neck. "Let me see him. Is he really mad? Will he bite?"

"He's one of those foreign dream witch doctors I told you about, who *must* see you or they'll die," said Helwan. "He bothered me at Nile Studios a few days ago. I don't know how he got in."

She came closer, her face gay and wild, her hands fondling the arm of her big escort, pelvis still jerking from the dance, eyes glazed with intoxication and wantonness. Up close her irises were purplish-black.

But as she looked at Blaine her expression changed. Her body slowly stopped moving. Her hands tightened on her escort's arm. A vague anxiety replaced the wildness on her face.

"Who is that?" she asked a little breathlessly. "Is it—?"

"No one, lady," said Helwan, and Blaine thought anxiety came into his face too. "A fan who got in without an invitation."

But Aida was staring at Blaine, her brow puckering.

The parlor to which the bodyguards escorted them was arch-ceilinged, with scalloped plaster walls, antique brass lamps, and a charcoal brazier. Though it was nearly midnight, a smoky, deep blue dusk came through open windows that looked out over old Cairo's narrow lanes and tiny shops, its minarets and domes, walled gardens and *mashrabiya*-screened windows. There was a haziness in the room that seemed partly mental, like opium smoke or a kind of field that affected the nerves directly, so that the outlines of soft, opulent furniture, the cool, nostalgic smell of jasmine, and the light tinkling of a wind chime seemed both vague and intense, dreamlike. The woman sat on a divan by the windows, and Blaine stood on thick Persian carpets in front of her.

Her face was uneasy. She rubbed the knuckles of a clumsy, slightly shaking hand over her eyes, then studied him. The two bodyguards lounged against the wall a few steps behind him, and the man she had been leaning on before, very tall and athletic and darkly handsome, stood next to her. His face was congested with some intoxication, eyes slitted. Helwan sat slumped in a chair; he was sweating and still breathing heavily, as if half-stunned by whatever drug he was on. A fifth man, a small, thin, bald Euro with nervous, bony hands and an ill-fitting suit, hovered a little way off.

The studio PR type fluttered near Aida. "Lady, the Deputy Minister would like to see you before he leaves. He has an important meeting with the Prime Minister, but he's waiting for you in the ballroom—"

"Are you—the one who called me?" Aida asked Blaine shakily. "From the—? What—what do you want?"

"What does he want?" Helwan said, struggling upright in his chair. "Sister, this man is a mental patient. Why are you talking to him?"

Blaine cleared his throat tremblingly. Now that he was here he realized that everything he had prepared to say to her was vacuous, absurd. He had come to her as a lover, he realized, to save her from the assailant beating her in the Kraima garden, to hold her broken hands—

"You called me Buthaina," she said as if slowly remembering, her voice trembling. "Where did you hear that name? Where could he have heard that name, Hussein?" she demanded shrilly.

"I don't know, my life," said the tall, handsome man. He giggled. "Let's go back and dance."

"I dreamed about you," Blaine forced himself to say, his voice dry, croaking. He was so nervous that he was scarcely aware of what was coming out of his mouth. "Your name was Buthaina. You climbed up on a wall and—someone pulled you down and beat you—and then there was an earthquake—"

The woman's face stopped him. She put trembling hands to the sides of her head.

"What?" she hissed, her face contorting as if he had said something awful, the worst thing she had ever heard.

Her eyes fearfully searched some place inside her head.

"Oh, Lord, in the name of God!" rasped Helwan, standing up. "No! No! You'll not start this again, in the name of God!"

The woman paid no attention to him. Her chest heaved.

"But the dreams aren't real," she whined. "I shouldn't worry about them."

The little European sidled toward them.

"You are upsetting Miss Aida," he hissed at Blaine in heavy, Slavic-accented English, though everyone else had been speaking Arabic. "You must leave now."

Her hands were trembling fists. "Hussein, the dreams aren't real, are they? No, they aren't. But he saw it too." Her fluttering eyes looked at Blaine again, and he felt their dark, desperate heat.

Helwan stood near her now. "You need to take your

medicine, darling," he said softly, shaking rhythmically as though his effort of gentleness in the face of his drug were causing a physical malfunction.

"No."

"Yes, darling. Are you feeling well? Look, you're trembling. You know what can happen next. You need your medicine."

"I don't want it now," she said. "It makes me hear the voice."

"But look at you—you're sweating," said Helwan. "You're getting symptoms. Your medicine will make you feel better, prevent something worse from happening."

The little Slavic doctor had taken a flat plastic syringe from his pocket. "You really must take your shot, Miss Aida," he said in surprisingly fluent Arabic. "You know how hard it is to get back on an even keel once you let yourself go. Remember last time? Remember the hospital?"

She looked up at him with sudden fear.

"No," she said weakly. "I have to talk to this man. He has something to do with the thing that's coming, the things that are happening to me. He reminds me of something important from my dreams."

"Reminds you of what?" asked Helwan bitterly. "That you're a prophet sent to warn the world against earthquakes? Is that it? Isn't that what it was last time? Don't be absurd, darling. Take your medicine. You could lose your mind again, don't you understand? Don't you remember last time?"

She looked up at him, silent, eyes full of doubt. The little European took her wrist and pulled it toward him.

"Hold still, Miss Aida," he said gently. "Hold still, or Mr. Helwan will be angry."

She stared at Blaine with troubled eyes but let the doctor straighten her arm, find a vein, and press the syringe against it. There was a tiny chirp as the syringe sonically read the depth of the vein, inserted its retractable needle, and released a measured dose of whatever they were giving her.

Her eyelids fluttered. She took a deep, shuddering breath. The wrinkles and strain of worry in her face relaxed. She took another breath and giggled. The little doctor put his syringe away. Her eyes were languorous and mocking, her body suddenly all inviting curves and muscles. She pressed herself back on the divan and giggled again, a thick, lustful, stupid giggle. She flicked her hand at Blaine.

"I'm tired of him," she said. "Hussein, let's dance."

Needing no further urging, the big, intoxicated man pulled her giggling from the divan.

The last thing Blaine saw as the bodyguards marched him out was a glimpse of Munir Helwan's face. It was distorted with hatred. But he wasn't looking at Blaine. He was looking at the big man Aida called Hussein.

—

The big, lantern-jawed bodyguard conducted Blaine to the elevator. Blaine's mind was a whirl. He barely noticed the ride to the roof, the pieties of the little old bellman, the courtesies of the chauffeur. Yet as the VTOL lifted with faint vibration into the murky darkness above the Tower of Dreams he thought he saw an abrupt movement in the smog below. There it was again, a silent orange flash; it could have been an explosion down in one of the poor neighborhoods around the feet of the skyscrapers, some riot or firefight between government security police and a militia, but he couldn't be sure.

—

It took half an hour of circling before they were cleared to land on the Nile Meridien. Though it was one in the morning the roof platform was as tense and crowded as when Blaine had left, and now there were government soldiers in combat gear, half a dozen sandbagging a corner of the roof, others peering over the parapet through some kind of intelligent optical device. A small metal table had been set up just outside the door to the transit lounge, and military police were taking thumbprints of everyone heading out to the airport. As far as he could tell, Blaine was the only party they had seen coming in all night. They pulled him aside.

The lieutenant who interrogated Blaine as he stood next to the table was fortyish and martially handsome, with a manicured mustache and hard, humorous eyes. He looked carelessly at Blaine's thumbprint-summoned passport on his desert camo laptop. "You are coming from a party?"

"Yes."

"How do the streets look from the air?" asked the lieutenant curiously.

"Hazy."

The lieutenant grunted. "Are you leaving Cairo soon?"

"Why should I leave? Officer, I've heard about the political issues, but will there really be difficulties? After all, the National Armed Forces are on duty, and . . ." Blaine shrugged innocently.

"There are 'difficulties' already." The lieutenant held up a finger quickly: "You didn't hear that from me. My advice is to leave as soon as you can. And if you don't, stay in your hotel."

He cleared his laptop and held out his hand with a flourish, inviting Blaine to proceed inside.

Down in his room a priority message was blinking on his wall screen, the stats showing the sender as Jenny Chan. Blaine hit Decline and turned off the phone, but not before he had rung down to room service for a pot of boiling water. Yet it wasn't until he had actually begun combining the powders and dried leaves from his herb pouches at the Louis XV desk that it occurred to him what he was doing. He interrupted the chant he had been murmuring automatically while he worked—the chant the ancient texts said was to propitiate the gods, and that Icon's researchers said put the unconscious into a receptive state for Image work—and sat back in his chair.

There was no need to jump off this cliff, he reasoned with himself. It wasn't as if dreaming would necessarily tell him what was happening in Cairo: translation of Image-dream metaphors into recognizable messages was complex even for the applications experts in L.A., and that wasn't his part of the business. Another dream would likely tell him no more than the others had: that the actress Aida was full of some kind of power, and that she was in some kind of trouble.

And another Image dream was likely to be unpleasant. Haseeb Al Rahman himself, a man Blaine would have thought stable enough to dig in Auschwitz or Hiroshima, had gone down under the weight of an Image he had dreamed in Cairo, and one that probably had to do with Aida.

On the other hand, he knew in a vague but urgent way that what he had seen at the Ehlam Towers required a reaction, some kind of psychological counterpunch. To creep into his soft hotel room and try to forget or rationalize the woman Aida's terrible beauty, the field of imaginal energy that surrounded her, to submit to his dismissal by the drugged goddess, would be to return to his controlled, dissociated life as a Senior Field Neurosocial Prospector, his numb life as Jenny Chan's paramour, emotionally and spiritually castrated, like the godless Westerners that so horrified the taxi driver Shukri.

The Nile Meridien, with its hermetically sealed Western atmosphere, would be about the worst place in the city to dig Image, Blaine knew; there was no exposure to the weather, sounds, smells, conditions that fed the people who skated unawares on the surface of the collective unconscious, and who fed it with their life-energy, no place to tie in your neural anchor where it would do any good. Maybe that would save him; dreaming in the hotel without electronics should greatly weaken any killer Image he might tap.

He leaned on the desk where he had been working the herbs, listening. The hotel was very silent, perhaps emptied by now of most of its guests. He started chanting again, crushing and combining the herbs with practiced, steady hands. Their dusty, potent, intoxicating smell came to his nostrils.

Because there was one other thing too, something he thought he had imagined, but that he couldn't get out of his head. At the second the syringe had chirped and Aida's eyes had fluttered, Blaine thought he had heard something: a gurgling, screaming laugh—the laugh of the devil-man who had pulled the dream-girl Buthaina from her wall and beaten her, and whom Blaine had seen in Darb Al Ahmar.

—

The exilaration and clarity hit him in the solar plexus and spine the way you never get used to, and he was riding the lucid dream that carries Images up from the collective unconscious. He came awake looking down a narrow dirt street in the thick heat of day. His exhilaration turned to dismay when he realized that he was in Shafa'i, the City of the Dead.

Its stench came to him, cooking smoke and open sewers, filthy bodies and the organic grime that builds up in slums over years. He looked around and nausea came over him. Along one side of the street skeletal, rag-clad bodies lay in the shade of decaying mud huts.

A figure was approaching down the middle of the dirt street, clothed in black from head to foot, making a welcome, solid shape against the filthy gray and brown of the slum. It walked slowly and gracefully, a veiled Muslim woman in the traditional black *lefeh*, only her hands and dark, kohled eyes showing. She might have been on her way to market or to visit relatives, except for her terrible surroundings.

Her eyes were fixed curiously on Blaine as she drew near, with the innocent, direct stare of a peasant. But when she was within about ten meters she faltered. She looked around quickly, as if she had just noticed where she was. Her eyes grew large with horror, and one braceleted hand went up to her veiled mouth. Blaine could hear her gasp from where he stood.

The woman in black stood looking around desperately, trembling. Small moans came from her, and stifled invocations to God. She swayed on her feet as if she would faint.

Finally her trembling fingers, desperately working, tore open the front of her black robe, baring her breasts.

They were milky white, plump and fertile.

A rattling rasp came from his right, and Blaine jumped, terrified. One of the skeletal beings that had been lying in the shade of a mud hut was moving, pulling itself painfully to its knees with scrabbling, claw-thin hands. Its face was a horrible dried skull mask of starvation; Blaine couldn't tell if it was a man or a woman. It staggered toward the woman in black until Blaine's terror almost made him unconscious.

But the skeleton-human only dropped to its knees before her. She cradled its desiccated head in her trembling arms, and gave it suck from her white breast. It sucked greedily, desperately, its dry lips clacking horribly.

Now there were more rasping sighs and other skeletal figures were moving, clawing and scrambling to their feet, staggering toward the woman in black. She took another on her other breast, cradling it in her free arm. But now there were dozens of them all around her, pulling weakly at her and at the two already nursing, trying to pull them away, get at her, tearing her robe farther apart with their desiccated fingers, crawling and climbing over each other like horrible insects, screaming dryly in their need.

The one she had first started suckling, in its starvation and the panic that it would be pulled away, bit her.

Blaine saw the blood running out of its mouth, crimson purplish-black. The woman shrieked. Her black clothes were being pulled off her and her long tresses fell over her shoulders.

He wanted to cover his ears, turn away, but he couldn't move, couldn't close his eyes. He wanted to die rather than see—

The two on her breasts had fastened there now with their rotting teeth, and her dark blood flowed down her white body, and she writhed, screaming. Her veil was pulled away. It was Buthaina. The other skeletal beings in their starvation frenzy were biting her now on all sides, eating her. She would have fallen but they pulled her in every direction, clawing, devouring, drinking her. Soon she stopped screaming and he saw one of her arms come off. Then they had her body opened up: her ribs split open with a tearing sound and a fantastic gush of blood and organs slid to the ground, eagerly eaten up by the ones down there on their knees. Soon she was just a pile of broken bones and gristle in a blackish pool of blood soaking into the ground, and a few smashed, inedible organs. Her long, blood-caked hair was thrown like an animal pelt a little way off.

The skeletal beings slowly got up from their feast and staggered back, some nearly covered with drying blood. It was hard to tell if they were aghast at what they had done.

A gibberish scream and shout of laughter came. A misshapen man was jerking and shuffling down the street. He was naked, covered with sores, his eyes bulging and fishlike with infection, his hair and straggling beard matted with filth, his mouth full of rotten black teeth grown horribly long. Lengths of string and cord were tied from his arms and legs and waist, and things dangled at the ends of them—the skulls and bones of small animals.

It was the devil-man from Darb Al Ahmar.

His swollen, infected, imbecile face was lit with an exultant smile. He screamed with laughter, saliva gurgling from his mouth. His bare feet crunched on Buthaina's bones, splitting and breaking them, and they cut him so that his own noisome blood mixed with hers in the dirt of the street.

Blaine had lost all thought, all track of who he was, his

personality, history. He was a locus of terror and nausea and anguish twined together.

Then the earth began to shake.

It was the rumbling of the Nile breaking its banks, he knew, and it persisted even when he found himself in his bed in the Meridien, lying stiff and soaked with sweat, the hotel shaking around him, giving its little cracks and harmonics. He lay too terrified to move, remembering the building crashing into the water the night before.

Slowly the sound and vibrations receded, faded, until there was silence except for the faint hush of the air system. Blaine forced his body to relax enough so that he could move, get out of bed, go to the window and look out, trembling violently, wondering if it had been a real earthquake tremor or part of his dream.

Everything looked normal: the dark glare of smog-haloed streetlights, the Nile dark and mysterious between its banks, the flashing navigation lights of a vehicle heading away above the hotel toward the airport.

He relaxed a little more. The sheets on his side of the bed were wet, so he moved to the other side, lay on the soft pillows fighting nausea and fear. Diggers were trained to deal with intense dreams, of course, and he had tranquilizers, hypnotics, even neuroleptics in his first-aid kit, but Haseeb had always said never to use those. The one thing never to do, he had always told his small group of protégés, was to try to *fight* an Image. Images were creatures of the collective unconscious, which was to the digger's psyche as the ocean is to a drop of water. Trying to repress an Image, or forget an Image, or change an Image to your liking, aside from losing you commission money, could damage you or worse. You couldn't fight an Image any more than you could fight a tsunami, but you could *ride* an Image, even a wild one. There were many ways to do this, Haseeb had told them. His prescriptions were: first, not to try to forget or change or ignore the Image—you had to give it as much attention as it demanded, staying obsessed with it for as long as necessary to cathart it from your nervous system; second, not to take drugs to cover over your feelings and perceptions, since that would violate rule number one; third, not to be afraid to go to sleep again after an Image dream—the body needed sleep and a chance to release the stress of the dream, perhaps right away, in order to avoid damage; fourth, to talk about the Image—not to anyone outside the Company, where it could be stolen or its power dissipated, but to friends inside, other diggers, to Haseeb himself if need be.

Tears ran down the sides of Blaine's face and onto his pillow as the thought came to him that now Haseeb was out of reach, lying in some mental ward, probably drugged out of his mind.

Which maybe meant that his ideas on how to stay sane shouldn't be made the subject of a religion. Yet now that Blaine had been fired from Icon there would be no one else he could talk to about this.

He forced himself to relax in the softness of the hotel bed. If Haseeb had gone down, that meant there was only Blaine to deal with Blaine's problem, just as Haseeb had had to deal with his own problems when he was a young Image-digger, back before there were experienced diggers around to give advice.

Before he knew it he had fallen back to sleep. His sleep was uneasy and disturbed by dreams, until his net link woke him again in a frenzy of fear. He crouched in his bed cursing, letting the pounding of his heart settle down before he got up and answered. He started asking the official-looking face on the tiny screen what the fuck it wanted before he realized it was recorded and was reeling off another U.S. Embassy message: "We regret disturbing you at this early hour, but the following is an urgent communication from L. P. Symington, American Ambassador to Egypt, to all U.S. citizens in the Greater Cairo Area. A Travel Advisory has been issued by the U.S. Department of State for Egypt, especially the Greater Cairo Area. Rioting is reported in the northern and northeastern parts of the city, and is spreading quickly, with isolated clashes and attacks by extremist groups. It is the opinion of the U.S. Department of State that the Egyptian internal security and National Armed Forces may be unable to control the situation. All American citizens are urged to depart Cairo immediately. Should you need assistance arranging transportation, please contact the American Embassy immediately. The American Embassy will be unable—"

Blaine broke the connection, opened the glass door, and stepped in his bare feet onto the cool, gritty bricks and acrid, damp air of his balcony.

There wasn't much to see in the foggy darkness, just the usual tiny fires flickering in the boats on the Nile and the diffuse orange glow of the sky, but he imagined that the vast roar of the city had taken on a different tone now, hot and angry, as if a million voices just beyond the edge of hearing were shouting in rage. Far away he could hear sirens, more than the usual number, he thought. And as he stood listening, the boom of helicopter rotors became deafening above him, and what must have been a convoy of military-sized craft passed over the hotel and down the river. After they had gone, faint but distinct came the abrupt, sky-muffled *crump* of a distant explosion.

13

One more day.

One more day was all he could allow himself in Cairo, he knew that morning as he ate without tasting the stale fava bean dish a cheerful waiter had brought to his room five minutes after he had ordered it. The Nile Meridien Hotel was empty now; aside from the unusual promptness of room service, Blaine could feel it, though nothing had changed in the hush of his suite. From his balcony, the traffic crossing the two visible Nile bridges that faded into the smog had visibly diminished, and big police boats cruised slowly up and down the river in place of the pleasure boats. That was a little unnerving in itself, but then the room service waiter had gotten to him. The little man had been chipper and cheerful. CNN and the other major news sites were still blocked off the hotel feed, and he hadn't had time to get on the net, but the waiter had told him that everything was calm, that the National Armed Forces had things well under control, and that there was nothing to worry about, not even the slightest thing. On the assumption that these protestations were hospitable reassurances to a guest's sensibilities, Blaine had concluded that things were very bad. This coming on the heels of his dreadful Image dream, he had begun to lose his nerve.

So he had given himself one more day. He would try to see Aida again and tell her about the dream and see what came of that, and then he would leave Cairo. Logic told him that she would leave also, along with the rest of the upper class, if she hadn't already; that when things calmed down he could return and resume his quest; that unraveling her mystery wasn't worth risking his life; but somehow in his heart he didn't believe any of these things. Somehow he felt sure that she was at the axis of some vortex of events that included the rioting and the Images and the earthquake tremors, and that when this vortex took Cairo gurgling down whatever drain was underneath it all she would go too, and she would be lost.

But the terror of the dream and the cheerfulness of the little waiter had chilled him to the point where he was ready to retreat again to the logical part of his mind. He had booked a flight for the evening, then left a message on Aida's phone saying that he had dreamed her again. Somehow he was sure she would send a car.

And she did, in the late morning when the call to prayer was echoing through the sky over sporadic distant machine-gun fire like a last humble entreaty to God. When Blaine got to the roof platform through the now-deserted transit lounge, Abu Tayib, Aida's chauffeur, was arguing with the soldiers at the checkpoint, which was now sandbagged on three sides. Big complicated guns mounted in spidery cybernetic targeting rigs and cabled to laptops had been set up on three corners of the roof parapet, and were also heavily sandbagged. Two drab gray combat helicopters sat on the tarmac, rotor blades drooping. Several dozen soldiers sat stiffly leaning on sandbags, sweating in their plastic armor, dirty smog-masks, and helmets that buckled uncomfortably snug at the chin, holding machine guns across their laps, watching Blaine or watching nothing. The sense of waiting was suffocating. Even the wind had died, so that the platform seemed to float in a hot, acrid cloud, far removed from whatever disasters might befall the city below. No civilian hotel attendants were to be seen, and Abu Tayib's big black Mercedes VTOL was the only civilian craft on the platform.

The soldiers were telling him that Blaine couldn't leave the hotel, and that he himself must leave at once or be arrested. Blaine joined the argument loudly. In the end Abu Tayib dropped enough names of high military officials and bureaucrats who were friends of his boss that the soldiers uncomfortably let Blaine pass.

Abu Tayib smiled at Blaine under his large mustache as he held the VTOL hatch for him, and they floated off the roof in a muted hum of rotors. They flew high and kept to the middle of the river, but nevertheless Blaine heard the dull *chink* of something small and high-speed hitting their fuselage.

"Stray bullet," said Abu Tayib's voice through the intercom. "Please make sure your seat belt is fastened, and stay calm, Mr. Blaine."

A minute later the VTOL banked and dived. The maxed-out roar of the rotors was loud even in the cabin, and inertia gravity pressed Blaine into his seat as the limo rushed for Ehlam Towers before any hostile fire that might be on the riverbank realized they were within range.

The wrench of the rotors coming around to reverse thrust yanked Blaine against his seat belt, but they touched down gently. Abu Tayib opened the passenger hatch with a worried expression, as if concerned that Blaine had been shaken up too much, and helped him out.

There was one other VTOL on the platform, with a crowd of twenty people around it, and Blaine could hear raised voices of heated Arabic argument as the rotors of Abu

Tayib's craft wound down. Half a dozen of the people around the other VTOL broke away and came toward Abu Tayib's at a trot.

"Welcome, effendim," the dark, impeccably groomed man in the lead tossed to Abu Tayib. "Let's go. To the airport," he commanded. He and the others, some minked women and another groomed man, started to get into the limo, brushing Blaine aside with murmured apologies and pleasantries.

"I'm sorry, sir, but this is the lady Aida's car," murmured Abu Tayib. "It is impossible to move it from this spot."

"Brother, look," said the man who had been getting into the VTOL, getting back out and facing Abu Tayib heatedly but still reasonably. "We are just going to the airport, and then you can come back, straight back." He smacked one of his hands onto the other to illustrate how quickly Abu Tayib could come back. "I will pay you enough for the lady Aida to buy another entire car. Here, look, how much do you want?" He took out a leather-covered bank terminal.

"Impossible, sir, impossible," murmured Abu Tayib in an embarrassed voice, waving the terminal away.

Then they were all around him gesticulating and arguing, the men heatedly asking him to be calm, the women clutching their minks at their throats wide-eyed and asking him with the peasant melodrama of their language if he wanted them all to die.

Blaine headed for the roof lounge, out of whose shiny doors another half-dozen beautiful people were hurrying. The other VTOL's motors whined up to a hooting bellow behind him, then roared, lifting off in a gust of gritty wind.

The door of Apartment 21C emitted a gush of people as Blaine neared it. One was the woman Frieda, her eyes bright with excitement. "National Army units have turned against the government!" she called to him as they passed. "We're paying the most shocking price for a taxi to the airport—!"

In the foyer, still radiantly dark, the autohuman cyber-clash was still chugging deafeningly in subtly shifting patterns, but no one was there except two youths lying drugged or dead on a couple of sofas. Half a dozen others danced frantically in the room beyond, lights strobing down on stray clothing, medication wrappers, half-eaten food, and other debris strewn over the empty floor. In the buffet room one thin, dark man who looked marginal for a high-flying partyer, and might just be a delivery person or domestic who had put on some of the cast-off clothes around the place, was filling a plate hungrily from an elaborate, freshly laid buffet that seemed to have hardly been touched. A handful of other guests, dressed for travel, hunched anxiously on the edges of armchairs and talked in low, tense voices. One of them shook his head mutely when Blaine asked for Aida.

He went through the big apartment cursing himself, palms sweating. He'd brought along his palmtop to keep up with the news, but there was no place to mount the aerial where it could see the sky. There were still a few goggled youths playing computer games, even a couple copulating on a sofa, but the apartment was emptying out rapidly. He was in a small, cozy library when he heard Aida laugh.

He went quickly toward the sound. A hall led to an empty ballroom with gilt decoration on the walls and ceiling. Aida, barefoot and wearing a very short black dress that gave glimpses of narcotic skin patches on her inner thighs, stood in the middle of it, arms held stiffly at her sides, fists clenched. She wore a cold, supercilious expression. She studied the dozen or so partyers who had apparently straggled after her into the room: a few ragged, heavily intoxicated Eurokids, a couple of young Arab men barely of shavable age with prominent Adam's apples, the skinny man Blaine had seen heaping his plate at the buffet, her two bodyguards, and a handful of others. She didn't glance at Blaine. Her face was twisted with distaste.

"Are you the only ones here?" she asked contemptuously. "*You?* Where is everyone? Where are they hiding?"

"The city is burning, doesn't your presence know?" said one of the young Arab men. "Everyone is running away. But we—"

Her eyes were suddenly disturbed.

"Running away?" she asked, and her fists clenched tighter. She looked around, jaw set as if she had decided to take firm action.

She screamed full voice.

It was a terrifying sound, insane and desperate, and in his head Blaine seemed to hear undertones like the bellows of monsters and the howling voices of the dead. She was looking around in agitated confusion.

Two men broke through the ragtag of partyers, her bodyguards moving aside for them. They were Munir Helwan and the thin, shifty Slavic doctor with his nervous, veined, bony hands.

"Munir, where is everyone? Where have they gone?" Aida asked, her voice shaking. She looked around with wild eyes. "I was playing with Hussein, and when I came out it was all empty."

"Never mind, darling. Never mind," Helwan said. He looked sober, businesslike now. Behind him the doctor had slipped a syringe out of his pocket.

"Where have they gone?" she asked agitatedly. "Who will I dance with?"

"There's an emergency," Helwan said to her gently. "The Deputy Minister asked you to leave with him, don't you remember? We must go now. Your car is upstairs. . . ."

The doctor was sidling toward her.

The thought came to Blaine that if they goofed her again she wouldn't be able to talk to him. He stepped forward.

"Sister," he said.

She whipped her head around as if astonished and

frightened by the word. The violet-black chasm of her eyes gave him vertigo, though there was a glaze over their midnight and they jerked dizzily.

"Sister," he said again. "Buthaina."

He was aware of Helwan's raging curses, and hands took hold of him roughly. But vague recognition came into the woman's eyes. "Yes?" she said faintly.

This close he felt the force-field that bent all his senses upon her, so that the things around her grew dim, distant. At the same time there was a feeling in his body that he recognized. Standing close to her was like diving dream, he realized, the surge and pressure of the collective unconscious humming in his spine and solar plexus. It was as if *she* was an Image, he thought confusedly, an Image thrown up somehow in living, breathing form.

"Who let him in here again? Throw him out," Helwan yelled at the bodyguards furiously.

"Let go of him," she said. The hands hesitated, then went away.

He noticed a movement next to her. It was the doctor, sidling up with the syringe.

Her head whipped around to follow Blaine's glance and her face twisted with rage. She hit the doctor full in the face with a clawed hand, and he sat suddenly on the floor.

Helwan cursed. He and the bodyguards bent over the doctor.

"You left a message," she said to Blaine, as if remembering with difficulty. "On the telephone. About a dream." Her face was troubled.

"Yes."

She was silent, but her eyes compelled him.

In the background Helwan was snarling at the doctor to stand up, the bodyguards arguing heatedly. Blaine told her the dream. When he was done he felt nothing but her eyes on him, and he remembered the hands he had held in the wadi in Kraima, the cold, distant feel of them, the eyes staring sightlessly at the moon.

She giggled then, and her giggle made the hair stand up on Blaine's head.

"Let's go then," she said. She was covered with sweat suddenly, arms clutched tightly across her stomach, and she rocked her body autistically.

Helwan spun to face her. "We can't go anywhere, don't you understand?" he screamed. "We have to get to the airport!"

"To Shafa'i," she said. "To Shafa'i to see if this man is telling the truth. This man has the dreams too. If they're real, I'm damned! I'm damned to hell, you understand?" Her laughter had turned to frenzied screaming, and her face was terrifying. "I'm a devil, you understand?" She knocked away Helwan's hand, the syringe he had taken from the doctor rattling away across the floor. "I'm a devil and I have to go to hell! To hell! To hell!"

"My God!" Helwan gasped, staring at Blaine, his eyes protruding from his head. "He said this to you? He told you this?"

The doctor, who had finally gotten to his feet and was touching his bloody face delicately with his fingers, came forward and whispered in Helwan's ear.

Helwan listened to him and his color slowly subsided.

He turned to the gasping, trembling Aida. "All right, we'll take you to Shafa'i," he said, and turned on his heel. The party onlookers blanched and slunk away.

⸺

Blaine sat by the middle left window of Aida's VTOL, behind the seat where she sat herself. She had insisted that they revive Hussein Falwa—whom Blaine gathered was in some kind of coma after "playing" with Aida—and he had come out with dilated eyes and a raging color in his face, as if they had used some powerful stimulant on him. The chauffeur

Abu Tayib was gone when they got to the roof—fled probably along with the rest of the domestic staff—so Falwa flew the VTOL, leaving an empty seat in the passenger compartment.

Blaine was pretty sure, as they lifted off, that they were going to the airport despite Aida's orders. Helwan had had a private conference with Falwa before takeoff; then too, Helwan and the big, lantern-jawed bodyguard they had brought along looked as calm as if they were going club-hopping. The shabby Slavic doctor's eyes were shut, his head back against the seat, his bandaged face neutral, as if asleep.

Yet the time for calmness was over now, Blaine had realized as soon as they had emerged onto the roof platform. The voices of several kinds of machine guns echoed between the buildings from the street far below, and the scorched smell of explosives was in the air. Between bursts of fire they could hear what sounded like the distant roaring of a mob and an incomprehensible bullhorn, and in the far distance air-raid sirens.

Aida had decked herself in movie-star finery: a blue-black double-breasted suit that showed lots of fetching, white-stockinged leg, spike heels, sunglasses. Blaine had no idea what her concept of Shafa'i was, or what going there meant to her. Did she think seeing it would confirm the reality of the dreams that had been disturbing her? Had she had the same nightmare as Blaine?

The Mercedes climbed with a vigor that pressed him down in his seat. Out his window the rooftop platform quickly contracted to a postage stamp in the clutter of the city before smog obscured it. Falwa, handling the VTOL with a fighter pilot's abrupt precision, took them up high fast, then banked, and they were going at what Blaine guessed must be the craft's top speed, the rotors roaring, his seat vibrating.

A few minutes later, just as suddenly, they dropped like a stone. Blaine clutched wildly at his armrests, the thought that they had been shot down tearing through his chest, but the rotors were steady and their descent stable: after a few seconds he guessed that Falwa was bringing them down fast to reduce their target profile.

Helwan, in the seat opposite Aida's, roared, and the bodyguard behind him yelled. Helwan fumbled for the intercom button on the panel above his head.

"What are you doing, you dog?" he yelled.

There was silence from the cockpit.

"I told you to go to the airport, son of a dog!" shrieked Helwan apoplectically. "Do you want to kill us, and the lady as well?"

Aida's laugh was both wild and brittle. Helwan's face went white and he shot a glance toward her, and at that moment Blaine saw that being made a fool of in front of her was worse to Helwan even than the dangers of Shafa'i.

Then everyone was silent, staring out windows.

From the gray haze Shafa'i appeared and rushed upward for a moment at sickening speed, and then there was a roar and a surge of heaviness and they were flying swiftly above the slum at third-story height, Falwa looking for a place to land—hoping, Blaine guessed, that anyone with a gun had taken it away to fight the government in the parts of the city where the government held sway.

Shafa'i was called in English the City of the Dead, and had been an entire quarter of the old city of Cairo—twenty-six square kilometers—devoted to them, a great, dilapidated graveyard of silent, dusty streets running between endless rows of roofless stone enclosures around family graves and the tiny, ornamental buildings where the living had sat in shade on their occasional visits. In the 1980s and '90s, when Cairo's population had begun to far outrun housing, people had started moving into the graveyard: it was, after all, full of houses with walled yards. By the turn of the century 2 million people lived in the tombs of Shafa'i, and after that no one knew how many; during the *intifadahs* the government had lost control of the slum and had cut its losses by leaving it to the fundamentalists and militias, content to patrol its borders, closing them when an epidemic or rioting broke out in the filth and overcrowding.

Blaine had seen pictures of the villages of Somalia and Ethiopia, their lanes of parched gray dust trampled with trash, where gaunt, naked children played outside hovels of dried mud and corrugated iron, and packs of wild dogs prowled, rooting for food in the garbage. He could have been looking down at one of these villages now, except that this was a city. Hovels were packed and crammed together like carelessly stacked mud crates in what had been the streets, leaving only narrow lanes between, and other hovels were built in the grave enclosures themselves, and at intervals among them were the old tomb houses, grimy and decrepit, though here and there showing ornamental stone- or ironwork, a graceful column marked with graffiti, a spired dome holed and cracked, a carved frieze pocked and defaced. They flew over the ruins of a mosque, its leaning minaret broken off at the top.

The VTOL's rotors kicked up dust even twenty meters off the ground. Crowds of ragged people were coming out of their hovels to look up, but no one shot at them. They flew over lanes and streets scattered with trash, dirt blackened from cooking fires. The slum went on and on, kilometer after kilometer, until Blaine felt sick, and the demonic voice of the screaming cretin from Darb Al Ahmar crept into his head, filling him with its contagion, its assurance that life, real life, was this unending misery and filth, that all the rest was a brief illusion.

They were now following a wider dirt lane, and then ahead was a square or at any rate a wide place where several lanes came together. Falwa didn't hesitate: they went down with a great uprushing and billowing of dust and trash. With a bump the VTOL became still, and the rotors began to wind down.

"Shafa'i," Falwa announced through the intercom.

In a minute he swung the hatch open from outside, and the smell of the place came into the passenger compartment:

the stench of rotting bodies and uncollected filth, of dust and open sewers and suffering beyond comprehension.

Helwan, snarling curses, jumped from his seat and went for Falwa.

Falwa stepped back quickly from the hatch and Helwan's rush brought him stumbling foolishly onto his hands and knees in the stinking dust outside.

Aida gave her brittle, wild laugh. Falwa grinned at her.

Helwan's face was dead white and his eyes a frightening red. He was trembling so hard that his hand fumbled getting a small pistol from his jacket pocket.

Falwa, with a curse, kicked him viciously in the head. Helwan sprawled on his side in the dust and lay still, the gun limp in his hand.

The bodyguard got out, muttering a prayer. Blaine could smell sweat under his aftershave. He seemed to barely notice Helwan lying in the dirt, twitching slightly, the glitter of his eyes visible through slitted lids. Blaine followed him out.

Falwa helped them into the thick heat and stench. The whine of the VTOL's rotors had died, and it was almost silent, the kind of silence that rings in your ears. The bodyguard had a compact machine gun out and was reflexively tracking it back and forth, straining his eyes into the clearing billows of dust.

Falwa helped Aida from the VTOL. She stumbled with her spike heels on the uneven ground and he supported her, peering around anxiously, a pistol in his free hand. Aida's face was hard to read in her sunglasses.

The square where they had landed was twenty-five by twenty-five meters, its walls the crumbling, filthy, graffitied walls of tombs, heaped along one side with a noisome mound of desiccated trash and offal, lined along the other with a pitiful caricature of a market where ragged merchants almost black from sun sat in the shade of the wall, their wares spread out before them on cloths in the dust: piles of old clothes, rusted minor car parts, some meager food surrounded by flies. The square was filling with people now, people who had run and limped and hobbled to come see what the commotion was, why an opulent sky vehicle worth more than all the property in their quarter had landed there. They were not the awful skeleton-people Blaine had seen in his dream, but they were wretched. There were many skinny children, naked or wearing rags, bare feet gray with dust, their faces serious and uncomprehending as they looked at the strangers. A woman held a baby, its lolling head shaved to keep off lice, one of its eyes monstrously swollen and pussy with some disease. A feebleminded youth goggled at them, closing his eyes and wagging his head, then opening them again and squinting incredulously, dozens of flies feeding at the saliva dripping from his mouth, his clothes dark with dirt and sweat. A man came leaning painfully on a stick, one of his feet huge and dry and hideous with elephantiasis. A leper's face and shaking hands were mottled greenish-gray like a lizard's.

Blaine heard an intake of breath. Aida was staring around, her lips parted, forehead wrinkled. She swayed on her feet and Falwa steadied her. She lifted trembling hands to the sides of her face and her sunglasses fell off. Her eyes were wide and filled with horror.

Falwa mopped his face with a tissue that he held clumsily in the same hand as his pistol. "All right, now we have seen this, God be merciful to us," he said. "Do you see it, my lady? Are you satisfied? All right, then, let's go. Come on, let's go."

But her face was trembling, mouth working. It took Blaine a minute to hear what she was whispering, over and over: "To hell. To hell. To hell." People were still coming in from the lanes and streets and paths around the square, hundreds of them now, all staring silently, and she screamed to them suddenly, her hands held out: "To hell! *To hell! To hell!*"

As if enraged at her blasphemy or emboldened by her despair, someone in the crowd yelled and a rock banged the side of the VTOL behind Blaine. There was a moment of shocked silence; Blaine's eyes swept the faces before him, a mosaic of fear, confusion, anger, surprise. Then the bodyguard fired a burst into the air, and after that Blaine's perceptions were a blur: there was a hail of stones and fire around him; he was clawing desperately among a hundred people to get back into the VTOL; the rotors roared and the raging faces and arms and fists outside the windows were suddenly lost in billowing dust and crushing gravity.

There wasn't time to get to his seat. Everyone fell in the limited space of the passenger compartment as the VTOL bucked its way upward through the unstable air. Blaine hung onto a seat-back for dear life. Helwan lay in the narrow aisle. As the VTOL steadied and his fear ebbed a little, Blaine realized that he was looking down at Aida draped across her seat unconscious, a trickle of saliva coming from the corner of her mouth. Her suit and ripped stockings were filthy with gray dust, and her shoes had come off.

The bodyguard was yelling: "To the airport, Hussein, my brother! Straight to the airport right away!"

And Falwa over the intercom: "We don't have enough fuel after this takeoff. We're going to have to risk a stop at the Towers."

The bodyguard cursed hoarsely and loudly.

As Blaine watched, mesmerized, Aida began to stir, tongue quickly wetting her lips, shoulders twisting uncomfortably. Then her eyes fluttered open and she looked up at him.

For a second her eyes were dull and indifferent. Then they widened with an unspeakable horror.

Sweat sprang out on her face and she began to tremble. Her hands scrabbled shakily at her neck as if trying to find skin patches. Her lips moved convulsively. She was trying to say something. Blaine leaned down to hear.

"My medicine," she rasped shakily. "I need my medicine."

Her voice was ashen, the voice of a demon far beyond the forgiveness of God.

With a sharp *thwack* and a puff of dust a piece of carpet peeled back in the aisle near where Helwan lay, and a perfectly round half-inch hole opened in the ceiling above it.

Helwan sat up abruptly. His face was dead pale and sweating under the black bruise of his swollen eye and cheek. He was still holding his pistol. He lifted it and pointed it at Blaine, the tendons of his hand tensed, arm trembling.

"Get away from her," he gritted.

The VTOL was steady now. Blaine hesitated, then pulled the woman upright roughly, his heart pounding, half-expecting to feel a bullet tear through him. Touching her was intoxicating, electrifying, as if some kind of current ran through her. He pulled the seat belt across her and buckled it. Then he stepped carefully past Helwan without looking at him, got into his seat, and fastened his belt.

Behind him the bodyguard was cursing and talking to himself hoarsely; next to him the Slavic doctor with his bandaged face still lolled back on his seat, hands clutching his armrests the only sign that he was conscious. Blaine looked out his window. From the haze below pale streaks of tracer bullets snapped upward. The VTOL's rotor cowlings were turned almost horizontal for maximum lateral thrust. A tiny spot below burgeoned suddenly into a blur, and, yelling involuntarily, Blaine caught a glance of the sleek, finned shape of a precybernetic ground-to-air missile fishtail past the VTOL ten meters away.

They passed over the river, wide and dark. The roar of the rotors deepened and gravity pulled Blaine to the side. The Ehlam Towers roof platform tilted below them. They were circling it so that Falwa could figure out if it was safe to land, Blaine saw. Except for some smoke and a small flash from a street far below, the building looked the same as when they had left.

They descended. Nothing was audible in the passenger compartment above the hum of the rotors, but as soon as they touched down and the hatch was popped sounds came to them: machine guns, the snap of sniper fire, and from somewhere in the middle distance the roar of voices chanting and shouting. Thick, acrid smoke rose from the street.

Out the hatch Blaine could see Falwa tapping the keypad on a fuel pump, then pulling its retractable hose toward the VTOL. The clunk of the hose being attached and the hiss of liquid came through the fuselage.

Helwan got to his feet, holding the seats on both sides of him, his pistol sticking out of his right fist. He stepped shakily out of the hatch. There was a pause. Blaine, too dulled with trauma to realize what was happening, leaned back in his seat and closed his eyes, listening over his thrumming blood to the firing and chanting from the street. Then he became aware that the bodyguard had hustled desperately out of the VTOL, and he heard him yell outside: "Mr. Munir! For God's sake! Mr. Munir!"

There was a shot. By the time Blaine got out of the VTOL Falwa was writhing on the ground and Helwan was standing over him and very deliberately shooting him, again and again, the little pistol jumping in his hand, until Falwa lay still, his face an inhuman mask of what had been anguish, a thick rill of blood running out from under him and along the baking blacktop.

Cursing, Helwan began kicking the body, his white, sweating face distorted. The bodyguard, his incongruous tuxedo now stained with sweat under the arms, stood aghast, watching him.

The mob sounds had ebbed for the moment, and only a few machine guns spoke in the hot, windy silence, at different distances. They were of different kinds, Blaine could hear: one fired relatively slowly and made a *pock pock* sound like a bouncing Ping-Pong ball amplified a thousand times; another roared fiercely, rounds coming so fast it was impossible to distinguish the successive shots.

A coldness had come over Blaine in the hot, windy, smoky air. It was a chill that never quite left you after it had gotten inside you, he would find out later, but sometimes welled up again from nowhere, leaving you not afraid exactly, but believing that nothing could ever work out for the better in this world.

Helwan turned to Blaine and the bodyguard. "The robot pilot," he rasped. "We'll use the robot pilot." His face was gray, dripping, the eyes inhumanly narrow. He looked ancient, stony, like some idolatrous god.

They moved out of his way so he could walk around the nose of the VTOL to the pilot's cabin. After a pause, the bodyguard said: "When we get to the airport we'll call the police. But now we have to help him with the controls so he doesn't kill us all."

He headed after Helwan. A sheet of smoke blown by the wind covered the roof, and Blaine coughed, closing his eyes against sparks and cinders that smelled of gasoline and burning plastic. When he opened them again Aida was near the door to the roof lounge, walking without shoes across the broiling tarmac in her ruined stockings.

At the same second the VTOL's rotors turned over with a click and began to wind up, rising quickly to a hooting roar.

Blaine yelled, his voice inaudible over the rotors. He was torn for a second between the VTOL's open passenger hatch and Aida; then he sprinted across the roof after her.

With a rush of wind and shriek of rotors the VTOL lifted off behind him. Blaine spun around, waving his arms wildly and screaming: "She's here, you dogs! She's here, come back!" It came vaguely to his mind that the bodyguard was in the cockpit with Helwan, which was why they would fly all the way to the airport before they found out that Aida, for whom Helwan had just killed a man, wasn't with them. If they made it to the airport.

The VTOL rose slowly and clumsily, wobbling, its rotors booming. But it kept its balance, floating up until it disappeared in the haze.

Blaine opened the door of the roof lounge. There was no sign of Aida. The air-conditioning felt arctic on his cold sweat; he guessed city power was gone by now but that the building's backup generators were working. He touched the Down key on the elevator.

14

The long, plush hall was silent and empty, but music still boomed faintly as he neared the door of 21C. It opened when he pushed it—the lock had been either broken or turned off. The foyer was deserted, but the music hammered and pulsed as if a party was going on. The midnight room next door was still full of blinding 'thump but nobody danced there now; beyond that the elaborate buffet offered its exotic delicacies to no one. No one was in the ballroom, and no one was in any of the rooms or halls where he looked until he came to the silent, softly lit parlor. He knew before he saw her that she was there, by the fragrance of dread and yearning that filled him.

She stood very still in the middle of the room in her filthy movie star's clothes, looking at him. Her dark eyes seemed steadier than before. The only sound was the faint ring of wind chimes outside the windows that looked down on the serene, old-fashioned town of Cairo, the Cairo of an adman's dreams.

"You," she said. Her voice was almost a whisper. "Can you get me on the Cairo net? My server is down."

"What?" She was insane, the thought came to him. "The television stations are all down. The only way to give the warning is through the net."

Had she seen the VTOL take off? "You know someone who can get us out of here?"

She seemed unsure what he was talking about. Finally she said: "You don't understand. If it's too late now, then I've failed, I've—" She stopped, as if she couldn't think about that. "My memories, the dreams—They told me they weren't real. They gave me—" Sweat broke out on her. "But I shouldn't have listened to them. I didn't really *want* to remember. I wanted to be a movie star, a goddess, you understand? But if you get me on the net right now there might still be a chance. A tiny chance. You understand? I might be able to save my soul."

This was insane. They had to get out of here before the mob on the street overran the building or burned it. "You—you have a satellite jack?"

It was built into a musty antique table inlaid with silver and mother-of-pearl. With shaky hands Blaine took the palmtop case from his jacket pocket, slid the machine out of it, selected a cable from a side pouch. He jacked in, fanned the screen, climbed NetStar II to Beirut, Declined two Urgent messages from the U.S. Embassy and three from Jenny Chan. He clicked a couple of Cairo server sites he had bookmarked. Both were down. He did a search for operating Cairo-located sites. Except for a couple of foreign embassies and corporate branch offices, closed to access for fear of sabotage, he got the same message over and over.

"The Cairo net is crashed. Power hits, probably, and maybe infrastructure damage."

He looked up at her. She stared blindly down at him, a statue of ivory with eyes like ultraviolet suns.

Finally her trembling lips formed words: "I need my medicine."

She went to an antique chest in the corner of the room and began to ransack it desperately, throwing things on the floor.

Blaine tried to get himself to think. He had to figure out what to do now. He had to cast himself as the young Haseeb Al Rahman and figure everything out for himself.

Only one thing was possible, as far as he could tell: go up on the roof and broadcast a distress call to the skies. Maybe the U.S.A. or someone else sympathetic had vehicles overhead or stations listening to Cairo, and they would pick them up or at least tell them what to do.

The woman turned away from the chest holding a syringe. Her eyes were full of dull shock. She armed it with trembling fingers, pulled her jacket and shirtsleeves up her left wrist, pressed the syringe against it. It chirped.

She dropped it on the floor. Her breath came in a long desperate gasp, then another, languid and ecstatic, as if she had been removed from this planet and transported to the region of heaven.

Her eyes fluttered, and he saw that they were hazed again, occluded, unsteady, the eyes of the demented movie star. She came toward him. She seemed to move in slow motion, as he had seen her in the dance room, in utter silence. Her hands burned him where she touched him. "Dance with me," she said. Her voice—soft, throaty, intoxicating, and full of tears—seemed to be piped directly into his chest.

He tried to think over the bursting of his heart, the rush of neurotransmitters.

—

They were dancing. He wasn't aware of it at first, just of movement somewhere, which had a rhythm, a pulse inside his body, and that became stronger, thunderous, and then music emerged from it, and he was moving, dancing, a gut-thump marionette tangled up body and mind with another dancer who was a shadow of deepest black and blinding light, a panther, a skeleton, an angel, a demon, and, eventually, the woman. He faded in and out of lucidity, thrashing with unconscious, violent grace, sometimes unsure which of the dancers he was, sometimes thinking he was her, and then his vision seemed to expand, and she seemed to stand on a high place like a mountain, and all around her vast windy spaces, and the green and brown–rivered earth far below stretching in endless perspectives of clarity and exhilaration; but as the exhilaration reached its peak ghosts surrounded her, millions upon millions of them pressing upon her with their mummified bodies, the stench of their mortality, their harsh, screaming voices, their terrible suffering and the suffering of their children, and suddenly their faces burst upon her, real and three-dimensional through the curtain of neurochemistry she had hung around herself, their eyes crucifying her with their pain, and she turned and dived into the darkness of a room where crashing music tore her insides—

All was confusion then, until he realized that she had broken off the dance though the music still crashed and drove, and she was kneeling on the floor as if in pain, and giving herself another shot.

She threw the syringe away from her and stood up gasping with joy. And at that second, dimly through the coerced orgasm of the 'thump, Blaine thought he heard something.

A laugh. A screaming, gurgling laugh.

He looked around in shock, his terror bringing a sudden sickening sobriety. The dance room was empty except for him and Aida: there was no sign of the spastic cretin devil-man.

Aida was starting to dance again paroxysmally, laughing, but his fear kept him for the moment from going under. He had no idea what time it might be, or what might have happened outside the building. He grabbed the woman and dragged her from the dance room.

She let him drag her, the shot making her for the moment indulgent. Once out in the reception room she pulled away from him. "What are you doing? I want to dance."

She threw her head crazily this way and that, hissing a tune under her breath. They were standing in front of a big window that showed sedate, picturesque streets many floors down.

"We have to get out of here. There's fighting downstairs, a revolution going on in this town, don't you remember? If it succeeds, people like us are going to eat shit."

She danced close to him, eyes half-closed, lips smiling in neurochemical bliss, nuzzled him. "Let's eat shit," she whispered. "Let's die."

With sudden rage he grabbed her shoulders, yanked her so that her dizzy eyes looked into his.

Down on a street of ancient cobblestones an old, robed man rode a donkey slowly in the shade of an ornate mosque, his feet almost touching the ground. Palm trees stirred in the afternoon sunlight. A scarfed woman beat a rug on a balcony above a narrow, shady alley where fruit-sellers called their wares.

Under their feet came a dull vibration, as if an explosion had rocked the giant building far below them.

"We have to get out of here!" Blaine screamed at the woman.

"How? To where?" she laughed wildly. "I want to dance," she whispered.

Blaine tried to calm himself, think. "Listen," he said. "If they hit the building we won't be able to dance. The electricity's going to go out and there'll be no music. You understand? No music, and you won't be able to find your drugs in the dark. Just darkness and emptiness and nothing to do but think. We need to find some music and a party somewhere else. You understand? We have to get out of here."

A vague, faraway concern flitted across her face.

⎯⎯

Blaine could smell smoke in the silent hallway outside the apartment. All three elevators had "Out of Service" signs it on them.

He wondered if they would find militiamen running up the building's emergency stairs, and he held the exit door ajar and listened until the woman shoved him aside and started to climb, raving about finding a party. It was four flights to the roof, and then the afternoon smog blinded them. Debris was burning near the fuel pumps, where a crumpled body lay, and a dark plume of smoke floated up over the parapet smelling of high explosives and burning rubber.

The woman looked at the scene dully, licking her lips. Blaine couldn't tell if she recognized Falwa's body. He pulled her out of the stairwell doorway into the hot, smoky air at a run, to the deserted roof attendants' kiosk, and they crouched there against the wall, listening to the crackling blare of a bullhorn and the roaring of a mob on the street below. If there was a revolution going on it didn't take much imagination to believe that Ehlam Towers would be singled out for attack as a symbol of decadent wealth in starving Cairo. Crouching against the kiosk wall Blaine unpacked his palmtop, then jacked his tiny, frail antenna and made it curve into a nondirectional transmitter. Then he entered a local communication protocol and said in Arabic to the palmtop's microphone: "Urgent transportation request. Two adults, strictly civilian, unarmed. American citizen. Generous risk bonus. Required immediately. Answer, please." And he broadcast it at the top of the little machine's lungs.

The woman crouched against the wall of the kiosk like some kind of affluent urban savage, with her smoke-smudged face, her filthy fine clothes, and the leather boots he had dug out of a closet for her.

The palmtop beeped with an incoming message.

Blaine answered.

"We have air transport," a voice came through the palmtop. It was tinny and there was no visual: whoever it was was using a trickle of bandwidth, perhaps to avoid some of the more sophisticated forms of missile targeting. "What are you offering as a risk premium?"

"God keep you, let's discuss it when you get here. I'm giving you our GPS coordinates."

"And may He keep you. It would be more convenient to discuss it now, if possible." The voice wasn't Egyptian; the man sounded Jordanian, maybe Syrian.

"Make me an offer."

There was a minute of silence. "Forty thousand American dollars."

"Forty thou—! For an air taxi ride? Are you crazy?"

"We have you on our scope, brother. We're right above you. It'll take us two minutes to get to you once we agree on a price, exactly two minutes, God willing." There was a moment of silence. "My partner is softhearted. He asks me to offer you our special price of thirty-five thousand."

"Special price? I'll never pay a piaster more than ten thousand! By God, as long as I live—!"

"Excuse me, but that may not be long, brother. We have you up now. You're on the Ehlam Towers complex. By God, I can't believe you're still broadcasting. The militias and rebel army units are all around you, and it looks like they've entered the building. They'll be on the roof in a few minutes, and then—"

"But to take advantage of this tragedy to cheat a fellow Muslim—!"

"Brother, I have children! These militias have missiles, they have antiaircraft guns, and they're crazy! I may die coming down to get you; then what will my children do, how will they put bread in their mouths? We'll take you out for thirty-two thousand."

"Fifteen thousand. Not a dollar more."

"Brother, do you want to die? They're loading missile guns down on the street to blow up your building! Tell me just thirty thousand and we'll have you at the airport in five minutes. Thirty thousand is less than we've charged anyone all day."

"I'll give you twenty thousand, but don't say another

word. Not another word! I can't afford more, my brother! I don't have it! Believe me, I'd pay it if I could. Do you think I want to die? Now come down, hurry, and God give you strength."

A tremendous explosion jerked the tarmac sideways under him, and burning debris tumbled up into the air over the parapet, followed by searing smoke. Blaine tried to become part of the wall, arms over his head.

"—just because we're friends and fellow Muslims, you and me," said the tinny voice from the palmtop.

"What?"

"Twenty-eight thousand. I can't go lower because my partner is right here: he flies the plane. He won't come down for less than that. He's Israeli, my brother, and he doesn't care either about Muslims or Arabs."

"Twenty-two thousand."

"Twenty-five thousand."

"OK, come down! You've cheated me, you son of a dog, now come and get us!"

"If you would wire me the money first, sir. I'm sending my form down to you—"

"Damn your father on your mother! You'll take my money and fly away, you thief! Come get me and then I'll pay you, you pig!"

"Calm down, sir! We'll escrow it. I'm sending you the escrow form. As soon as I see the money, in American dollars, at that very second we'll be at your service, God willing."

An escrow form from a Swiss bank appeared on Blaine's palmtop screen. He tried to concentrate as he filled it out, twice checking the number of zeros in the cash amount. He sent it, wondering if he had made enough mistakes for them to insist that he redo it, hoping the bank processors in Switzerland were having light traffic for a minute or two.

The sky fell.

The smoke around them scattered wildly, roaring.

laine yanked the woman to her feet, ran toward where the
elicopter was hovering three meters above the roof.

A harness swayed in the swirling smoke. Blaine shoved
ne of Aida's legs into it and one of his own, then held on to
he thin cord and on to her for dear life, muscles screaming as
ravity got suddenly very strong, and then hands were pulling
er upward, and he let her go, looked down, and the roof was
lready a hundred meters below, wreathed in black smoke
nd flame; he was swinging in the harness under the climbing
elicopter and he felt sick. Then hands took hold of him and
e struggled upward, scraping his forearms and shins on
netal, and he was inside; he heard metal close beside him,
naking the roar of rotors a little less deafening. His legs wob-
led, he hit his head on something, crawled awkwardly into a
lastic seat next to Aida. Someone put a flight harness into his
ands; he buckled it around himself. Then jump-jets on the
opter roared and they went up ten times as fast.

Your thumbprint, sir, if you please," yelled the man who
ad pulled them into the 'copter, over the roar of the rotors.
le twisted around as far as his harness allowed in the copi-
ot seat in front of Blaine and held out an escrow release
orm on the screen of a scratched-up military-issue laptop.
le was a mustached, pock-marked Arab with receding, frizzy
air, maybe in his fifties. An old but serious-looking scar ran
om his upper lip to his ear, making the left side of his face
ok oddly discontinuous and piratical.

The interior of the jet-'copter matched his laptop: worn,
ghtweight metal flaking some obsolete air force's regulation
ray paint and crammed with an airline cockpit's worth of in-
trumentation, as well as fire extinguishers, inflatable rafts,
tility flashlights, flares, night glasses, first-aid kits, and every
ther military necessity, held in place on the bulkheads by
orn metal clips. It smelled strongly of oil.

"Where are we going, the airport?" the pilot yelled for the first time above the thunder of the rotors. His Arabic was guttural, and Blaine glanced at him. He wore a tattered blue jacket with Star of David insignia on the sleeves: an Israeli air force flight jacket, if Blaine wasn't mistaken. His bulky heads-up display goggles hid much of his clean-shaven face, but his short, coarse hair was salt-and-pepper gray.

Blaine opened his mouth to say yes when a voice said: "No."

Blaine and the Arab in the copilot's seat looked at Aida.

"Not to the airport," she said. Her face and voice were dull, and she was barely audible over the roar of the 'copter.

"To where then, darling?" said the Israeli. He took a glance around at her. The Arab was studying her face and long legs. If he recognized her he didn't say anything. "Don't you want to get out of here?"

"The airport is still open, but in a few more hours it may not be," said the Arab. "The last trip we took, there were still jets on the ground. I'll bet you've got some money left." He grinned at Blaine curiously.

"Take him to the airport," Aida said, gesturing at Blaine. "I'm going somewhere else."

"Where?"

"Wadi Sel."

"Wadi Sel? You don't mean the oasis in the Western Desert? No one lives there, lady."

"Out of the question," said the pilot. "Too far."

"There is one village there," said the woman.

"We can't take you there," said the Arab. "Too far. That wasn't included in the price. We can take you to the airport or at most to Fayoum. No farther."

Aida dug her hand under her flight harness and pulled a card-thin bank terminal from her jacket pocket. She tapped it and thumbprinted it, and fifteen seconds later did the same thing again. It chirped.

"Do you have paper?" she asked. The Arab dug in his pocket and came up with a limp Egyptian hundred-pound note. She took the worthless paper and pressed the terminal against it. Blaine could see the fluorescent orange printing when she handed it back to him. "And the same again when you get me to Wadi Sel."

The Arab looked at the printing and handed it to the pilot, who looked at it too.

"We have spare fuel on board," said the pilot.

"What are you doing?" Blaine gritted at the woman.

"We can refuel at Qara on the way back, eh?" said the Arab. The pilot nodded. One of his hands tapped at a keypad.

The woman tried to smile at Blaine, failed. "I remember Buthaina now," she said. "I remember all about her."

"We are under your commands, lady," said the Arab politely. "Shall we take the gentleman to the airport first?"

"No," said Blaine.

"Go to the airport," said the woman. She seemed so weary suddenly that she could hardly talk. "This is not your death."

"Then come with me."

She closed her eyes, shook her head.

"What's wrong? What's happening?" Blaine demanded.

"Go away. Escape," she whispered without opening her eyes.

"The airport is north, and Wadi Sel is west," said the pilot.

"Tell me what is going on," Blaine said to the woman, the goddess slumped before him.

She didn't answer, didn't move.

Blaine cursed. "Wadi Sel," he said. "I guess we're going to Wadi Sel."

The Arab stared at them curiously. The pilot banked the copter gently, and the sun came around ahead of them; his goggles darkened.

Aida lolled in her seat, eyes closed. She was very pale.

From time to time Blaine thought he heard a buzzing over the roar of the rotors, and saw flecks of light around her.

The Arab was watching them. It occurred to Blaine that it would be better if their rescuers didn't know the identity of the woman they had picked up. He asked a question to preempt the curiosity he felt building: "Are you guys Israelis?"

He got "Yes" and "No" simultaneously. The Arab slapped the back of the pilot's head roughly. He ran a finger along the scar on his left cheek.

"In 1982 when the Israelis came into Lebanon, I was in Samsoun, in the Bekaa, fighting with the Fatah Hawks. The Israelis bombed Samsoun to gravel, and this man was the first one in the bombing squadron all the way. He killed most of my friends. If he had come one centimeter closer to me, he wouldn't have a business partner. And you know the one thing, the only thing that could make me go into business with a man like that? A murderer and war criminal?"

"Money," said Blaine.

The Palestinian laughed.

"It was a beautiful mission," said the Israeli. "Very efficient, very workmanlike. We destroyed the entire terrorist complex, meter by meter, in two hours. Nothing left. I felt very good about it."

"One still has to make a living even after there's no one left to fight," explained the Palestinian.

The two men sat quiet now, facing forward, as if preoccupied with their own thoughts, the Israeli making small adjustments to the controls from time to time. Aida was slumped in her seat, eyes closed.

In the late afternoon they landed in a tornado of hissing sand, the Israeli cursing the likely destruction of every moving part in the 'copter, and then he and the Palestinian got out and unloaded fuel cans. Blaine climbed down the folding metal steps to stretch in the hot, stiff desert breeze, squinting at a landscape like coarse, rock-strewn beach

stretching in every direction to a horizon gray from blowing sand, cloudless pale blue above, his ears ringing from
the roar of the 'copter in the gritty hiss of wind. The sun
was yellow-orange, low in the sky. He climbed back into
the 'copter and studied Aida as the creaking, thumping,
and gurgling sounds of refueling came through the ultra-
light metal. He was sure the men hadn't noticed the bursts
of light and static that erupted around her, but Blaine the
Image-digger could see them; they were being funneled to
his senses via his unconscious, he knew, Image material
so powerful that it penetrated even his waking mind, like
the episodes he had seen in Cairo, fantasies of her from
the collective unconscious, cast with unknowing human
actors. Yet other than the bursts of light she showed no
sign of life. Hesitantly Blaine reached out and took her
wrist.

It was like grabbing a high-tension wire. He threw it away
from himself convulsively and it fell limp across her body.

The Israeli climbed back into the 'copter. Without the
goggles he looked tired, and like he could have been from
New York City. He asked anxiously if Blaine thought the
woman—who still hadn't printed their bonus scrip—was all
right, but seemed reluctant to touch her, whether out of pro-
fessionalism, gallantry, or some subliminal instinct that she
was dangerous.

Anyway, the two men were in a hurry—to get back and
gouge some more desperate Cairo strandees while the fighting lasted, Blaine guessed. The Israeli checked systems while
the Palestinian clambered on top of the 'copter to make sure
the rotor bearings hadn't been fouled by sand. In a few minutes they were airborne again, the sinking orange sun glaring
through the windscreen. The Israeli seemed to be following
some map in his goggles; he made occasional small but de-
cisive adjustments to their course. They had been flying another hour when he said: "Wadi Sel."

Leaning forward to peer out the windscreen, Blaine

could see the depression below the cherry-red crescent of the sun, like a gigantic flat-bottomed valley the same color as the desert but full of shadow, a road winding down its steep ridges, and far ahead a deeper shadow of dark green, as if things grew there. All the oases in the Western Desert except Fayoum were at the bottom of half-kilometer depressions, near the brackish groundwater table.

"She says there's a village," said Blaine. Aida was still asleep or comatose.

"I have it," said the Israeli. They were heading toward the smudge of dark green.

The last sliver of sun sank abruptly below the horizon and everything became clearly visible for kilometers in blue evening light, a strange effect for those used to the smog-bound spaces of Cairo. Below them Blaine could see clumps of palms and dark green scrub interspersed with barren land. They flew lower and slower, and the clumps got closer together until they were cruising fifty meters above what looked like a dry savanna with patches of gray mud, the palms growing at a slant from the prevailing wind. They were following the desert road they had spotted before, Blaine saw, a narrow ribbon of asphalt.

Rectangular fields of muddy clods and green shoots appeared on both sides of the road, and they were descending. Ahead in the dusk Blaine saw the village, a city block–sized complex of single-story mud-brick houses all built against each other around narrow dirt lanes, windows blank and hollow in the evening.

The Israeli brought the 'copter down on the road a hundred meters from the village, both he and the Palestinian watching it with professional caution. The Israeli didn't kill the power, but left the rotors turning at an idling speed.

"Praise God for your safe arrival," said the Palestinian.

Aida opened her eyes.

"Evening of jasmine," murmured the Palestinian to her.

God willing, in goodness." Blaine could tell that the two men felt uneasy, eager to get their money and go.

With trembling hands she printed scrip on another limp Egyptian bill, and then, murmuring polite thanks and pieties, the Palestinian unfolded the metal steps.

"Where are you going?" the woman asked Blaine as he followed her down. The solid, dusty asphalt felt strange under his feet. "Go back. Take him back with you," she called to the men in the 'copter, who sat looking at them; then the Palestinian gestured him to come on board.

"I'm coming with you," Blaine said to her over the rhythmic grunt of the rotors.

"You can't. No one can come where I'm going."

"I am."

The woman's eyes were wild in the dusk. "Then you'll die."

He just stood looking at her.

"Sister, we have to leave!" the Palestinian yelled. He was leaning out of the 'copter, one brawny hand on the lever that retracted the steps.

"What do you want with me?" she asked Blaine.

"Not you. Buthaina. To see that she's all right."

"She's not all right. She's dead." Her hands were shaking. A sudden drool of spittle went down her chin.

And if he went back without her—? Even if he could return to his job at Icon, what would it mean? Jenny Chan his "lover," Haseeb gone, his travels around the world digging for illusions, feeling nothing, believing nothing—

The woman turned and walked away into the dusk. He followed her.

"In peace," the Palestinian called behind them. The rotors roared with a rush of wind, then receded upward.

15

After the 'copter had gone it was very quiet. A breeze whispered, bringing the smells of water and earth. A nightingale sang somewhere at the edge of hearing. It was almost night now, with the quick dusk of the desert.

White flames suddenly enveloped Aida, roaring three meters into the air. Blaine leapt backward. Through confusion and terror the thought blared in him that she had torched herself with gasoline, was committing suicide right in front of him. She shrieked, clawing at herself on her knees in the road, and her screams seemed to echo on nonexistent mountains.

That was when the first men reached them, running from the village holding torches, wide-eyed, sun-blackened, mustached peasants wearing *gelabiyahs* and white cloths wrapped around their heads.

The flames suddenly went away from Aida. She was unburned, unharmed. She staggered to her feet. The pounding of Blaine's heart almost made him faint. When the village men saw her they fell back a few paces, muttering prayers. Other men and a few women were running up behind them in the dark. Their torches lit the scene flickering orange.

It seemed to take Aida a minute to focus her eyes, but when she saw the villagers she spat on the road, her face convulsed. "What's the matter, pigs, don't you know me?" she cried slurringly.

They recoiled wide-eyed, as if they would run. She strode forward, yelling: "Don't you know me? Don't you know me?"

"Of course—of course we know your presence," said one man fearfully.

Roaring fire leapt from her again and she fell down shrieking. Blaine could feel the flames' intense heat on his face and hands.

Most of the people ran. Blaine couldn't tell whether they saw the fire or were just terrified by her screams. In a minute the flames died down. Blaine crouched over her prone body, not daring to touch her. After an interval she stirred and pushed herself shakily and with difficulty into a half-sitting position, her legs in their tattered stockings splayed out on the road as if paralyzed.

"Where is the 'umdah?" she demanded harshly but fully, as if the flames had injured her.

"The 'umdah—the 'umdah is coming, lady," said the man who had spoken before. "Here he is."

Out of the darkness hobbled an old man with two younger men flanking him, and a crowd of fifty or sixty people at his back, some of whom had fled a minute ago. The old man wore a gelabiyah of rough beige material and had a long white cloth like a scarf around his neck whose ends hung almost to the ground. One old, gnarled hand leaned on a cane. His face was hawklike, with the dignity of respected age. His eyes flickered in the torchlight as he looked at Aida. The eyes of the silent onlookers flickered less brightly around him in the dark.

"Lady, you have come back," he said.

"Yes, pig, I've come back. And I need a wedding. Tonight. I'll pay, as usual."

The old man looked troubled. "Again, father? Has God not yet touched your heart?"

"No, the devil has touched my heart!" she screamed at him. "Hell has touched my heart! But you will give me the wedding, won't you!"

"Yes, lady. Yes, lady, we will give you the wedding," said the old man, backing up fearfully along with the people as the woman staggered drunkenly to her feet.

"I warn you not to thwart me! Not to get in my way! I haven't taken any medicine! I don't have any medicine! I may lose control!"

"Whom will your presence marry, this man?" asked the 'umdah, gesturing at Blaine.

"Yes, this man. Unless he takes his last chance to escape he will marry me tonight."

"Yes, lady. Under your commands, lady. At once, lady."

⬤

As soon as the 'umdah, the village headman, announced the wedding, the atmosphere began to change. The women were told in ritual words to take Aida and prepare her for her wedding, and they surrounded her, fearfully at first, taking care to keep their distance; but as they approached the village Blaine, walking among the men a hundred paces behind, heard wedding ululations ring out from among them, and a few even started chanting a traditional song. It was as if the cultural category "wedding" had taken over the villagers' minds, driving out the strangeness of the context and the suddenness of the announcement.

The men were cheerful too, and excited, a wedding

being the local equivalent of the circus coming to town, since, Blaine guessed, the *mulid* circuits didn't make it out this far. They had deep, rough voices, open, innocent faces, and they smelled pleasantly of sweat and garlic, and were intensely curious about him. Once they realized he spoke Arabic they peppered him in their peasant accents with polite, intrusive questions about where he came from, who his family was, how much money he had, whether he had other wives, whether he knew what to do with a woman, and so on.

He tried to answer them, but his mind was a whirl. He had never seen anything like the flames that had leapt from the woman's imaginal body. What did they mean? *Who or what was she?* How did these villagers know her? Why did she want to marry him, and was he going to go along with it? His fear and confusion must have showed, but if so the men put it down to the excitement of a groom on his wedding night.

But what was she? A living, breathing Image, he answered himself, though the answer made no sense. Human beings couldn't be Images any more than archetypes could walk and talk and shoot pool. Yet somehow the collective unconscious had filled her—a single human individual—with enough imaginal energy to power an Image stronger than anything he had ever heard of. Was that what a prophet was? A "warning variable" thrown up by the collective unconscious and filled with psychic energy so that the conscious world would listen when she spoke? But what had she spoken of that made any sense?

They walked past rice paddies, water glittering among the shoots in the torchlight, past fields of corn and a grove of towering date palms with orange trees planted under them for the shade, past hobbled water buffaloes sleeping patiently until tomorrow's work, over a narrow, glass-still irrigation canal. The land was wide and flat around them, stars sparkling and bright, the air mild and dry and delicious, with scents of citrus, jasmine, and damp earth. Palm fronds whispered in the breeze, and far away dogs barked and a donkey brayed in its sleep.

The asphalt of the road petered out into a rocky, trash-strewn lot in which two ancient, battered jeeps sat by the mud-brick walls of the village's outermost houses. Narrow dirt lanes opened between the houses; the men led Blaine down one of them, earthy, dusty-smelling walls with pane-less windows and worn wooden doors pressing close on both sides. Lantern-light came from some of the windows. There was a stir about the place; children in a state of high excitement peered at them openmouthed from windows or ran after them, staring at Blaine. The chanting of women came faintly from somewhere in the village, and from some-where closer the cooing of pigeons. There was some joking and jostling among the younger men.

A man stood outside one of the houses in the lane. Its front was whitewashed, and over the open door a rough, bright mural depicted the *hajj*, the pilgrimage of one of its oc-cupants to Mecca and Medina. The man was middle-aged, with gray in his hair and mustache, his *gelabiyah* prosperous-looking, gold rings on his dark fingers. Using ceremonial phrases he invited Blaine and his retinue inside. His face was troubled as he studied Blaine, but he said: "Welcome to the groom. We are honored."

"In the name of God," Blaine murmured, entering the man's house.

Inside the front door was a small courtyard floored with gray flagstones, stars shining in the deep, cool blue above. Some children and adolescent girls squatted giggling by a pigeon-cote, watching Blaine and a few of the older men come in. The rest of the men stayed out in the lane, milling around and laughing, a few now and then breaking into loud, masculine chants.

At the inner end of the courtyard yellow light came through another door. Inside was a large, square room floored with more flagstones, walled with mud brick hung with tapestries and household goods like trays and pots, and roofed with dried palm fronds laid across open beams. It was dimly lit by a lantern and furnished with uncomfortable-looking, heavily shellacked wooden furniture; it smelled of kerosene and antique wood. A dozen men stood in the room and shook hands with Blaine as he entered, murmuring "Congratulations" and studying him curiously with their frank, dark eyes. Their hands were rough and strong from field work. Women and girls peered with intense curiosity from the next room around a slightly open door.

The few men who had come in with Blaine were followed by the middle-aged man who had greeted him, murmuring, "Welcome" and "We are honored." As soon as Blaine had shuffled around the circle of well-wishers and shaken every hand, the man faced him. "We are your family," he said loudly, gesturing, as if Blaine might not understand Arabic.

"God keep you," said Blaine, using a polite expression appropriate when you weren't sure what the other person was getting at.

"Are you a Muslim?" the man asked him.

"God be praised."

"God be praised," said the man, relieved, and the other men murmured, "God be praised." This wedding was hard enough to swallow without adding the prohibited circumstance of a Muslim woman marrying a non-Muslim man, Blaine guessed.

"We are your family," repeated the man. "I am Mohammed Fahlawi. We will be your family for the wedding ceremony."

"I am very, very honored, hajj Mohammed" said Blaine, and the other men murmured piously in welcome and approval. Blaine wondered what pecuniary or other inducements had been offered to the Fahlawi clan for risking its honor to sponsor a foreigner in a questionable wedding.

After a second his curiosity got the better of him. "Can anyone tell me anything about my bride?" he asked.

There was an uncomfortable silence. "You don't know her?" asked Mohammed Fahlawi. Arranged marriages were common enough in this part of the world, but not without the parties obtaining all relevant information about each other.

"I know her in some ways, but in other ways not at all, hajj," said Blaine. "For example, I didn't know she was from your village."

"The 'umdah can tell you about her," said Mohammed Fahlawi politely. "We know her very little as well."

"But does she often marry in this village?"

Female ululations and rhythmic clapping were audible outside.

"Here are the women," said Mohammed Fahlawi, clearly glad of the interruption. "We must arrange your procession of gifts to the bride."

The men had given way, and the lane outside the courtyard was now full of peasant women in their embroidered black *gelabiyahs* and colorful headscarves, their rosy, dark peasant faces, brilliant teeth, and bright, alert eyes shining in the torchlight. They chanted a responsive chant in their loud, frank voices.

"Look at the house of the groom!"
"We're looking!"
"Think of the life to come!"
"We're thinking!"
"Bless the children to be born!"
"We're blessing!"

When Blaine emerged from the courtyard door behind Mohammed Fahlawi the women burst into their wedding ululations, to the Western ear much like TV Indian war cries. Blaine was immediately surrounded by clapping, chanting women flushed with excitement.

Back in the courtyard woven trays had been laid on the flagstones and draped with bright cloths, and on these the women of the household were arranging cones of sugar, bags of rice and macaroni, piles of toffee, bunches of grapes, oranges, and dates. As Blaine stood and watched the proceedings other women wearing gold bracelets, necklaces, and headscarves sewn with gold coins came in from the lane and offered to bargain with him for these.

"Two hundred dollars," said a woman, holding up an ample dark arm, which under the sleeve of her *gelabiyah* was bangled with gold. Evidently even here the relative value of the various national currencies had not escaped the notice of the populace.

"Two hundred!" yelled Mohammed Fahlawi above the chanting and clapping, the beating on drums and ululations, and the general excitement in the courtyard and lane. "Sister, this man is kin! That bracelet is not worth fifty dollars!"

"I'll give you seventy-five dollars for it," said Blaine kindly, warming to Fahlawi's bargaining strategy.

Yet he was still apparently paying above market; in a few minutes the courtyard was full of women covered with gold jewelry—the savings of their respective families—and Blaine was printing out scrip at a reckless rate. Soon the women of the Fahlawi family were arranging a pile of gold jewelry among the fruits, sweets, and domestic necessities on the trays.

Soon the trays were passed over the top of the courtyard wall—since they were too big to fit through the door—and a great cry of approval went up from the women on the other side—"God is great!" "Light on light!" "O Lord of all the worlds!"—and then, with great drumming, clapping, chanting, and ululations, the excited procession moved off down the lane to deliver the gifts at whatever house had adopted the bride for this evening of solemnity.

"We are making three nights into one night," said Mohammed Fahlawi in Blaine's ear. "*Laylit il-gelwa, laylit il-enna,* and *laylit il-dukhla,* all in one night. So we must hurry. The lady Buthaina's relatives are inside to write the contract before the procession of gifts comes from the bride."

The name "Buthaina" made the hair prickle on his head. "Her relatives? Her real relatives?"

"Her uncle and his sons."

They were sitting in the inner room on the uncomfortable wooden furniture smoking hand-rolled cigarettes and sipping tiny cups of thick coffee from a tray brought round diffidently by a little boy dressed in a brand-new, light blue *gelabiyah*. They stood up to shake Blaine's and Mohammed Fahlawi's hands and the hands of the other Fahlawi men. The uncle was a large, dark, imposing man of about sixty wearing a rich man's turban, whose family name was Darwish. He and his equally large and dark sons maintained expressions of stiff, glaring dignity, glancing around fiercely as if to make sure that no one was questioning the honor of their family because of the conduct of their female relative. But since everyone in the room maintained an aspect of innocent congratulation, as if this was no different from the handful of other weddings that took place in the village every year, the Darwish representatives apparently could find no occasion for a quarrel. The uncle and sons reserved their most suspicious regard for Blaine, a foreigner who might be planning to disgrace their family with his degenerate Western ways. But even here, Blaine's obsequious and respectful greetings in his nearly perfect Arabic seemed to propitiate them.

A very old, white-bearded man stayed seated while the others greeted each other; Blaine guessed that he was the imam, the lay cleric who officiated over weddings and other solemn and religious events in the village. He was blind, his eyes blanked out by bluish cataracts. He murmured pieties as the men bent down to shake his hand. When the proper greetings were over and the men had urged each other to take their seats, and had sat down, there was a silence, and all eyes were on the imam.

He slowly chanted the Fatiha, the opening verse of the Quran:

In the name of God, the Compassionate and Merciful;

Praise God, Lord of all the worlds;
The Compassionate and Merciful;
Master of the Day of Judgment.

Thee do we worship, and seek Thine aid.

Show us the straight way,
The way of those on whom Thou hast
bestowed grace,
Those whose portion is not wrath,
and who do not go astray.

All the other men had sat with their palms upward in their laps while the verse was being recited, and now they cupped their hands over their faces in the traditional gesture of ablution, and Blaine did the same, as his grandmother had taught him many years ago.

"Who is the groom?" asked the imam. "Is he here?"

"I am here, grandfather," said Blaine.

"God bless you, child. Come and sit next to me."

The man sitting to the right of the imam vacated his chair and Blaine sat in it.

"And the representative of the bride?" asked the imam.

"Present," said the uncle, and came and sat at the left hand of the imam.

"Are you a Muslim, child?" the imam murmured to Blaine in his old, soft voice, turning his blind, searching eyes on him, and when Blaine said yes, asked him a few catechism questions, then questions calculated to disclose whether he was of marriageable age, unmarried, and otherwise eligible to marry, of sound mind, free of compulsion to

marry, free of serious disease, and so on. When he was satisfied, the old man turned to the uncle and had a murmured
conversation with him as well; from the scraps Blaine heard,
he gathered that the imam had already met with the bride
and obtained her consent to the marriage. As befitted a duti-
ful relative, the uncle raised the question of dower.

"Dower is unnecessary because of the financial independence of the bride," said the old man. He turned to
Blaine again. "Have you come to make an offer of marriage?"

"I have."

"And are the witnesses present?"

"Yes, grandfather," came two hoarse, strong peasant
voices.

"Make your offer, then."

It was all very sudden. Not that he had considered
changing his mind; for wasn't this why he had come to
Egypt, the antidote to his former life? And he doubted any
man could have refused her, however strange it was—

"I—I wish to offer, and I do offer to marry Buthaina Darwish, and live with her as husband and wife," Blaine said
awkwardly, and his voice sounded soft and light in that con-
clave of hardy peasant men. The uncle Darwish's dark eyes
shining in the lamplight held his.

"On behalf of my brother's daughter Buthaina, and having spoken with her and obtained her consent, I accept the
offer," said the uncle gravely.

"Then let it be so, and may God bless the union," said
the imam, and so Blaine and Buthaina were married.

"You and our sister and daughter Buthaina are now
married," said the imam to Blaine, his blind eyes searching
for him in the dim light of the lamp. "But listen to me," he
went on, cutting off the words of congratulation from the
other men in the room. "Listen to me before you go." There
was silence. "You or someone else in this room may believe
that because of the suddenness of this marriage, or because
your wife Buthaina is an entertainer from the great city, or

ecause in the West, God be merciful to you, as we hear, the
istitution of marriage is not respected—you may perhaps
elieve because of these things that this contract we have
ritten tonight is cheap or a mere formality or an excuse for
ebauchery or negligence or dishonor, but it is not. All the
bligations of marriage bind you and your wife, and any
hild born of this union will be legitimate and the offspring
f your blood. This marriage is blessed by God, and will be
idged by God on the Day. Do you understand this, child?"

"I do, grandfather," said Blaine.

"And does everyone else understand this?" asked the
ld man.

There was a murmur of assent.

"Then celebrate and go to your wife and consummate
ie marriage, and may God keep you and keep your chil-
ren. Listen, I think I hear the procession of gifts from the
ride." The old man laughed softly.

His hearing was perhaps a little weak; Blaine had been
earing for the past few minutes the rising sound of
hanting and drumming, clapping and ululation, as the
ride's procession neared the house. Blaine stood up and
1ook hands all around again, accepting everyone's con-
ratulation with pious responses. Mohammed Fahlawi
as in the inner room urging the women to even greater
ats of cooking—a smell of spiced meat and tomato
iuce through the open door reminded Blaine that he was
arving—and boys and youths were hurrying to and fro
iddenly with chairs and trays and folding tray-stands.
Vhen Blaine came back out into the courtyard he saw
1at chairs and trays were being set up there and in the
ne outside, and that christmas lights—dimly lit by con-
ections to car batteries—were being strung up, men and
oys calling to one another, their voices submerged in the
nanting of the women. The women of the Fahlawi house-
old stood outside in the lane clapping and drumming
id exchanging responsive chants with a long procession

of women from the Darwish household carrying on their heads trays laden with gifts.

"The house of Fahlawi is in honor!" chanted the Darwish women.

"And the house of Darwish in honor!" replied the Fahlawi women.

"The two houses are one family!"

"And the two houses are one blood!"

Then, with excited rhythmic clapping the Fahlawi women moved aside and the Darwish women came into the courtyard, passing their trays over the top of the wall as before.

The trays were piled with the same kinds of gifts that had been sent to the bride—sweets, Jordan almonds, fruit, all of which with effusive thanks to God and the Darwish women Blaine laid in the hands of his hosts and hostesses—but there was also a white *gelabiyah* and headcloth of fine cotton, which he took.

Guests were already being seated in the courtyard and in the lane, trays with cigarettes and tiny tumblers of mint tea were being carried around, and a four-piece orchestra was setting up in one corner of the courtyard. Above, the cool, dark air rose to the distant stars, but in the houses of men all was noise and festivity, the age-old ceremonies of marriage building a pressure in the collective unconscious that Blaine's trained senses could feel: an ancient, ritually induced Image that spoke of fertility, of growing things and children, of the earth and the sun and the cycle of the year, and the cycle of human life.

A hand plucked at Blaine's arm as he stood in a greeting line by the courtyard door along with Mohammed Fahlawi and other important people of the Fahlawi family and shook hands, it seemed, with everyone in the village. He looked into the face of a young man.

"It is time for you to be washed," Mohammed Fahlawi murmured in his ear, shaking hands with an old, tattered man who had come to give his congratulations and receive the alms and free meals that would be given out." "We are combining three nights into one, so you must hurry."

Blaine took his *gelabiyah* and headcloth and followed the young man amid cries and ululations and clapping. The young man led him through the inner room and the room beyond that—a large kitchen where a dozen women were cooking heavily but broke off and ululated deafeningly as he came through—then through a small, stuffy bedroom with a fastened wooden shutter and a board ceiling, and finally into a flagstone-floored bathroom with a drain in the middle, lit by three candles in a candelabra, where two other young men were pouring pails of steaming water into a large galvanized basin.

"*Mabruk*, hajj; congratulations, hajj," they said respectfully. Blaine had never made the pilgrimage that all prosperous Muslims were supposed to make to Mecca and Medina, but it was a term of respect, indicating the speakers' belief that he was a man both of substance and good religious faith, as well as being of a respectable age, older than themselves.

"May God congratulate you," Blaine responded properly. He put his *gelabiyah* and headcloth on a rickety table, undressed, and sat in the hot water of the basin. The young men poured hot water over him and scrubbed him with rough soap and loofahs until he glowed, chanting as they worked a man's marriage chant, a chant about work and health and wealth, beautiful wives and many sons, crops and livestock and honor. When they were done they toweled him off and combed his hair and splashed on an abundance of flowery perfume. They helped him on with his *gelabiyah* and wrapped his headcloth turban style. Then they led him to another room in Mohammed Fahlawi's mansion: a small room with a window whose shutters opened on a grove of shoulder-high orange saplings growing by the walls of the village, and above them the stars in the deep, scented jewel box of night. The young men brought in a kerosene lantern and then withdrew respectfully, closing the door.

The room had a prayer rug laid diagonally on the floor—facing Mecca, Blaine supposed. They were giving him a time for prayer and reflection before the consummation of his marriage. He stood with his arms on the windowsill, looking out at the stars and the land, unspoiled because it could support only a few hundred people, smelling the cool, quiet air, listening to the trilling of crickets and frogs. The sound of the door opening made him turn.

It was the old village headman, the *'umdah,* leaning on his cane.

"May God hear you," he murmured as if Blaine were at prayer. "May God give you peace."

"May He hear you and give you peace," Blaine responded.

The old man shut the door behind him and stood looking at Blaine, wavering slightly, whether with age or indecision Blaine couldn't tell.

Finally the *'umdah* said: "If you want to run away, it is still not too late. The marriage has not been consummated. Mahmoud Shakfi will drive you to Qara in his jeep for fifty dollars. She will not blame you. You heard her words."

Blaine studied the old man for a minute. "Do you advise me to run away, father?"

"If you were my son, I would advise you to run away."

"Why?"

"Do you not see how she raves and screams? She is possessed with *jinni* or demons, God forfend, she says so herself. And what of all the other men she has married, what has happened to them? They say they have all gone mad or died."

"How many has she married altogether?"

"Here in this village she has married six, father. I do not know how many elsewhere."

"Yet you continue to give her weddings."

"Yes, God forgive us."

"She is from this village."

"True."

"You must know her story, then 'umdah. Will you tell it to me?"

The old man stood wavering again.

"You see that I need to know it, father."

"I will tell you," said the old man, "if you promise to keep it secret. There are those in our village who would kill to preserve the honor of their families."

"I promise."

"Then listen to my story, father, and I will tell you. In the name of God, the Compassionate and Merciful.

"Thirty years ago, the richest family in the village was the Darwish family, and the head of the family was Omar Darwish, and his younger brother was Tawfik Darwish, whom you met tonight, and who accepted your offer of marriage on behalf of his niece. This girl, Buthaina, was the third child of Omar Darwish."

"Omar Darwish was a proud and masterful man, generous but short-tempered and haughty. His lands and livestock were fertile, and his children were healthy, and his daughter Buthaina grew into a bride of great beauty. Omar Darwish was proud of her, but jealous also that her beauty not call dishonor upon the family, and he guarded her closely as she grew older in a way that was tiresome for a young girl who was still in truth a child. So it was that she used to creep out when her father was sitting with the men or riding out to look at his fields, and she would run to the groves or the edge of the desert with her playmates.

"When Buthaina was fifteen, people began to gossip, and what they said was that the beauty Buthaina Darwish had lost her virtue with the son of one of the neighbor farmers. Omar interrogated Buthaina, and she swore it wasn't true. Yet the stories continued, until Omar finally called for the village midwives to examine Buthaina and prove them false.

"The next day one of my sons ran home sobbing. He

had been working near the edge of the village where the Darwish house faces, and he had heard over the wall of their courtyard Buthaina Darwish screaming as if she had lost her mind, and the equally insane screams of her father, and the lashing of a bullwhip.

"The girl denied and denied that she had committed the sin, and her father commanded her to tell him who had dishonored her so that he could kill him, but she denied it still, and no amount of whipping would make her say otherwise. So Omar Darwish, in a rage that only family dishonor can bring upon a proud and haughty man, had her head shaved and took her out to the palm grove by the edge of the desert, and had his hired men bury her up to her neck in the earth; he swore that she should have no food or water nor be set free until she told him who had dishonored her and the name of the Darwish family.

"Her mother and the women of her family begged him to relent. They told him that as a girl of thirteen she had been running and had tripped on a stone, and that when she stood up her legs had been covered with blood from her vagina, and that this was the explanation for her not being intact. But Omar did not relent. His love for his daughter seemed to have been overthrown by his rage.

"I tell myself that if the same thing happened again I would act differently. Perhaps everyone in the village tells himself that. But to the shame of the village, no one dared defy Omar Darwish. One of the village girls crept down to see Buthaina the third night after she was buried, and came back crying that she would die, that her face was the face of an old woman and she couldn't hold her head up, and she was begging, begging in a whisper for water, and repeating over and over that she was a virgin.

"This was in the year 1378, by the Muslim calendar, and in that year the great *zilzal* came, on that very night.

"It was terrible. Omar Darwish and both his sons and his wife died when their house collapsed on them. Those who

ere spared were busy digging others out of the wreckage,
urying the dead, rounding up and feeding the animals, so
hat we forgot Buthaina for a while. When we did at last remember, my sons and I ran to the grove at the edge of the
esert, but what we found was just a hole where she had
een buried. The *zilzal* had torn up the earth: it was humped
nd uneven, and dozens of trees had fallen, and a spring of
water had come up from nowhere. We hoped that the *zilzal*
ad somehow thrown her out of the ground, or that some-
ne had come down and dug her out. Anyway, she was nowhere to be found, and we never saw her again. Not for many
ears.

"It wasn't until months later that 'Aliya Lateef told me
story that at the time I dismissed as a hysterical woman's
le. She said that on the night of the *zilzal* she had been out
nasing one of her brother's horses, which had broken its
ther and bolted. Animals can sense the *zilzal* before it hap-
ens, they say. When the *zilzal* came 'Aliya was in open
round and she fell on her face with her arms over her head,
rying and repenting of her sins. When the tremors passed
he ran back toward the village, and along the road she says
he met Buthaina Darwish.

"'Buthaina, sister!' she cried. 'What has happened? Is it
he end of the world? Are you alive?'

"But Buthaina said nothing. She looked more alive than
he had ever seen her, 'Aliya said; she looked like a lioness,
nd her eyes flashed, but she said nothing. 'Aliya was fright-
ned and ran back to the village."

The old man paused, then went on.

"Five or six years later men from the village traveling to
ara went to a movie house, and much to their astonish-
ent there on the screen was Buthaina Darwish, grown into
woman and more beautiful than she had ever been.

"The people of the village wondered at this, and soon a
ay came when a big air car landed on the road, and when
he people ran out to see, Buthaina Darwish stepped from

it, and we were afraid. For it was clear that she was very rich now, and also very strange. A madness seemed to be upon her. She had only contempt for the people of the village, ordering us around like servants. And it soon came out that we *were* her servants: someone had bought up most of the village land in the previous few years, someone who had paid high prices but demanded secrecy, so that each landholder had congratulated himself that he had outsmarted the other families. But when she came to us that first time she showed us the deeds of sale, and we knew that most of the land we worked and lived on was now hers.

"A construction company came from Cairo and built her a house—a palace, by God—up the ridge at the edge of the desert, overlooking the grove where she had been buried years before. After that she would appear every so often in her air car and bring a man to whom she would demand to be married. We were afraid of her, and we did as she asked. The marriages she demanded were strange but not prohibited, we told ourselves. We owed her our loyalty as a village woman and as people who had failed her, we told ourselves. And we told ourselves that our children would have nothing to eat if we angered her so that she evicted us from our land."

The old man was silent, thinking.

"As to whether you should approach her as her husband, only God can help you decide. The men are coming in a few minutes; if they should find you gone—if you should, for example, slip out the window and meet Mahmoud Shakfi at his jeep on the road—no one would blame you, not even your bride, I think. God be with you."

16

The men found Blaine standing by the window of the prayer room ten minutes later, and with a great chanting in their deep, loud voices, and a great, fast clapping of their large, strong hands, with laughter and whistles and mock grabbing of his nonexistent beard, with back-slapping and arm-slapping, they hustled him from the room and carried him on their shoulders from the house and down the lane with beating on drums and the ululation of women, children running behind, and the dim stars far above, and carried him out of the lane into a crowd of men just outside the village walls in a wide space of scrub and crabgrass before an orange grove lit by torches. Now some of them, running, led a great white horse from somewhere, many hands laid on it to keep it steady in the tumult, and Blaine was hoisted atop it and given the reins. The crowd parted before him and he saw, barely twenty meters ahead, a crowd of women in the torchlight, and at the front of them stood Buthaina.

She looked unexpectedly like a Western bride, in a long,

frilly white gown and lacy veil. The women were clapping and chanting loudly for him to come to her, to take her, to be her husband.

Now came an awkward moment: Blaine didn't know how to ride a horse, and this one was huge and had no saddle; he gripped it hard with his legs, afraid he would fall off. But before it could wander or rear up someone slapped its rump and it trotted most of the way to Buthaina.

She came forward stiff and pale in her white gown, her face drawn as if she was in pain. But when he put his hand down to her she sprang onto the horse in front of him and grabbed the reins, as the women in front of them and the men behind laughed and ululated and clapped and whistled.

The people parted and she kicked the horse's ribs. It leapt forward as if electrified and they galloped off into the darkness, Blaine holding on to her to keep from falling, feeling the rhythmic tightening of muscles in her back and abdomen and sides, the strong slenderness of her waist, the beating of his heart, the jarring of the big animal under him. The electricity he had felt when he had touched her in the helicopter was gone, and there was no sign of any fire.

In only a minute they were out of sight and earshot of the village, galloping through fields in the deep cool of night pierced with silver from a full moon rising over a grove of twenty-meter palms before them, and then they were among the massive boles of the trees, the horse flying surefootedly, its hooves thudding softly on the fallen, dry fronds, and beyond the grove a wide land of scrub and salty mudflats ran to the sandy slopes of the ridge in the middle distance rising up to the desert plateau all around them.

She spurred the horse across the flat and Blaine held to her tight, jarring painfully in his ignorance of riding. When they hit the sand the animal slowed, but still she urged it and he could see above them, at the top of the two-hundred-meter ridge, the silhouette of a house against the moon.

The horse labored up the ridge, its sweat hot and prickly

on Blaine's bare legs under the *gelabiyah*. When they reached the top, the sand and rocks of the desert stretched away in the moonlight. They jumped off and Buthaina slapped the horse's rump, and it trotted away back down the ridge, sand sliding under its hooves.

The stone house before them was built on a rock shelf that thrust out of the sand at the very edge of the ridge. It had three stories, high arched windows, and a long, wide front stair, and was surrounded by a high stone wall.

Buthaina held out an old-fashioned metal key. Her hand was shaking. He looked closely at her. Her lips trembled and her eyes were wide. Sweat was on her face and her breath came in gasps. It had been ten hours since she had taken a shot, Blaine realized with a sinking feeling. With a habit like hers withdrawal would be brutal even without the enormous pressure of the collective unconscious that seemed to be building in her. Maybe she had more drugs in the house; he didn't know whether to hope so or not.

He took the key from her and, on an impulse, took her up in his arms with a rustle and flounce of wedding gown, and carried her. Her body was strong, lithe, her spine slender and supple under his hands. Her eyes were darker than the night. Touching her was strange; there was a tingle around her as if electricity had started to build up again, and there seemed to be a faint shimmer too.

A metal gate in the stone wall was ajar. Blaine pushed it open with a creak quickly blown away in the desert silence by the whisper of the wind. Then he climbed stone steps gritty with sand, fumbled with the key at the metal house door, and pushed it inward.

Inside it was dark and silent, so that the rustle of her gown as he carried her seemed loud. In the middle of a big dark room he felt a spasm of trembling come over her.

"Put me down," she whispered. Then whimpered: "Put me down."

He set her on her feet but kept his hands on her arms to

steady her, the gleam of her eyes like black jewels in the darkness.

"Let go of me," she hissed. Then in a sudden shriek: "Don't touch me! Get away!"

He jerked back, startled.

Blinding light burst up, a giant, roaring blowtorch of white-hot flame that scorched his face and hands.

It was worse than before. Flames covered her, devouring her, and she screamed, clawing, failing.

Then there was darkness, silence.

Blaine fell heavily on his rump. His mind seemed to go away. When he could think again, he didn't know whether the darkness was physical or a result of his faint. He was dizzy, unable to stand up.

Sobbing came from a few meters away. He crawled toward it, and his hands touched the brocaded sleeve of Buthaina's wedding dress.

"Don't touch me," she sobbed softly.

"Are you—are you all right?"

"I have to burn, don't you understand? I have to burn." Her sobbing was soft, and her body and dress where he touched her seemed undamaged.

The Image was now so powerful that it was consensual in real time, Blaine realized vaguely. The collective unconscious projected flames burning Buthaina, and Blaine saw the flames, and she felt them.

And suddenly they were roaring again, and she was shrieking with the insane laughter of agony he had heard in the garden in his first dream of her, and her prone body was burning, burning like a corpse cremated, and he covered his ears and squeezed his eyes shut, looked away, but wherever he looked, eyes open or closed, he saw her burning, heard her awful screams.

Then it was dark again, and her screams subsided, but slowly this time, as if the flames had left her unhinged.

"Buthaina?" he whimpered.

"It was real," her shaking, sobbing whisper came. *"It was
al what I dreamed all those nights, and the life I thought was
al was a dream. I didn't know—I heard Satan laugh when I
›ok the drugs, but they told me it wasn't real. But now it's too
te."* He crawled close to her again. She lay huddled, dark
air tumbled around her. He rolled her on her back and held
er in his arms. Her gown was soaked with sweat.

"It can't really hurt you," he said urgently, shakily. "It's
ot physically real, just a scene from the collective uncon-
ious. I know it seems real, but when it's dissipated it'll go
vay, I promise—"

She looked up at him as if slowly becoming aware of his
xistence.

"I thought perhaps God would have mercy on a bride
1 her wedding night," she gasped. "But I'm too evil. I have
› burn."

"Get that out of your head," he hissed shakily. "That'll
1ly make it worse. There are no prophets nowadays. No
1e can save people anymore; they've heard it all before.
1e scientists have already warned them."

He picked her up. Moonlight seemed to be coming from
›mewhere to his right. He carried her that way.

Moonlight poured thickly through an arched glass door
a luxurious sunken living room. The woman stirred in his
ms. He set her on her feet. She went to the door, opened it,
1d stepped out onto a decorative terrace of smooth stone
1d columns, drifted now with blowing sand. She stepped
ver a stone balustrade and walked in her bare feet into the
esert plain.

Blaine followed her at a little distance. The desert wind
1d moon played in her hair as she walked toward that vast
nptiness, her wedding gown fluttering a little. Finally she
opped and slowly raised her arms, stretched them out, as
she stood on the sand of a great, desiccated beach and
:ld out her hands to a ship that was sailing, sailing away.

Then the fire roared and she was burning like a torch, he

heard her shrieking laugh of agony, and it was the voice of Buthaina from his dream, and he ran madly toward her.

It was killing her this time, he saw, blackening and crisping and melting her to a grotesque caricature of a human while her bubbling mouth screamed—

"It's not real!" he shouted desperately to her.

Then his arms closed around her and his thoughts disappeared in pain so sickeningly brutal he would not have thought it possible.

He tumbled away in darkness, burning.

He saw a virgin buried in the ground, in ancient days it seemed, in pagan ceremony. For three days and three nights she stayed there, and then the earth moved, and when she came out she was no longer a human girl; something had entered her from the deep, molten heart of Earth.

And he saw the people of the Earth, saw filth and hunger and sorrow and sickness and the suffering of children.

And he saw leaning over a hole in the ground of the oasis palm grove, and over the tormented city of Cairo, and over the tormented Earth a great pale Angel with its wings folded and its head bowed—

The first thing he became aware of was the whispering of the wind. It went on a long time, and he knew it came from the desert; he looked out across the waste in his dream, and the wind blew toward him through an endless corridor of sand and moonlight, blew from the land from which all the world comes, far across a desert and an ocean, from a green coast dimly seen, and Blaine had seen it before in his dreams.

Slowly he woke up. The desert wind whispered around him. He was lying on cool sand.

Suddenly he remembered the flames, and he sat up and looked at himself in panic, but his body wasn't burned. His mind was burned, but his body was intact. He wondered at the feeling of relief that gave him.

He looked around for Buthaina but she wasn't there. He tried to call her, but he didn't seem able to talk.

He stood up unsteadily with sudden misgiving. The stone house was fifty meters away in the moonlight. He hurried back there. After the moonlight it seemed very dark inside. He wandered through the rooms looking for her. The house was empty. But on an ornate dressing table he found a pair of scissors gleaming in a puddle of moonlight, and scattered on the floor were locks of silken hair, thick and dark as shadows.

He stumbled out the front door and down the stone steps, out the gate. The moon was riding low in the sky, leaving the oasis below in thick, greenish shadow. In panic he started down the ridge, sand clogging his steps, sliding underneath him.

The quake came when he was nearly at the bottom. At first there was only a distant booming that seemed to subside, as if he had heard the thunder of some vast dry storm over the desert. Then the ground exploded.

He flew head over heels in the air, fell in a vast, hissing slide of rushing earth. He struggled in body-bursting panic, clawing to keep his head above liquid, flowing sand. Another explosion spat him into the air. The sand was rushing along the flat where he fell this time, and he scrambled up, tumbled, slogged up again desperately, and then he was clear of it and crawling in the wide, bucking plain. With a splitting roar like lightning tearing through the ground a jagged crack opened five meters from him, and he tried to scrabble away from it but found he could do nothing but clutch the ground. He clutched it.

After untold minutes he realized that he was lying still, or nearly so. He couldn't tell if the faint shaking under him was the earth still moving or his own trauma. The booming was distant again, like the echo of thunder.

He sat up, trembling uncontrollably, got to his knees and then with difficulty to his feet. He was numb, his body buzzing with adrenaline. He noticed dizzily that the vast sand ridge had slid catastrophically almost to where he stood halfway across the flat, like a fallen mountain. The rough hissing of sand still came from it as residual slides ran their way to the bottom. There was no sign of the house that had stood at the top. He realized then that he was seeing all this in something other than dark silhouette: the light of dawn was coming, smoky blue and still through dust moving in the air. The distant rumbling had died away now, and everything was very silent, as if every creature, every bird had been struck dumb by the earthquake, even the wind stilled.

The palm grove was barely a hundred meters from him, half the trees leaning or fallen. The scuff and crunch of his stumbling feet on rocks and dirt as he labored toward it came loud in the silence. He skirted a steaming crevice that smelled like a bomb had gone off in it, climbed humps and raw ridges heaved up in the flat. Among the labyrinth of fallen, leaning, and standing palms the earth was folded and torn too, and it took him a long time searching, climbing over massive boles, wending his way through the chaos before he found her.

The shovel she must have used to dig the hole lay nearby. He didn't know if she had filled it by pulling dirt onto herself, or whether the quake had shaken dirt in on her, but only her head showed in the ground between two standing trees, the hair cut off unevenly close to her head. She was dead, half-open eyes glinting in the light of dawn, an ooze of blood coming from one corner of her mouth. The frantic earth had crushed her in her hole.

17

The earthquake, epicentered in the Western Desert a hundred kilometers from Cairo, had been Richter magnitude 8.5, as big as the 1976 Tong Shun quake in China, he found out later. Tong Shun had killed 750,000 people; five times that number had died in Cairo, and as many more had starved or died of cholera and typhoid and dysentery in the weeks after. A million people had fled into the desert around the city, and years later relief agencies were still struggling to feed their ramshackle camp cities. The exclusive neighborhoods and the slums had alike been destroyed, and the Nile eddied in backwaters of collapsed and sunken buildings and streets, tangled reinforcing bar and concrete rubble.

Blaine learned all this from the U.S. Army hospital psychiatric ward in Wiesbaden, Germany, where he was admitted after a military rescue team mobilized to take Americans out of Egypt had responded to a call from the Wadi Sel villagers. They had found him two days after the quake, sitting in the palm grove and watching the decaying head of a

woman. Icon's Legal Department had made zealous efforts
to have him placed under Company care at a certain Swiss
sanitarium, but because his employment contract had been
terminated the Army refused to release him. He was diag-
nosed with post-traumatic stress syndrome, medicated and
then tapered off, so that two weeks later he was sitting on a
screened veranda overlooking a lawn, some trees, and a
loading dock in the watery German sunlight, wondering
what he would do when they checked him out, when a polite military orderly told him he had a visitor. It was a surprise, because he didn't know anybody in Wiesbaden, or in
Germany at all. The visitor was tall and dark, with a goatee
and shoulder-length black hair, and he glowered with burning black eyes at the unbalanced U.S. military personnel sitting on the veranda.

"Haseeb!"

Haseeb pulled up a chair and they hunkered with their
heads together so no one could hear them, ignoring the curious stares of the other patients and the orderly, and Blaine
couldn't remember when he had ever been so happy.

Haseeb glowered dourly at him. "When they letting you
out of this booby hatch?" he asked in his Urdu accent.

"Next two, three days. Man, I thought I'd never see you
again! They said you were fried, they said—!"

"Shh, keep it low. I was fried, nh. But the worst part was
those croakers in Icon's fucking sanitarium tried to keep me
under. Our former employer doesn't want anyone knowing
what happened to us, because someone might try to regu-
late their precious Image-digging. I had to palm a lot of pills
and say a lot of mantras to get my head straight. And they
still wouldn't let me out. Finally got a call through to my
family in Karachi, and they sent lawyers and bodyguards.
The staff couldn't decide whether they were going to shoot
the place up or sue the fuck out of them, so they let me
out."

"I was trying to find you! I had to sit and listen to that window fan that answers your phone—"

"Tell me about it later. I came here to talk business, nh? I got a job for you."

"I'll take it."

"Done. You want to know what it is?"

"Anything but working for Icon."

"There's not going to *be* an Icon when the mega-fucking-lawsuit we're filing against them gets going. I'm talking about honest work. You ever heard of Indonesia?"

"It's one of those Southeast Asian countries."

"Muslim country. Highest economic growth rate on the planet past four out of five years. Biggest per capita budget surplus in the world. Highest rate of capital formation, most rapidly increasing per capita income. They got everything except a genteel bloodline, but they're buying that too. Djokjakarta University is pulling top academics from around the world with big money, and they want to buy themselves a trendy religious studies program. Show the Euros who's boss."

"Religious studies? But how—"

"You ever hear of a guy named Chaim Maddox?"

Blaine paused. "You believe in that shit?"

"Don't you? Now?"

He looked into Haseeb's black eyes and it started to dawn on him. But as it started to dawn on him he remembered—His heart, which had been beating with gladness, collapsed into itself like a black hole.

His voice was choked. "Haseeb, man, I got to tell you what happened."

"I *know* what happened," said Haseeb, looking at him in that deep way he had. "When it happened to me I was using electronics and had been on the herbs for a month, so it took me down. You understand? That's one of the reasons we have to do this. I have Maddox signed up, and Boyle, and a dozen of the best diggers in the world." His eyes on Blaine were intense. "We can't just let it go at that. We can't let religion be just something they use to sell liquor to Third World teenagers. You get it?"

He got it. Djokjakarta was beautiful, but about as far from his beloved Middle East as it seemed possible to get. The weather was tropical, the people looked Polynesian, the food was Southeast Asian, and of course no Arabic was spoken anywhere. But he was too busy to get homesick for a while. They were putting together a curriculum and a research program that would have gotten them thrown out on their ears at most universities, but the more funding they requested the better pleased the Djokjakarta University administration seemed to be, as if it was a sign that their acquisition was the real thing, real Western academics with a penchant for spending huge money on unreal projects. Some of the money was diverted to pay vicious American lawyers to gut Icon, and they had already filed a formidable phalanx of razor-edged, booby-trapped, multi-million-dollar lawsuits. But the rest was for research, and research that, if it bore fruit, would change the way people thought about religion, advertising, psychology, and geoscience.

So it was exciting, and he was as happy as it was possible for him to be then, and he lived in a bungalow in a meticulously landscaped, intensely green faculty neighborhood on the edge of the huge campus, and every few days it would rain sheets and he would watch out his study window as his small yard slowly filled with water like a shallow bathtub. He didn't do the herbs and he didn't dig Image: they weren't ready to actually start research yet, and besides, some of them had been in or near Egypt and needed R&R. All of them had different words for what had happened, but no one wanted to talk about it yet.

Blaine didn't want to talk about it, but he thought about

it. He paced the floor of his bungalow into the early-morning hours, sporadically jotting notes, trying to erect an explanation, a rationalization, an interpretation to protect himself from the memory of her rotting head, the flies. He asked himself, for example, what sense it made that the collective unconscious—or some stratum of an even deeper Mind, if Maddox's theories were true—would send a prophet to warn of an earthquake in the early twenty-first century, when the scientists had already been warning of it for years? Could such a prophet be considered to have failed if she didn't give the warning? Or had it all been a mistake, a primitive reflex of the local collective unconscious that had filled an unfortunate human woman with a pointless compulsion and an unmanageable power, and then torn her apart when she didn't play it out, oblivious of the fact that it meant nothing in the modern world?

Or could it be that she had been meant not to save people from the quake, but to save their souls? To warn people to mend their ways and tend to the suffering of their brothers and sisters lest retribution befall them? Maybe it really was a devil whose laugh had accompanied the drug-induced diversions from her ministry. But again in that case it was almost as if she had been meant to fail, like most of the other prophets who had ever brought that message, crying in the wilderness.

On the other hand, the collective unconscious could fantasize devils and fire as symbols of its energies. Maybe the flames that had engulfed her and apparently driven her to kill herself were not a punishment for failure at all, but just imaginal energy that had built up in her to attract the attention of the masses to her prophecies—the same energy that had filled Cairo with fantasies of her, and which had to be dissipated in some way when she didn't use it. . . .

But neither those theories nor any others seemed able to ease his mind.

—

Until one morning he woke just before dawn, and a nightingale sang and stopped meditatively in the garden, and he was back in the tiny house in the Jordan Valley with the cool floor tiles and the still air perfumed with jasmine coming through his barred bedroom window. He got out of bed, trying not to wake himself with his fear and hope. The kitchen screen door slapped behind him as he went outside. He went down to the bottom of the garden full of deep blue and faintly purplish air like cool water, and stopped by the fig and orange trees next to the concrete wall.

From the next garden came the clack of plastic sandals. Blaine's heart was pounding, his hands slick with sweat. Before he could decide whether to speak there was the sound of something being pulled near the wall and a sound of climbing, hands appeared at the top of the wall, and she pulled herself up and was straddling it in her long black robe.

He looked up at her; at her thick brown hair, her strong, shapely shoulders under the robe, her long, graceful hands. Gone were the dizzy eyes, the wild numbness, the glaze of intoxication—or rather, those things had never been. This was the peasant girl who had climbed his garden wall in Kraima.

"Buthaina," he whispered. Please don't let her be beaten, he was praying. Please don't let her be pulled down—

But the girl twisted herself around and, lifting her other leg over the wall, jumped lightly to the ground.

He couldn't move. He was shaking.

Her bare feet stepped through crabgrass to the flagstone walk. She stood in front of him and smiled, and her smile was glad and joyful.

He knelt. He knelt in front of her, sobbing.

She put her hands on his head, ran them through his hair. She said softly:

There are Gardens,
Under which rivers flow.

Shade cool and ever deepening.

And beautiful mansions,
To dwell therein. . . .

He knew then that he lived still with his wife, in the other world, where dreams and death carry us.

ABOUT THE AUTHOR

JAMIL NASIR was born in Chicago, Illinois, of a Palestinian refugee father and the American daughter of the inventor of the fork-lift truck. He spent much of his childhood in the Middle East, where he survived two major wars, hiding in cellars and storerooms with his family. He returned to the United States and started college at age 14, studying hard sciences, philosophy of science, English literature, psychology, and Chinese literature and philosophy, finally graduating from the University of Michigan in Ann Arbor with a Bachelor of General Studies.

Between college stints he hitchhiked extensively over much of North America, working as a carpenter, assistant gardener on an estate, shop clerk, warehouseman, applepicker, and paralegal, among other things. He finally found himself back in Ann Arbor, where he got a law degree in 1983. Since then he has been employed part-time at a major Washington, D.C., law firm.

He has sold science fiction stories to *Asimov's, Universe* (vols. 1, 2, and 3), *Interzone, Aboriginal SF,* and a number of other magazines and anthologies, including Steve Pasechnick's 1990 best-of-the-year anthology *Best of the Rest,* and Dozois' and Dann's *Angels!,* a reprint anthology. He won a First Prize in the 1988 Writers of the Future competition.

Mr. Nasir meditates three hours a day, likes to cook, listen to music, play computer games, read, and walk. He lives in the Maryland suburbs of Washington. His first novel, *Quasar,* was published in 1995, and his second, *The Higher Space,* in 1996.

Come visit

BANTAM SPECTRA

on the INTERNET

Spectra invites you to join us
in our new on-line forum.

You'll find:

< Interviews with your favorite authors and
excerpts from their latest books
< Bulletin boards that put you in touch with
other science fiction fans, with Spectra
authors, and with the Bantam editors who
bring them to you
< A guide to the best science fiction re-
sources on the Internet

Join us as we catch you up with all of Spectra's finest
authors, featuring monthly listings of upcoming titles
and special previews, as well as contests, interviews,
and more! We'll keep you in touch with the field, both
its past and its future—and everything in between.

Look for the Spectra Science Fiction
Forum on the World Wide Web at:

http://www.bantam/spectra.com

SF 30 8/97